THE COSMIC ADVENTURES OF

ASTRID AND STELLA

STORY BY SABRINA MOYLE
PICTURES BY EUNICE MOYLE

AMULET BOOKS · NEW YORK

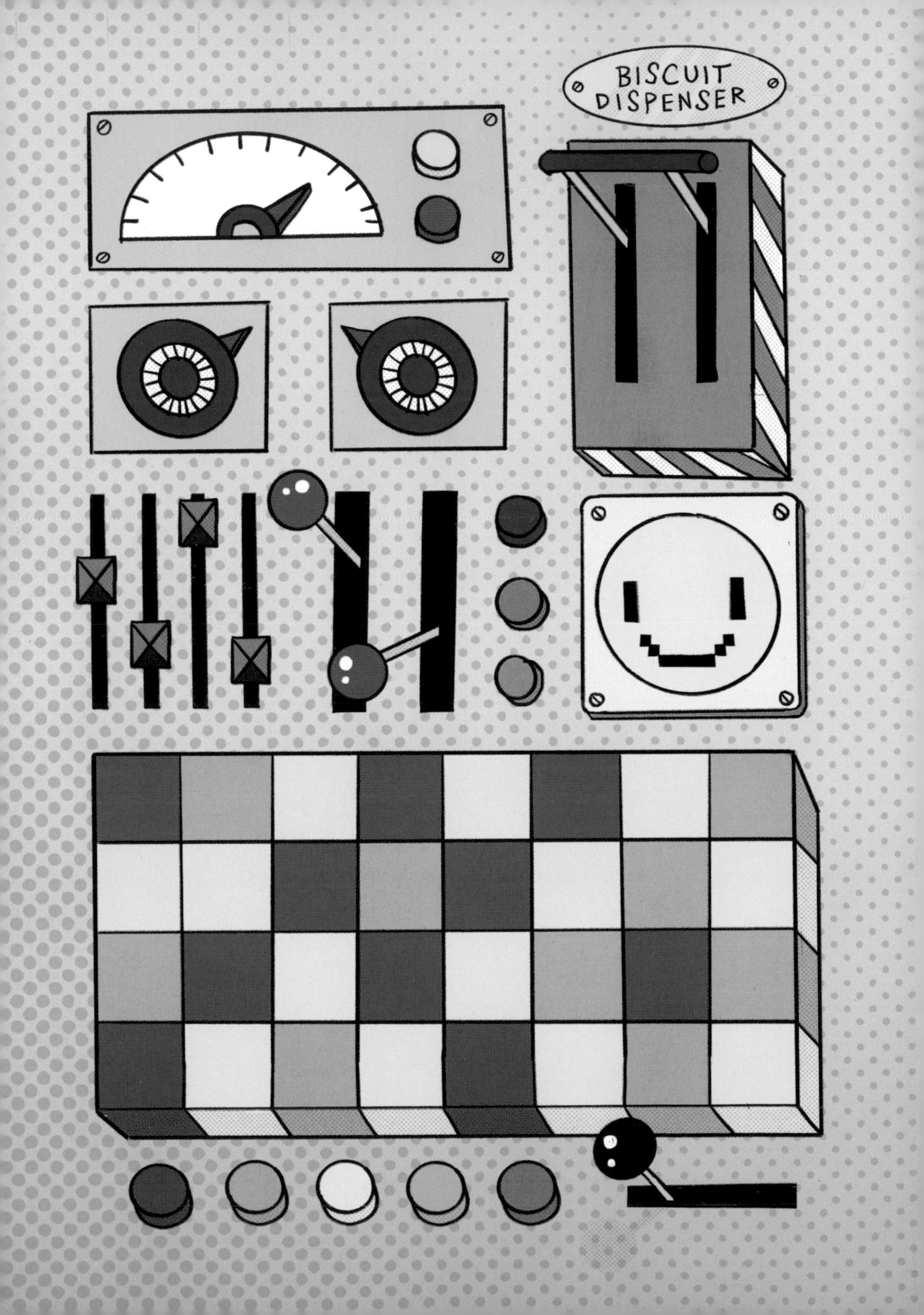
BISCUIT
DISPENSER

CONTENTS

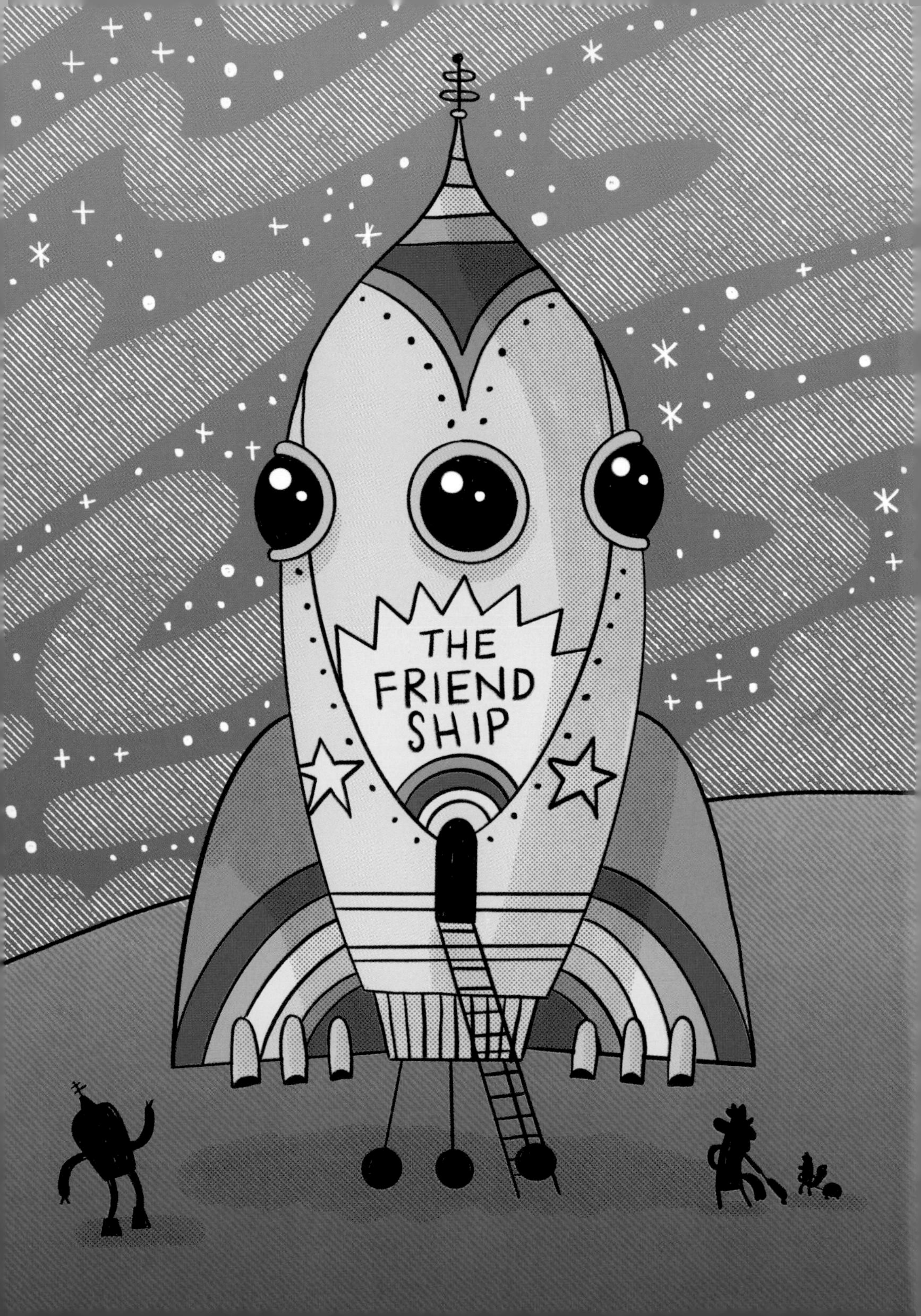
THE FRIEND SHIP

CHAPTER ONE

WHEN'S LAUNCH?

Today's the day!

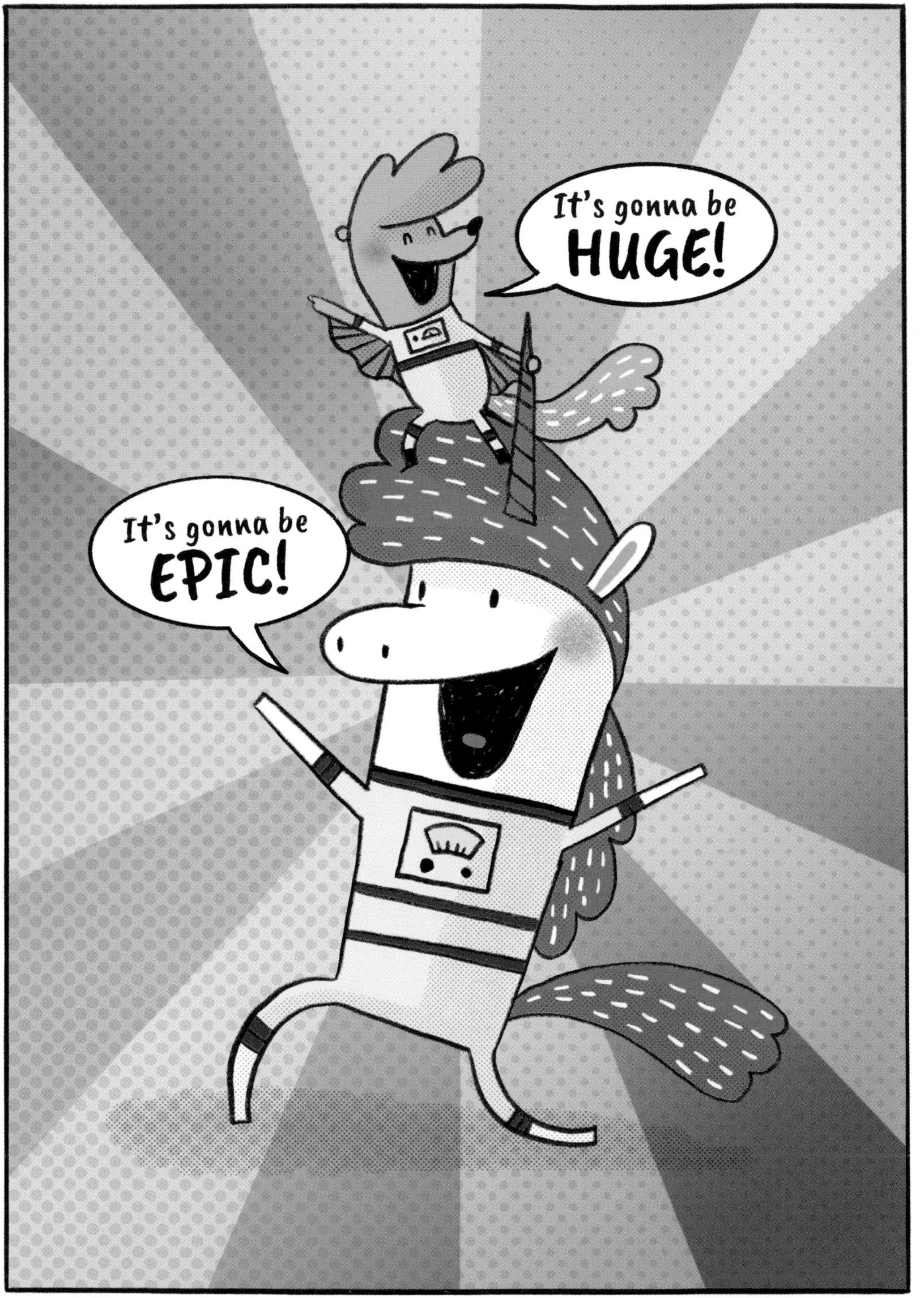
It's gonna be HUGE!
It's gonna be EPIC!

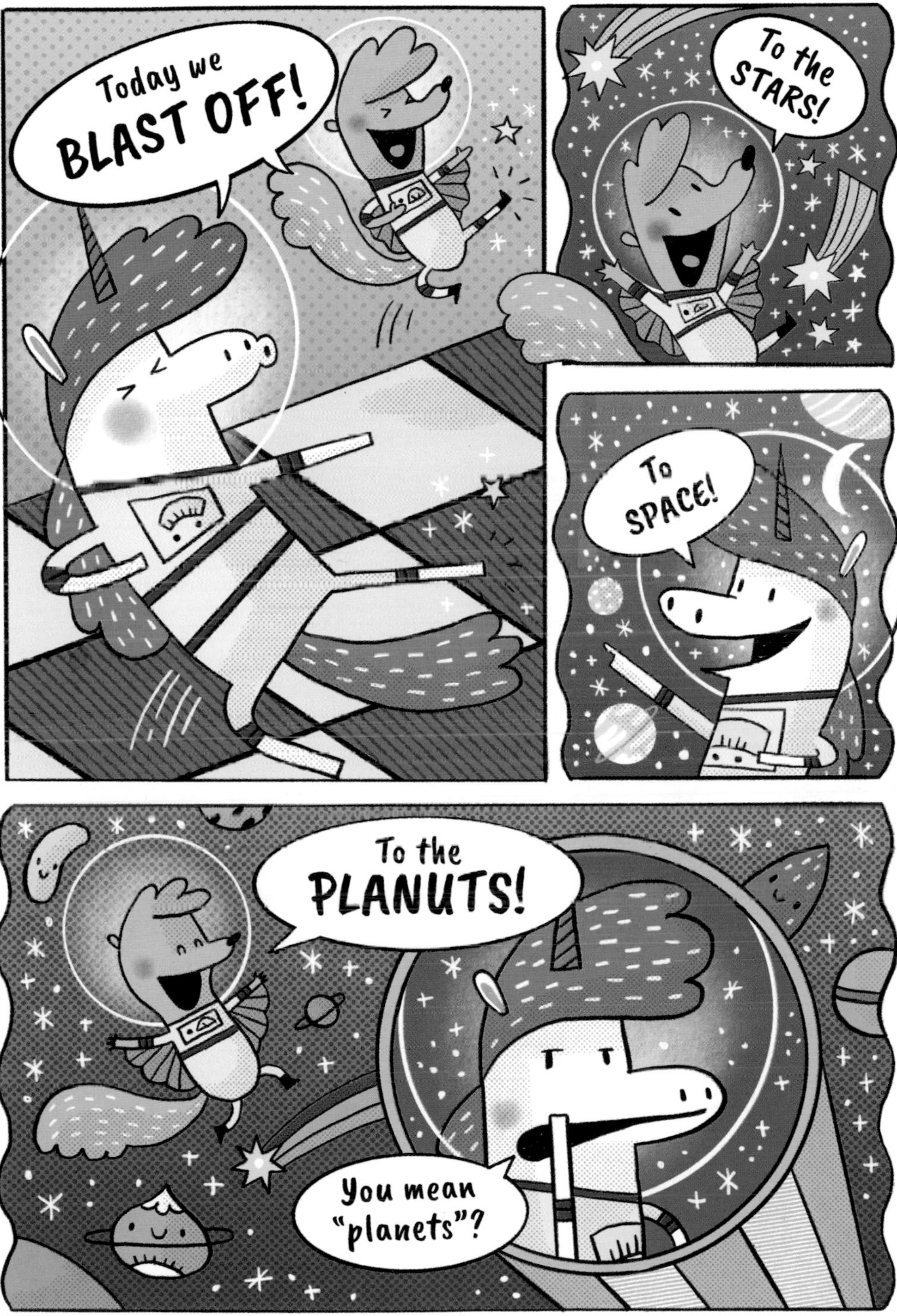
Today we BLAST OFF!
To the STARS!
To SPACE!
To the PLANUTS!
You mean "planets"?

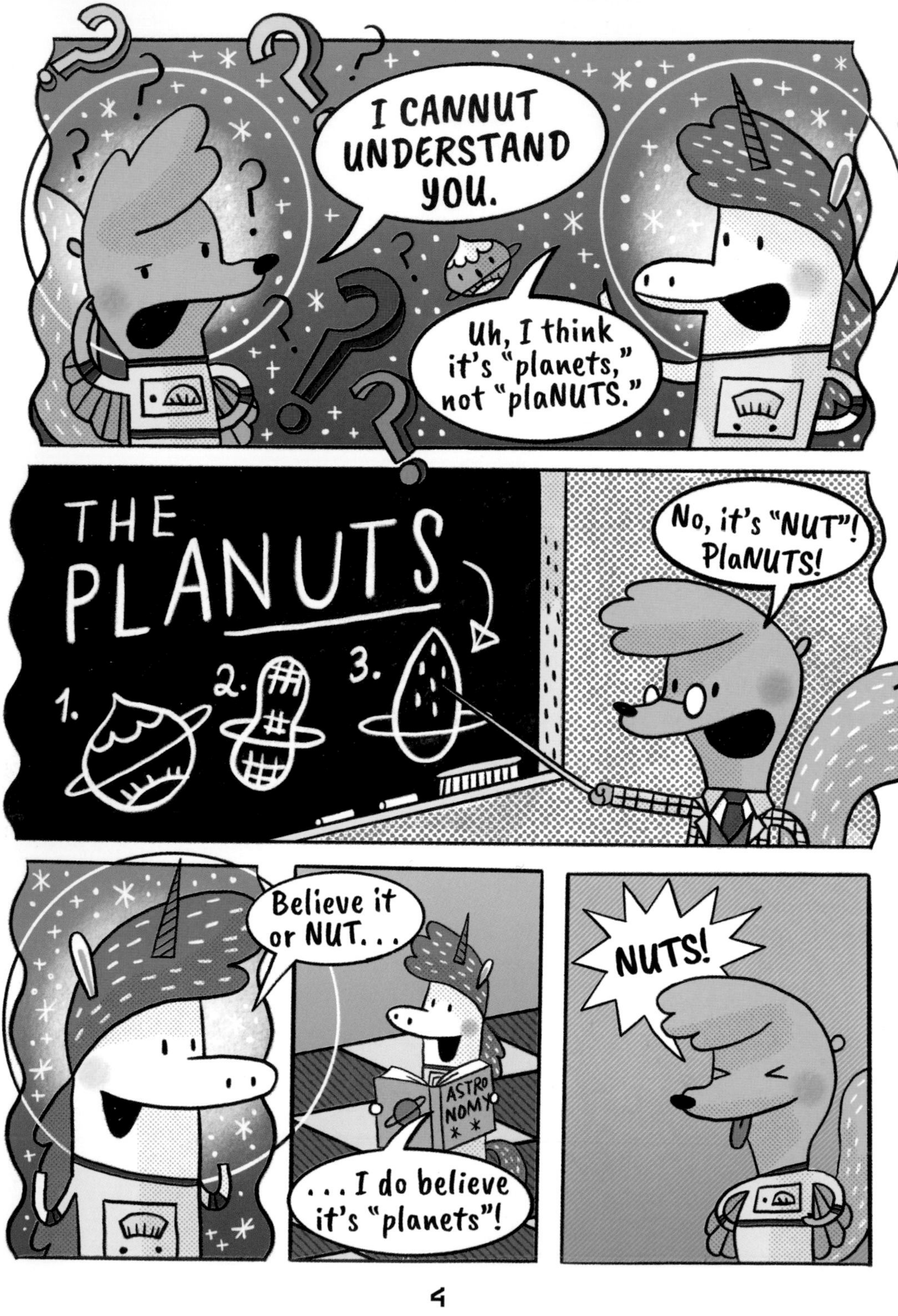
I CANNUT UNDERSTAND YOU.
Uh, I think it's "planets," not "plaNUTS."
THE PLANUTS
1.
2.
3.
No, it's "NUT"! PlaNUTS!
Believe it or NUT. . .
ASTRONOMY
. . . I do believe it's "planets"!
NUTS!

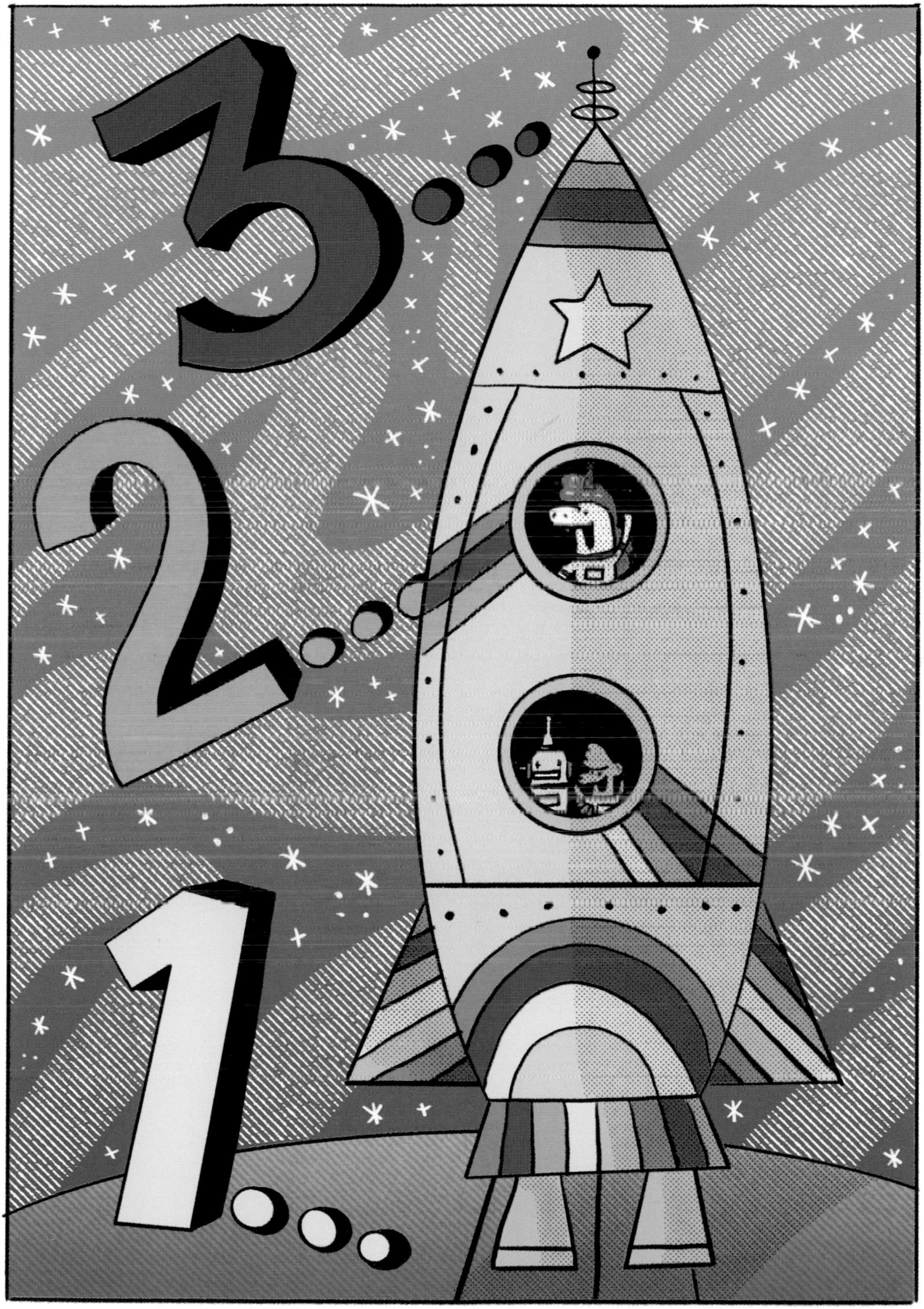
3...
2...
1...

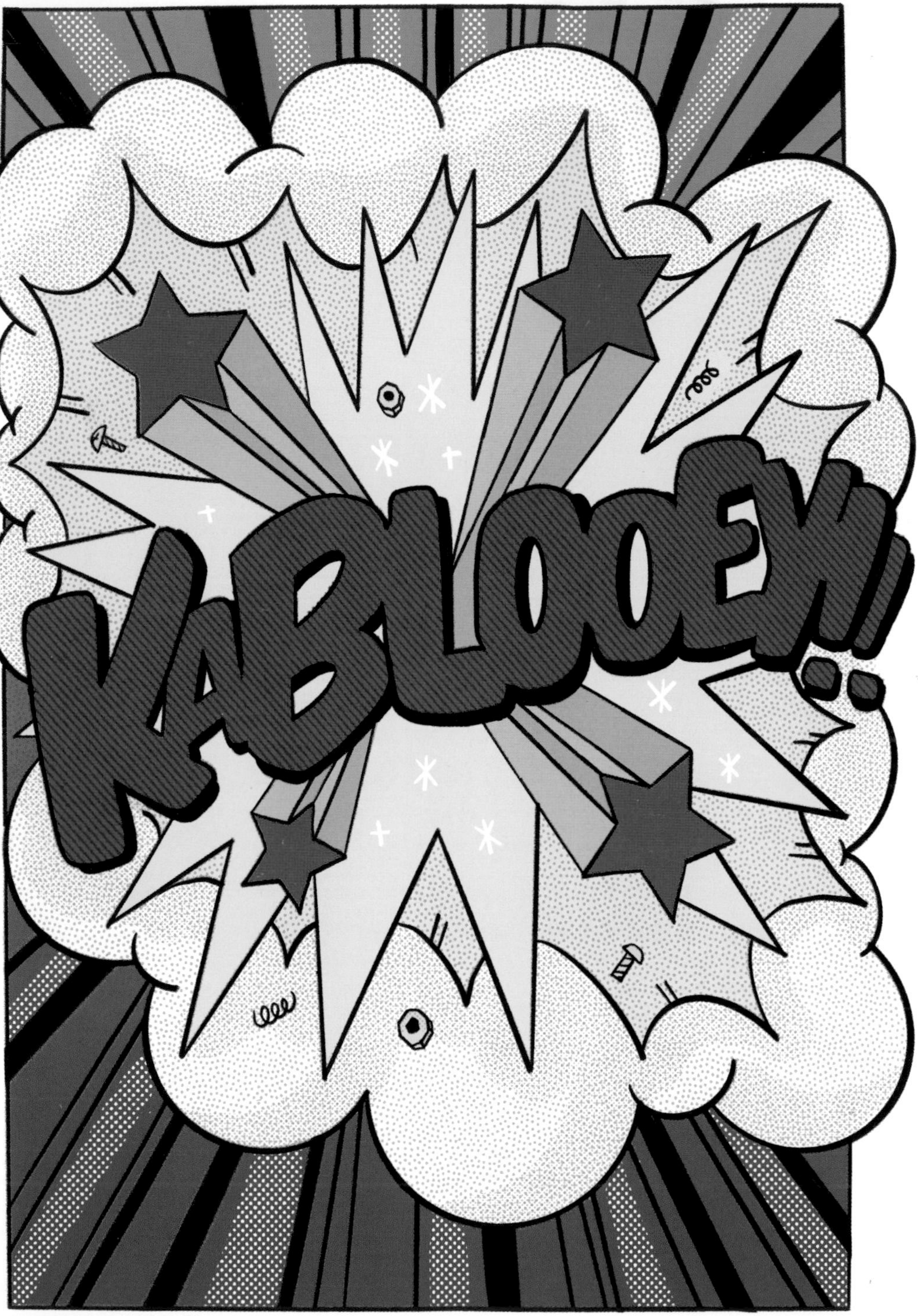
KABLOOEY!!...

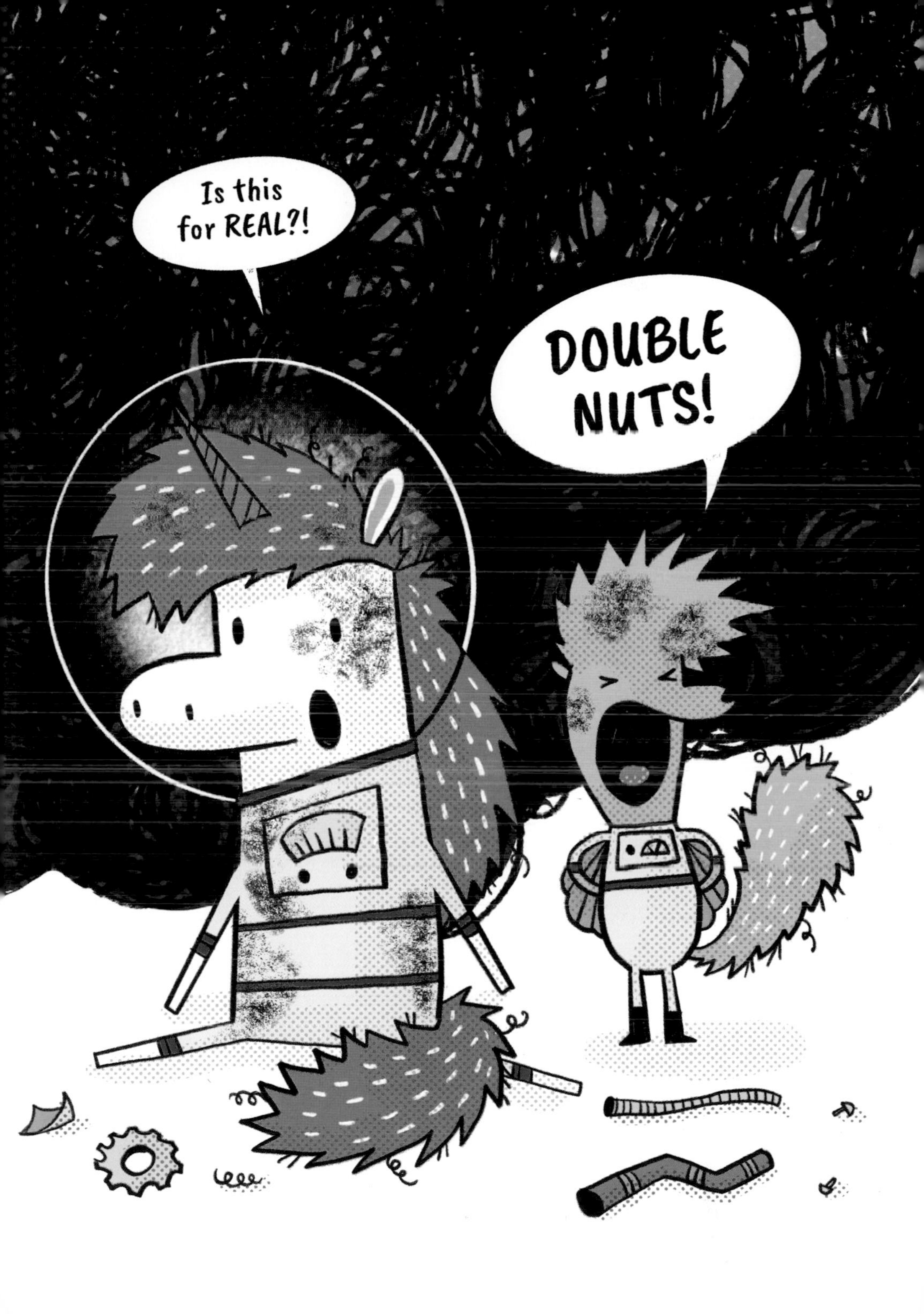
Is this for REAL?!
DOUBLE NUTS!

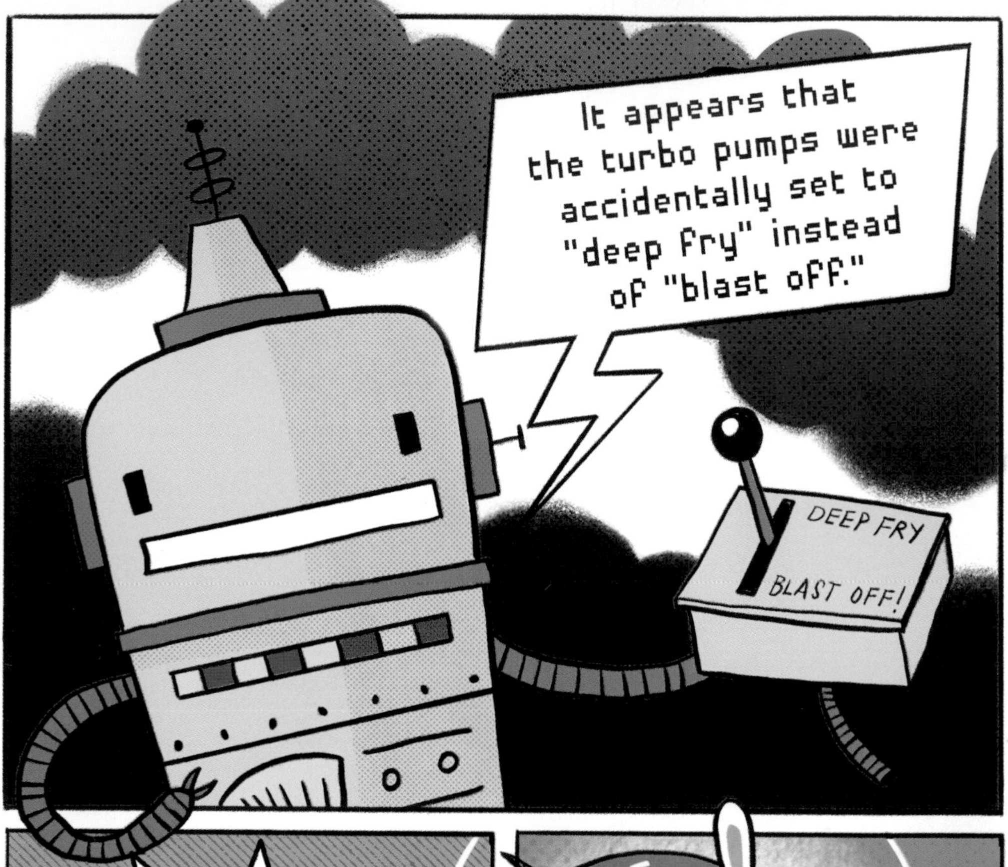
It appears that the turbo pumps were accidentally set to "deep fry" instead of "blast off."
DEEP FRY
BLAST OFF!

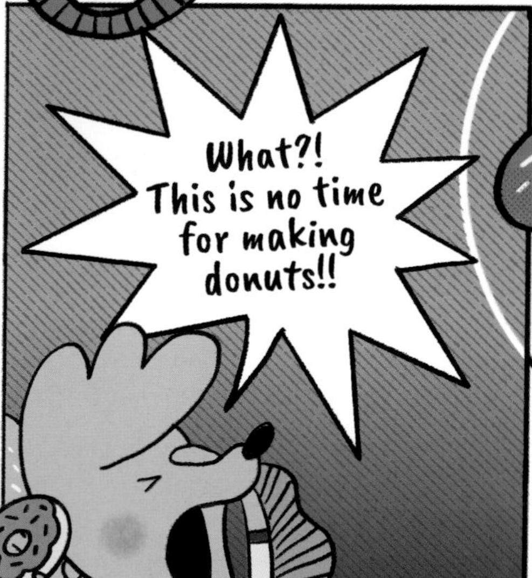
What?! This is no time for making donuts!!

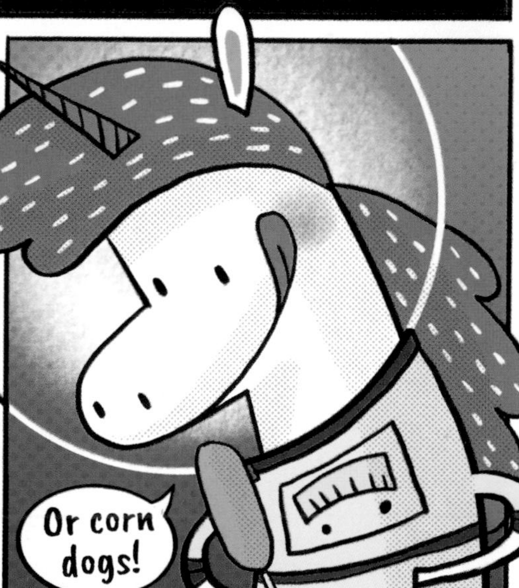
Or corn dogs!

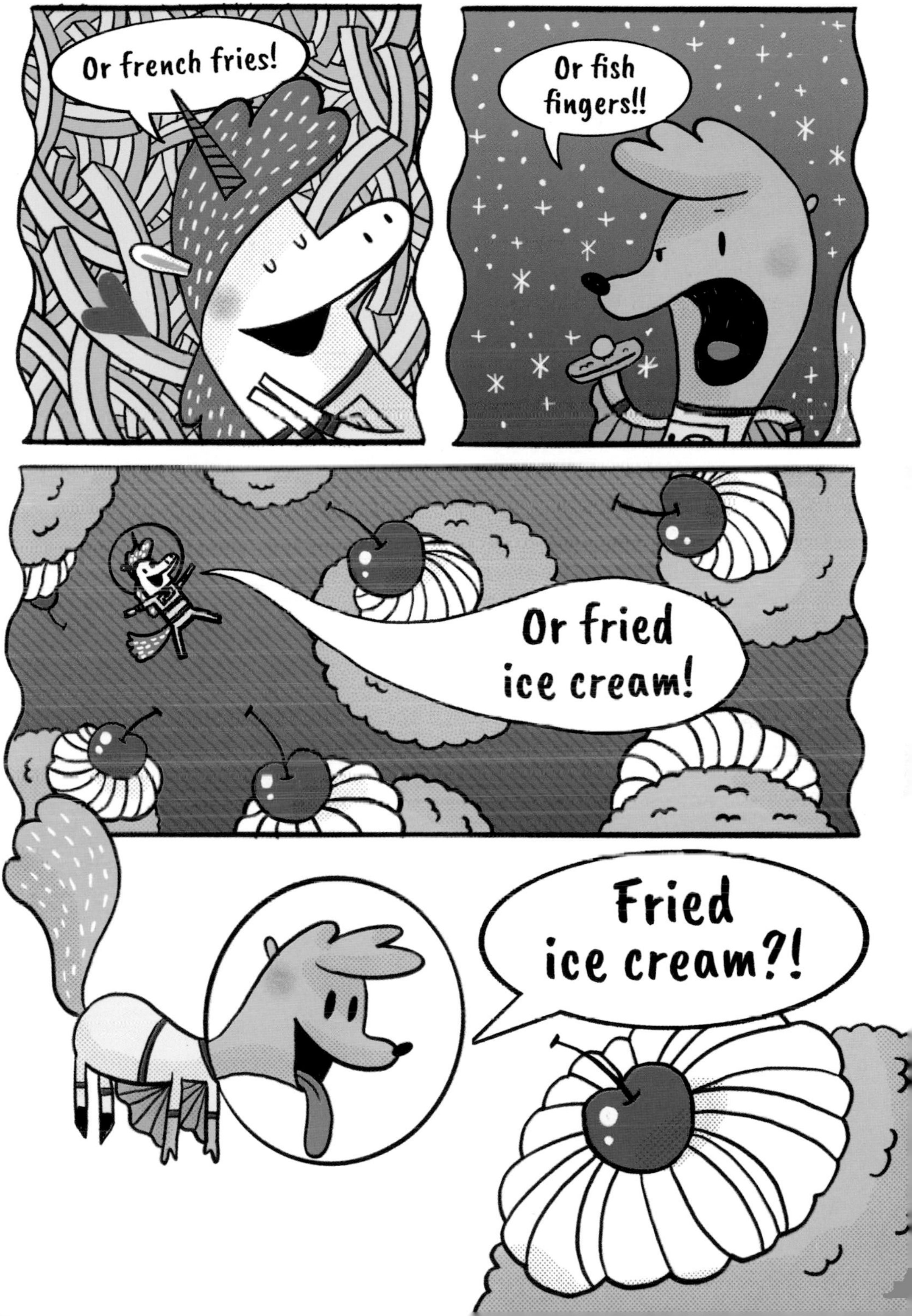
Or french fries!
Or fish fingers!!
Or fried ice cream!
Fried ice cream?!

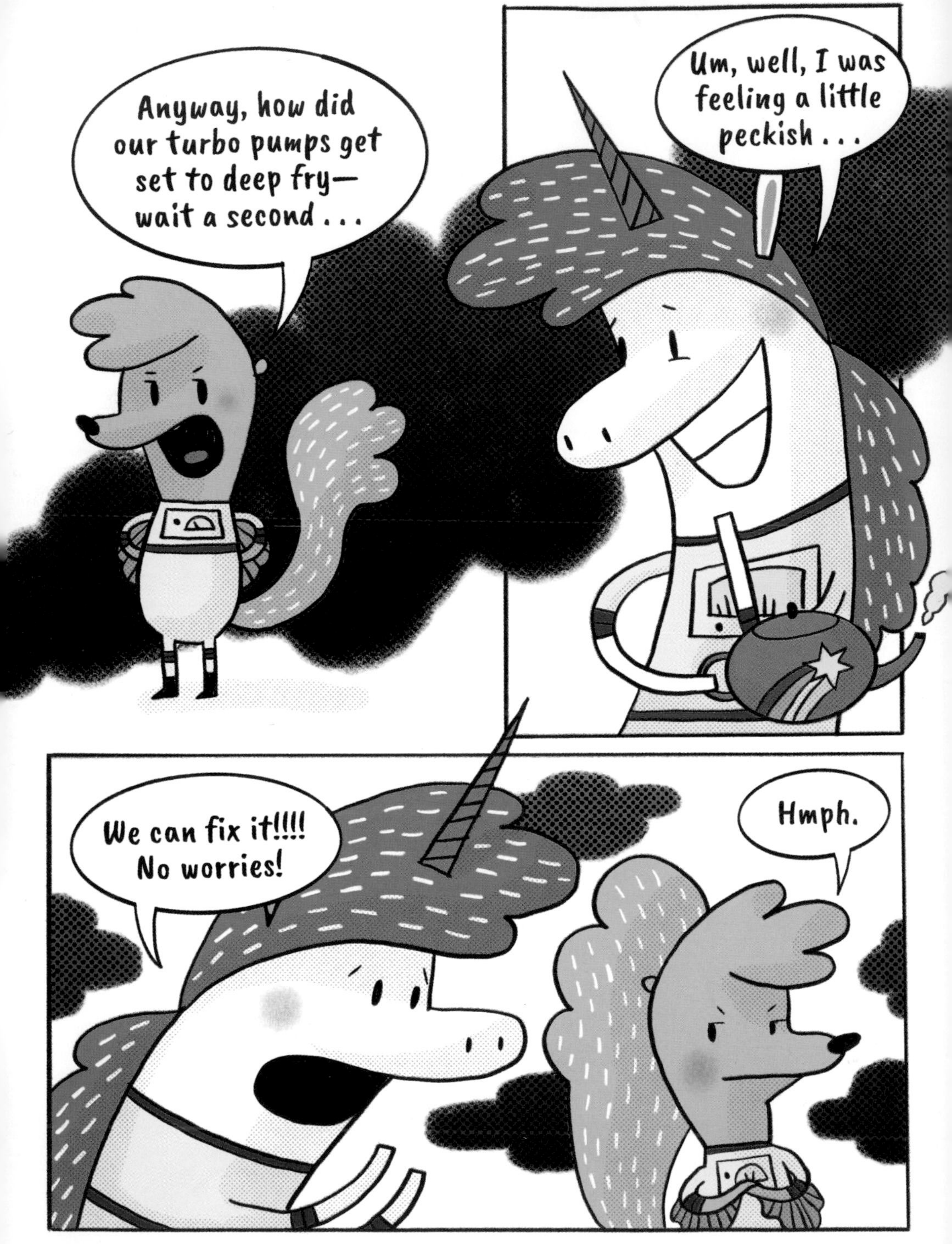
Anyway, how did our turbo pumps get set to deep fry—wait a second . . .
Um, well, I was feeling a little peckish . . .
We can fix it!!!! No worries!
Hmph.

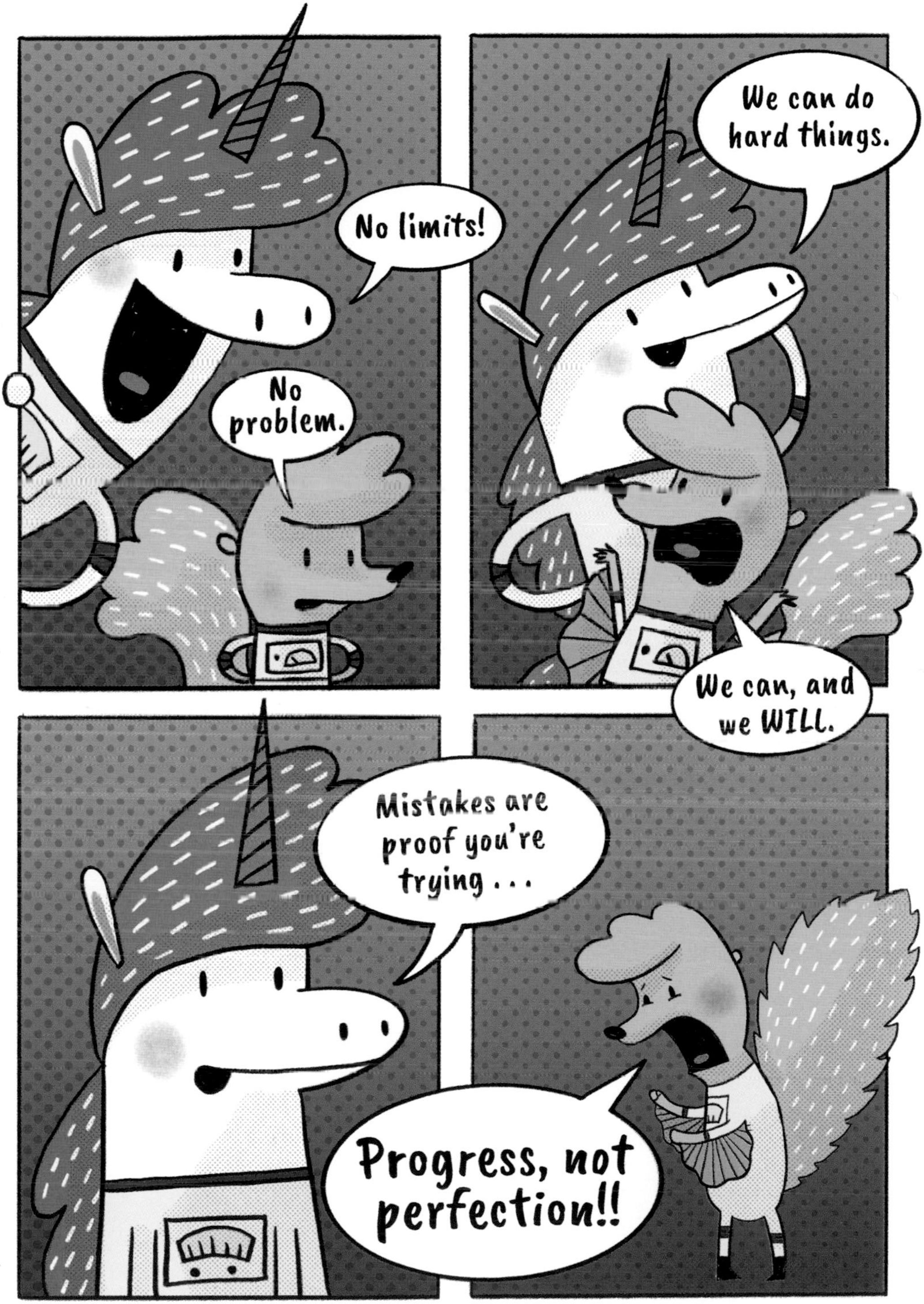
No limits!
No problem.
We can do hard things.
We can, and we WILL.
Mistakes are proof you're trying . . .
Progress, not perfection!!

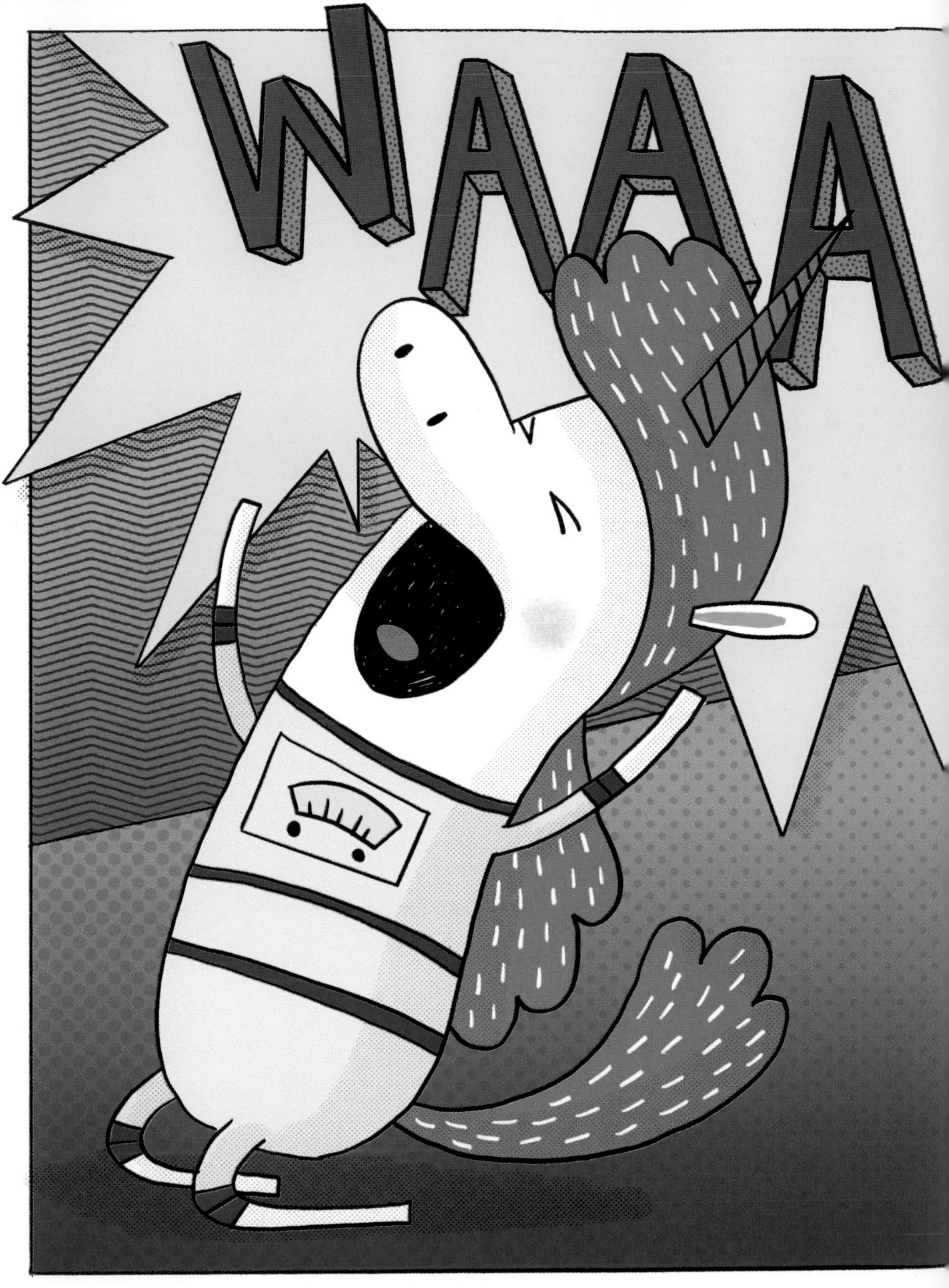
WAAAA

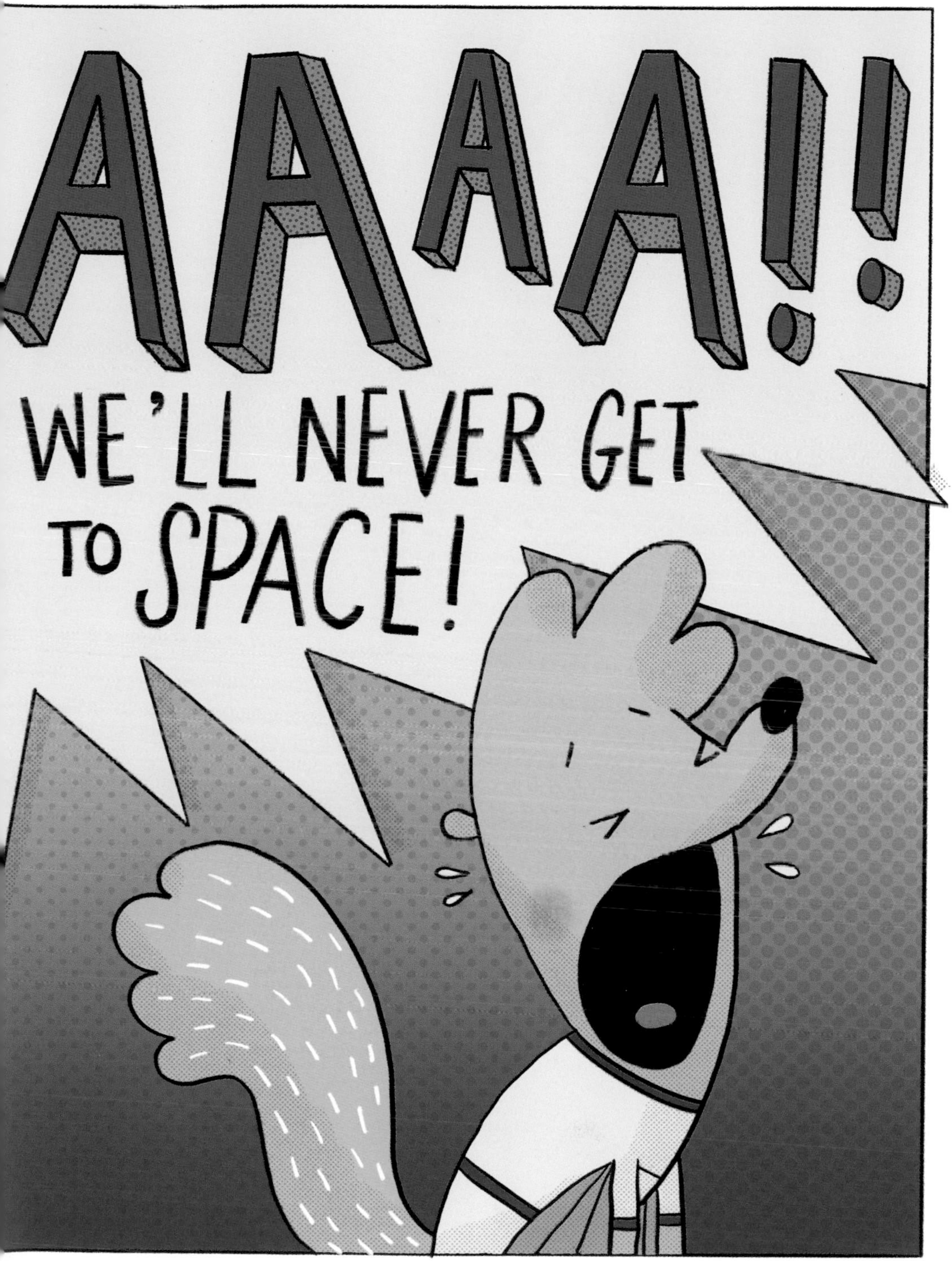
AAAA!!
WE'LL NEVER GET TO SPACE!

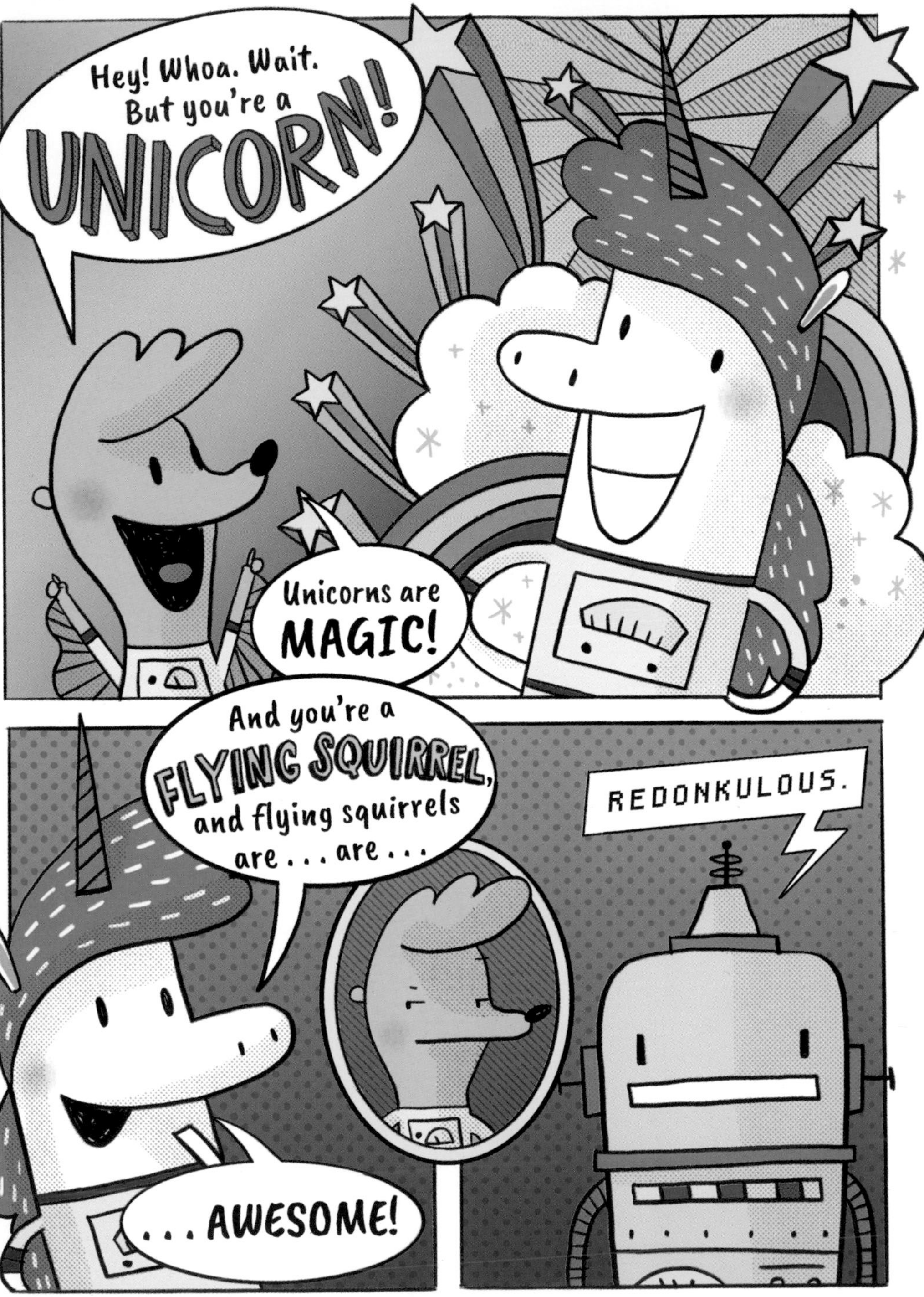
Hey! Whoa. Wait. But you're a UNICORN!
Unicorns are MAGIC!
And you're a FLYING SQUIRREL, and flying squirrels are . . . are . . .
REDONKULOUS.
. . . AWESOME!

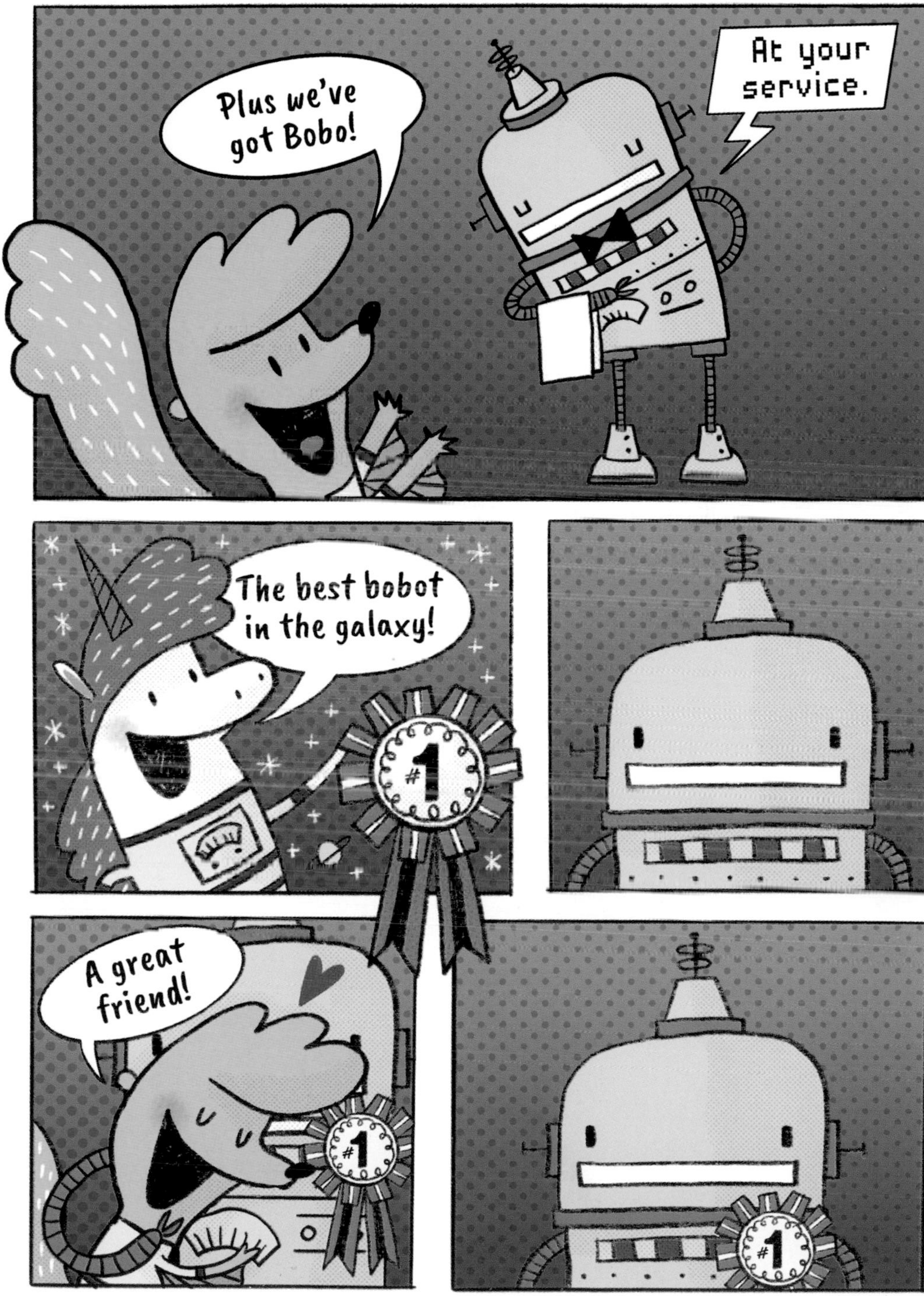
Plus we've got Bobo!
At your service.
The best bobot in the galaxy!
A great friend!

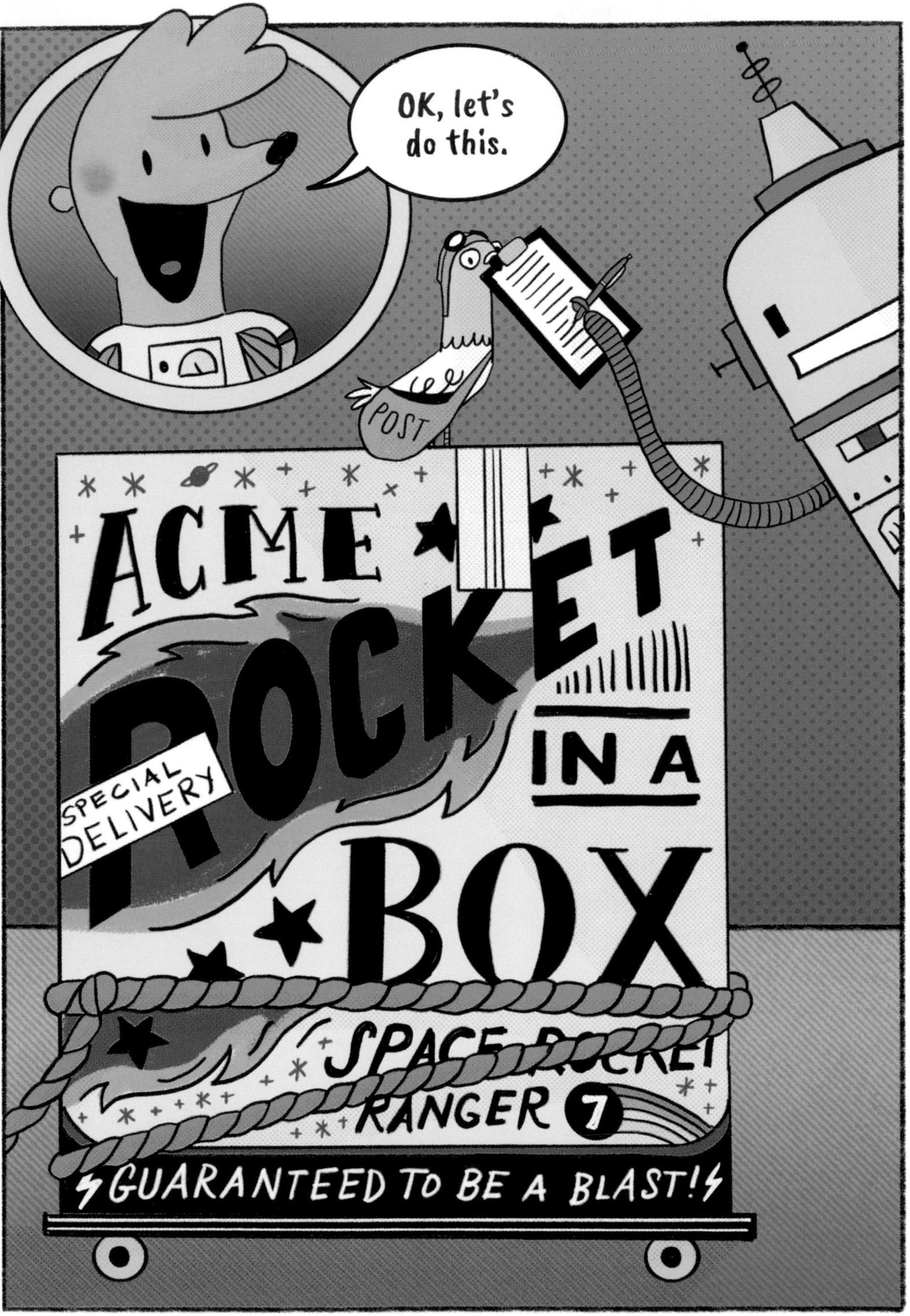
OK, let's do this.
POST
ACME ROCKET IN A BOX
SPECIAL DELIVERY
SPACE
RANGER 7
GUARANTEED TO BE A BLAST!

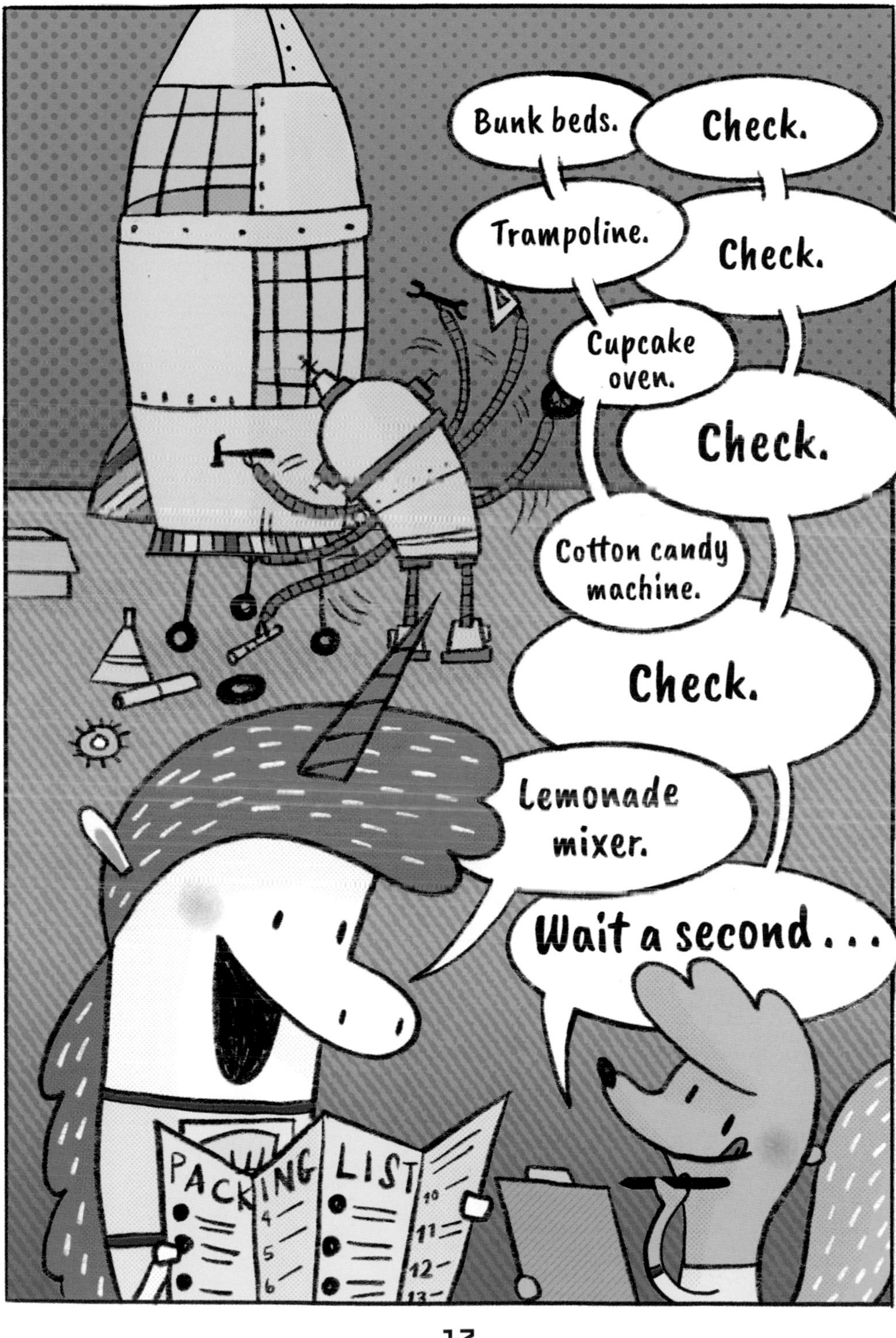
Bunk beds.
Check.
Trampoline.
Check.
Cupcake oven.
Check.
Cotton candy machine.
Check.
Lemonade mixer.
Wait a second . . .
PACKING LIST

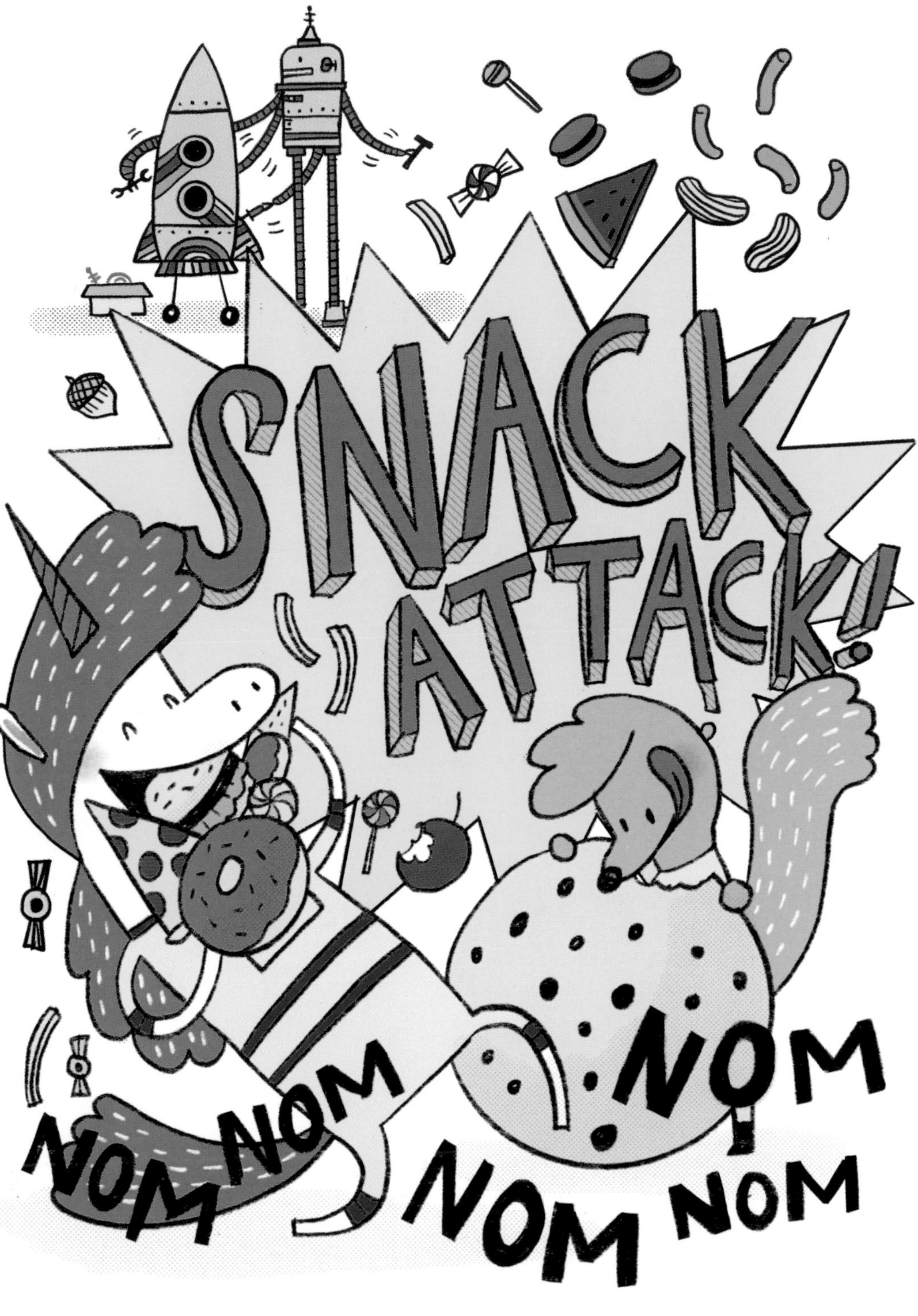
SNACK ATTACK!
NOM NOM
NOM
NOM
NOM NOM

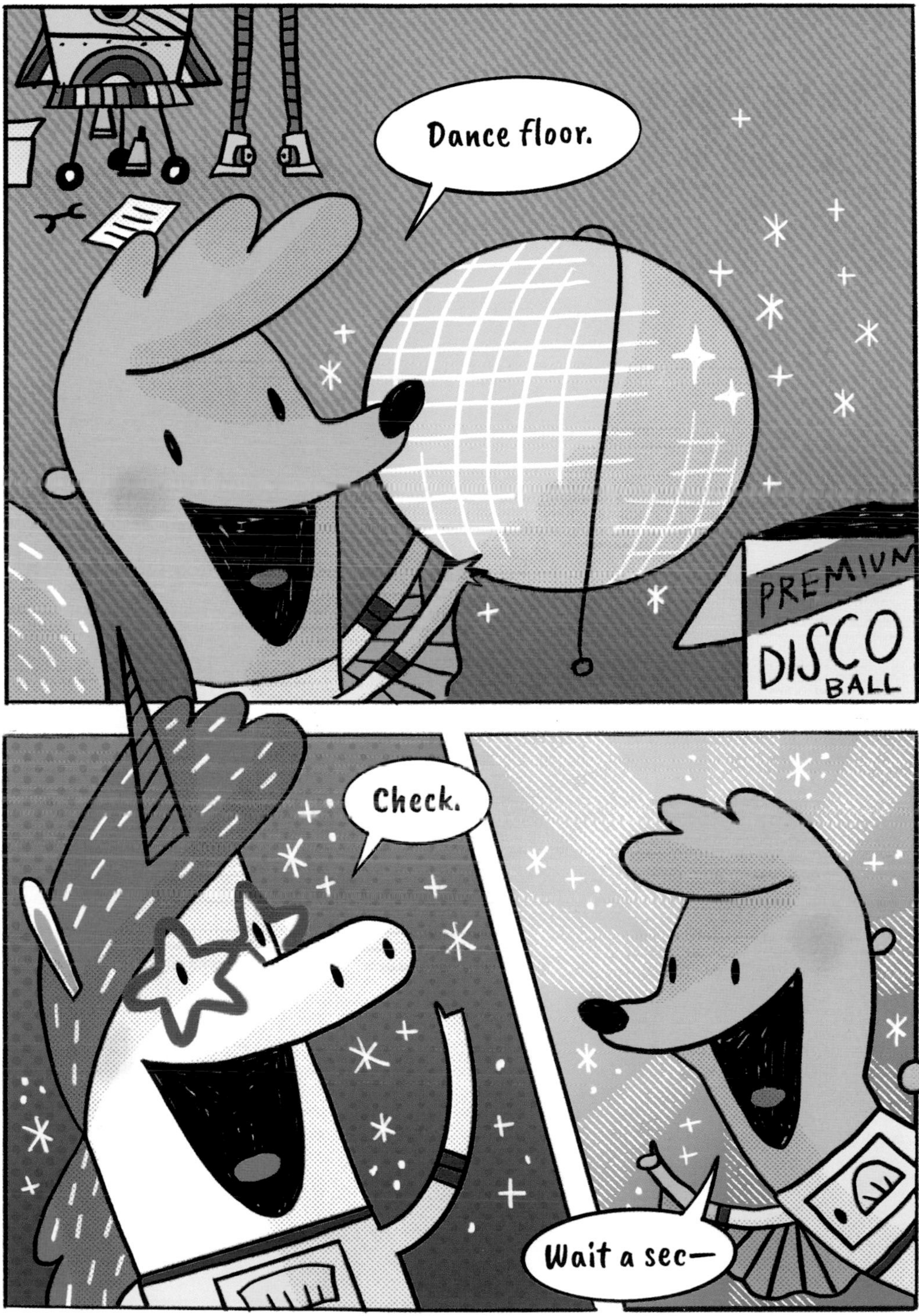
Dance floor.
PREMIUM
DISCO BALL
Check.
Wait a sec—

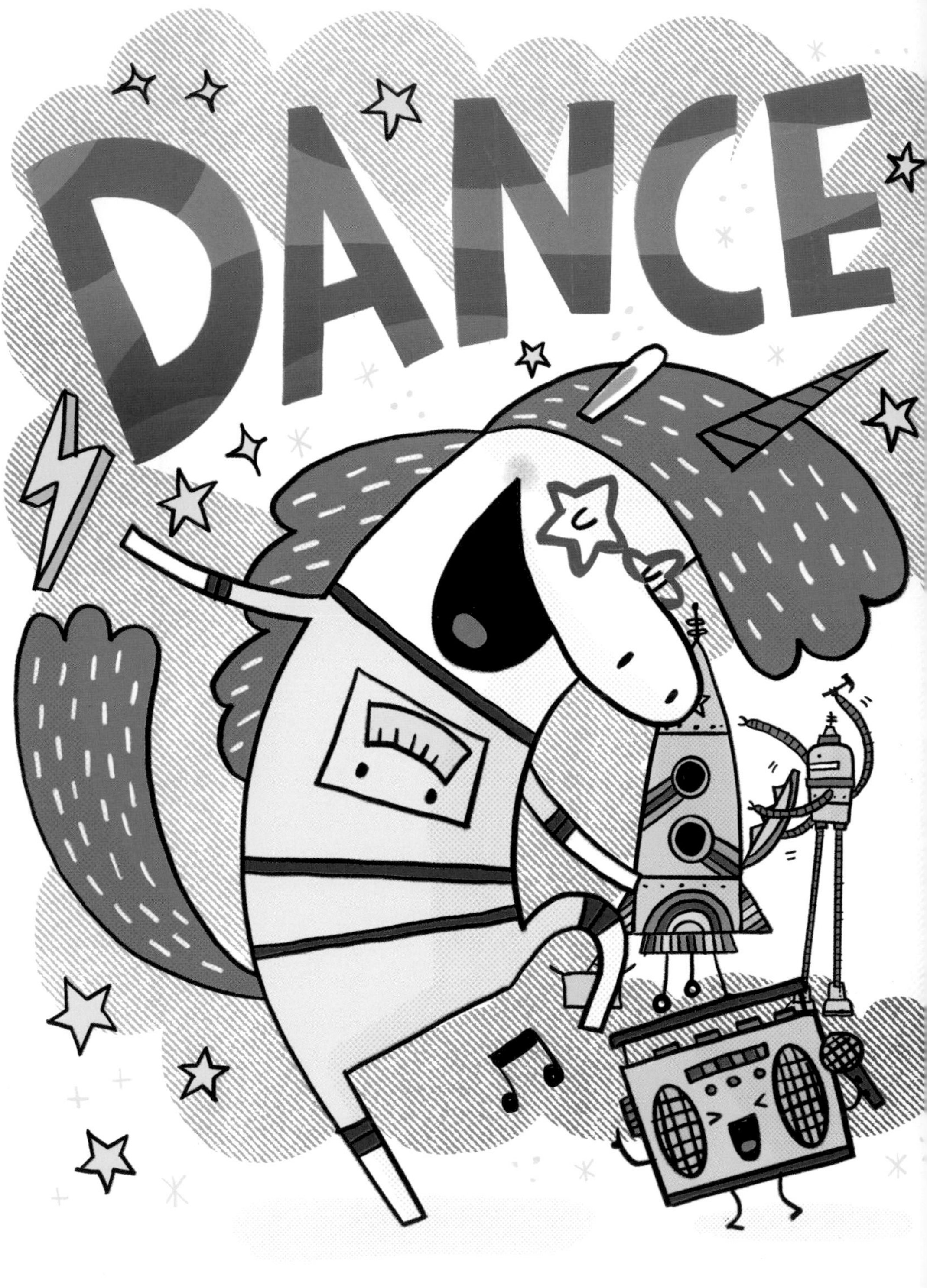
DANCE

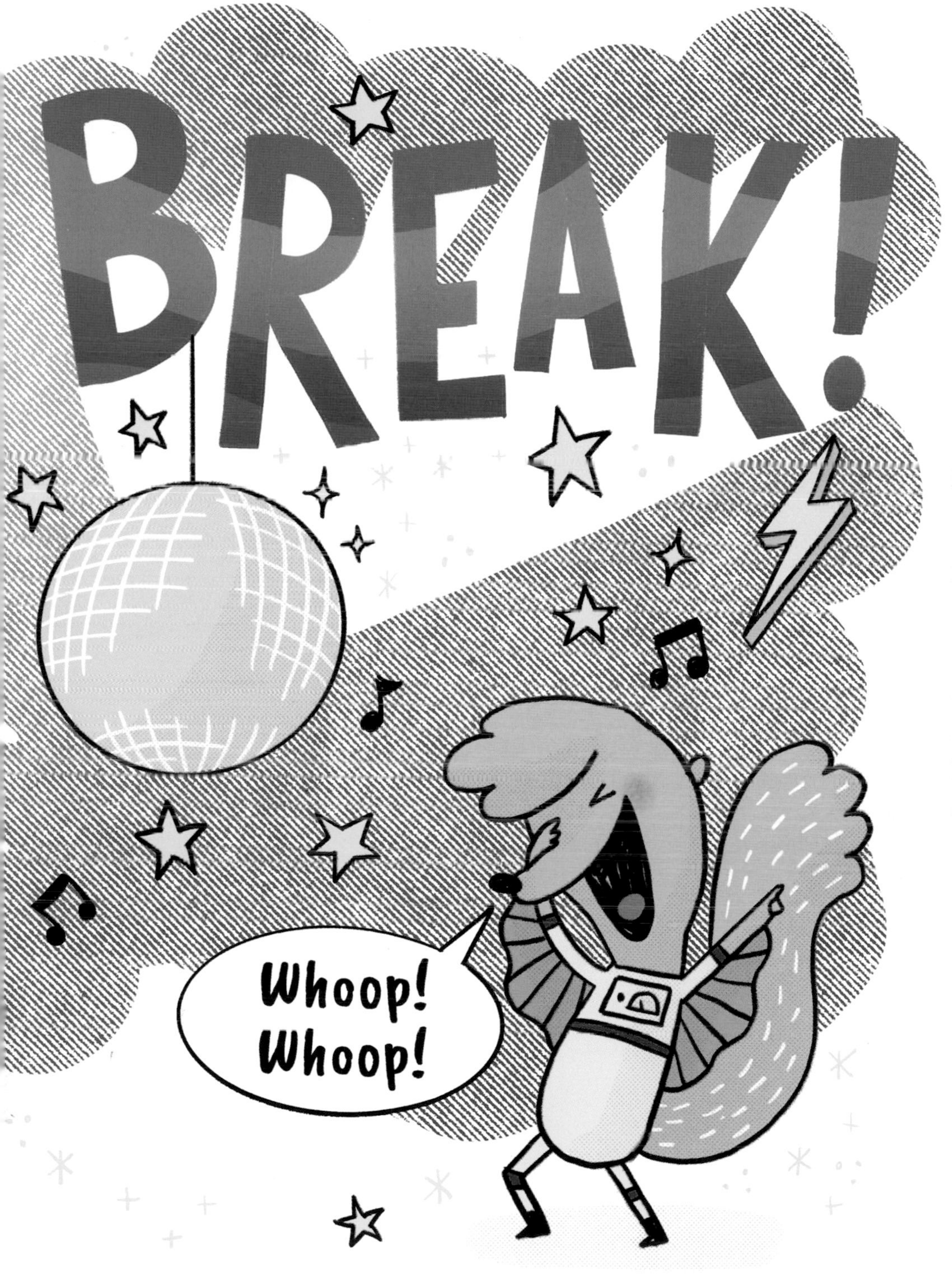
BREAK!
Whoop! Whoop!

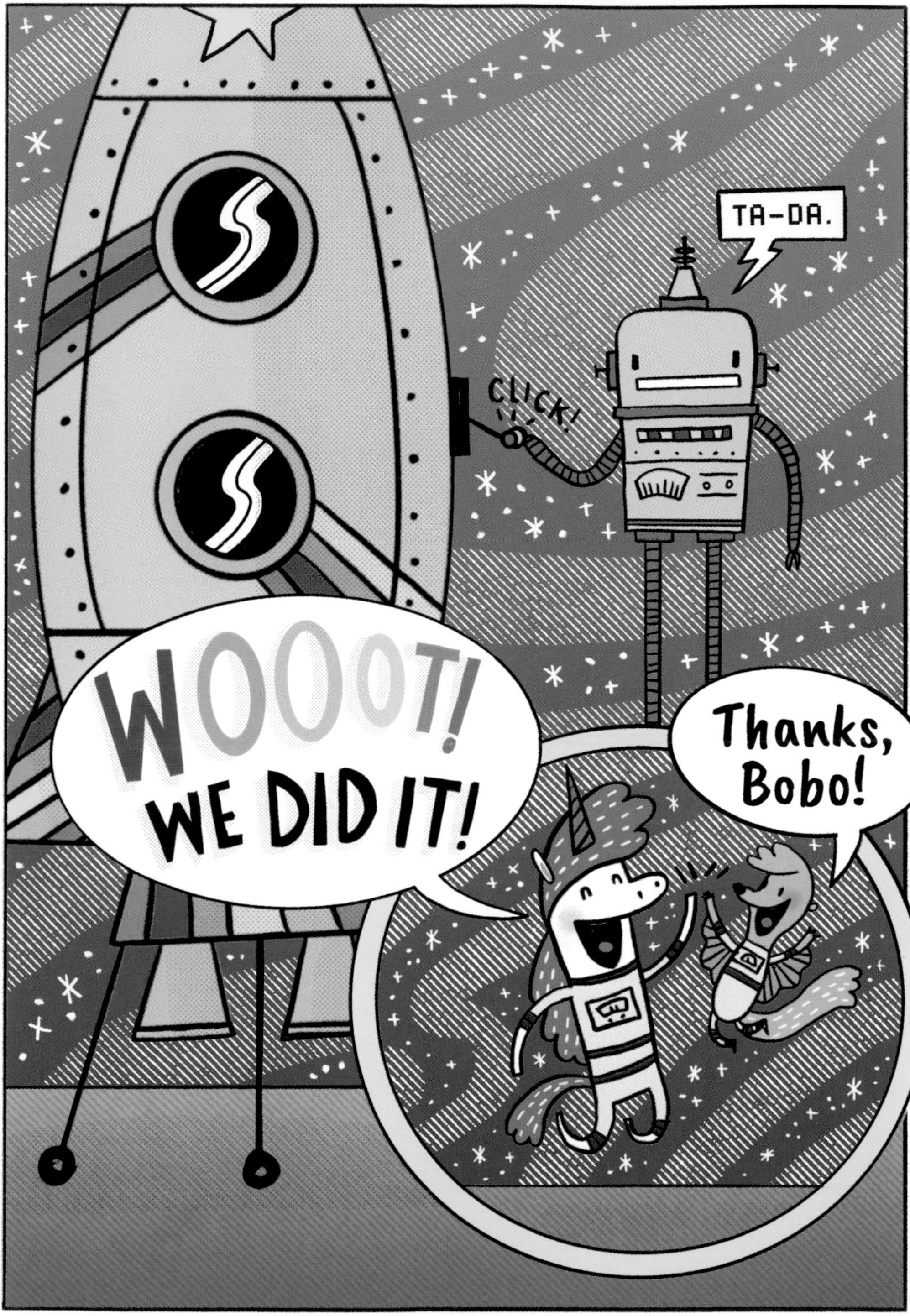
TA-DA.
CLICK!
WOOOT! WE DID IT!
Thanks, Bobo!

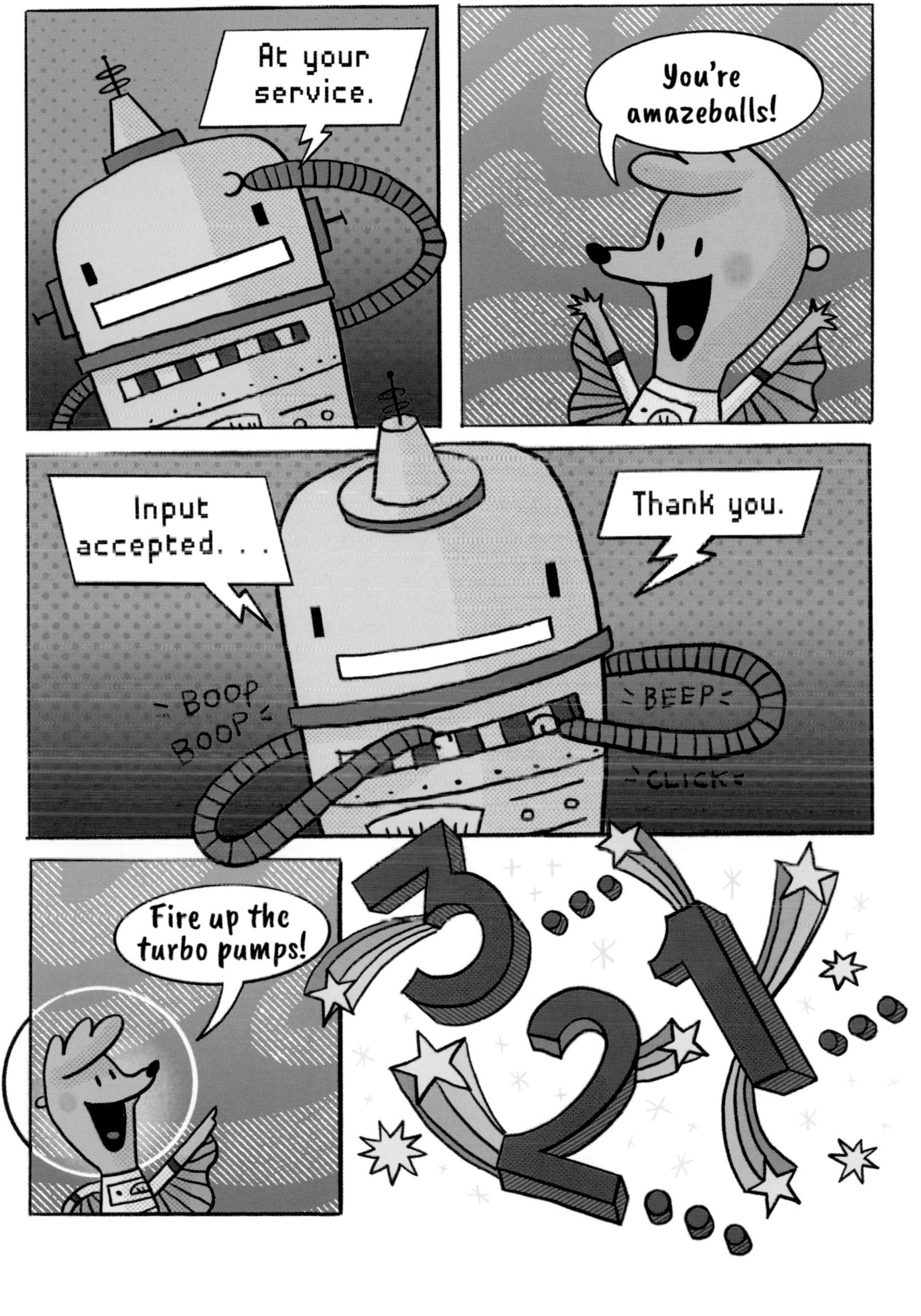
At your service.
You're amazeballs!
Input accepted. . .
Thank you.
BOOP BOOP
BEEP
CLICK
Fire up the turbo pumps!
3...
2...
1...

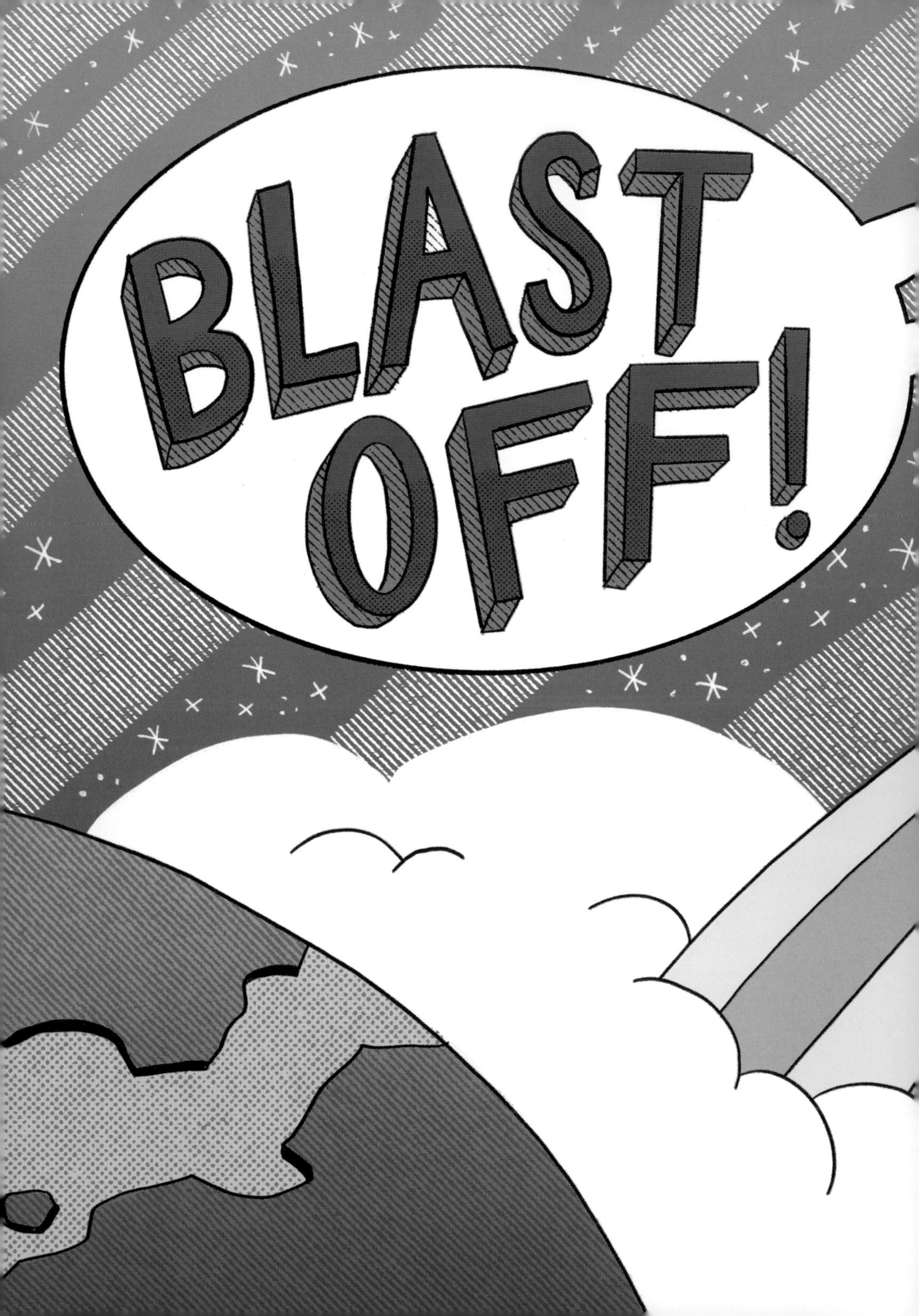
BLAST OFF!

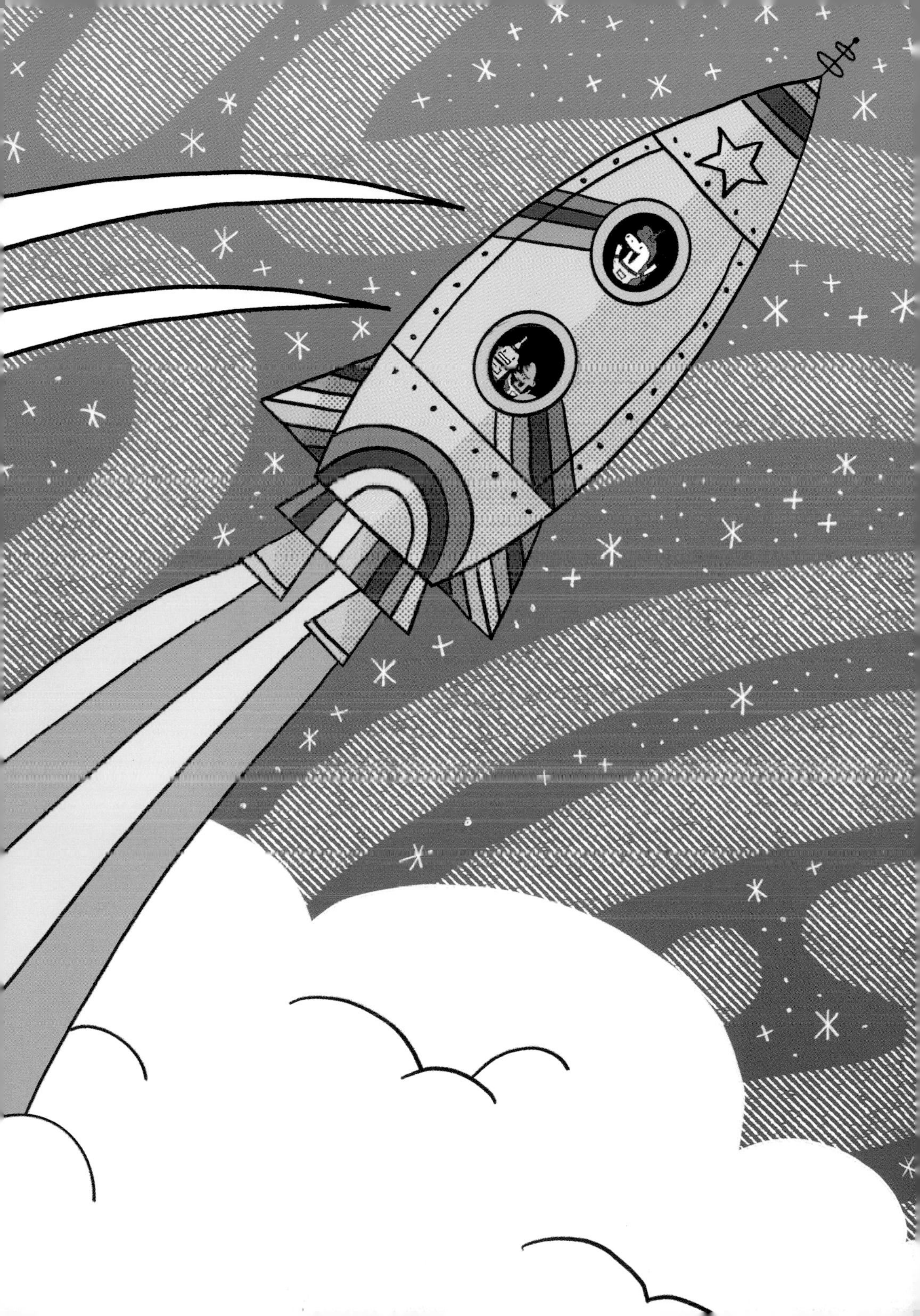

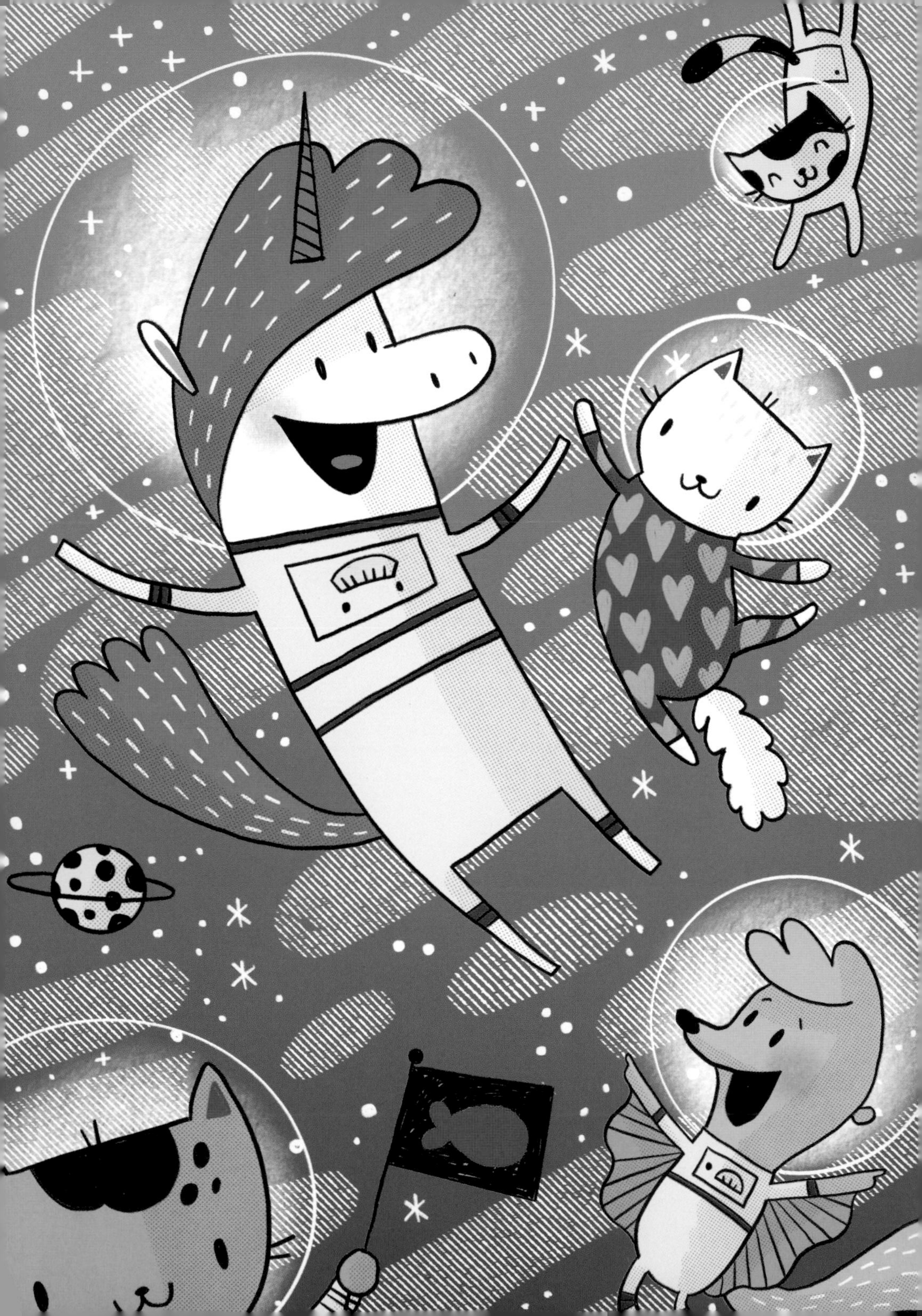

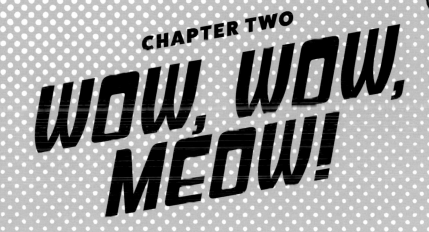

CHAPTER TWO

WOW, WOW, MEOW!

You're the cat's pajamas!

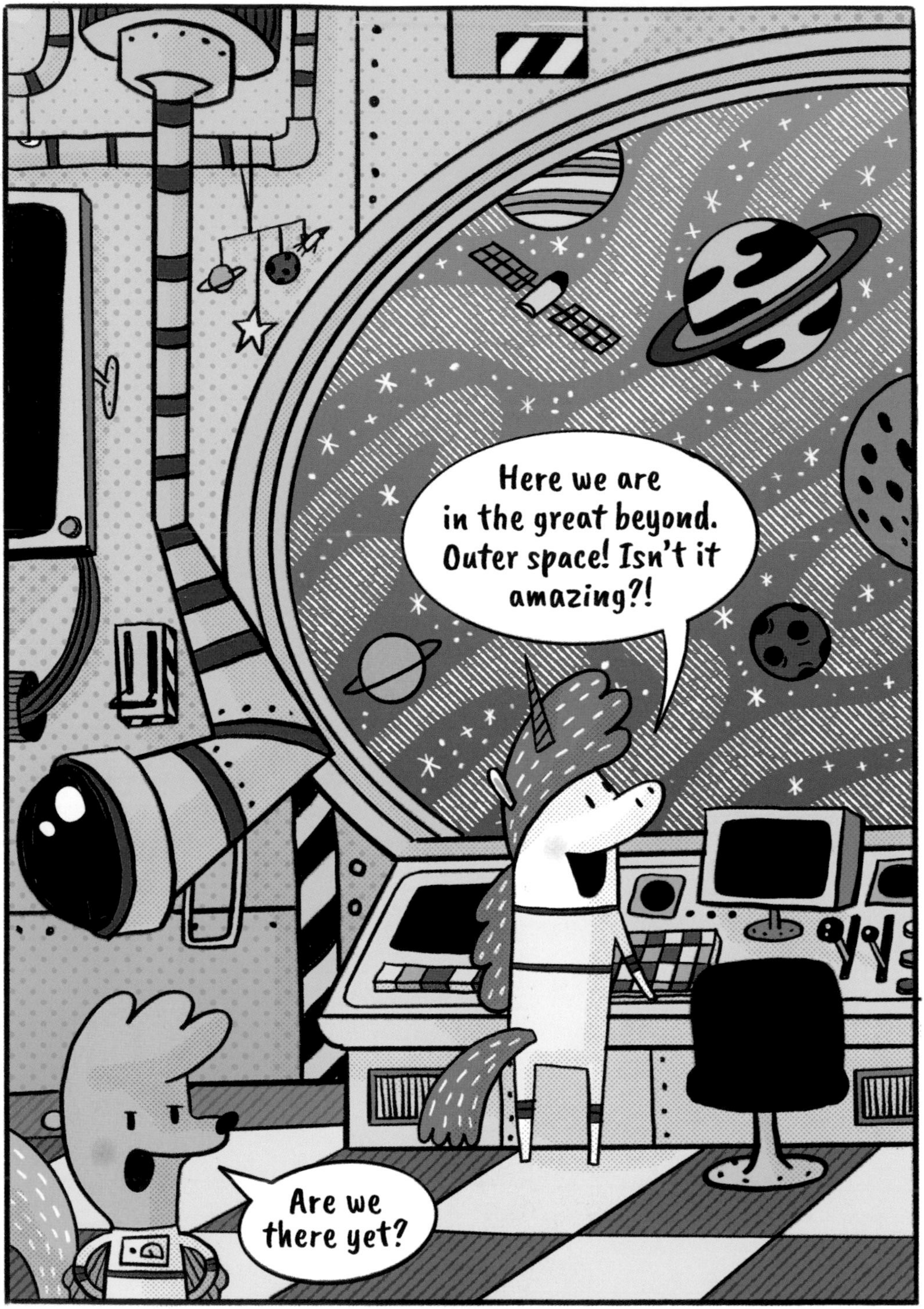
Here we are in the great beyond. Outer space! Isn't it amazing?!
Are we there yet?

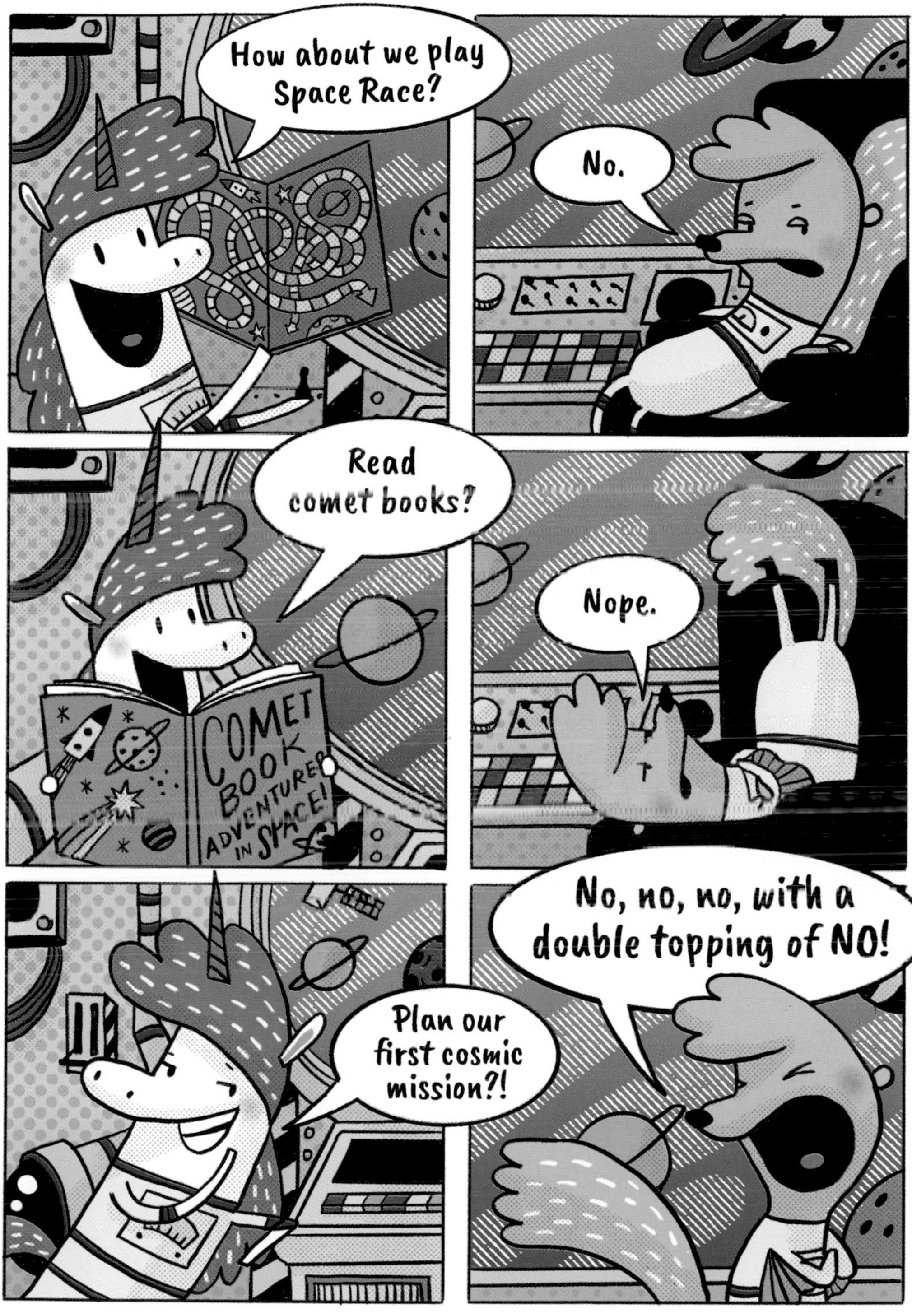
How about we play Space Race?
No.
Read comet books?
COMET BOOK ADVENTURES IN SPACE!
Nope.
Plan our first cosmic mission?!
No, no, no, with a double topping of NO!

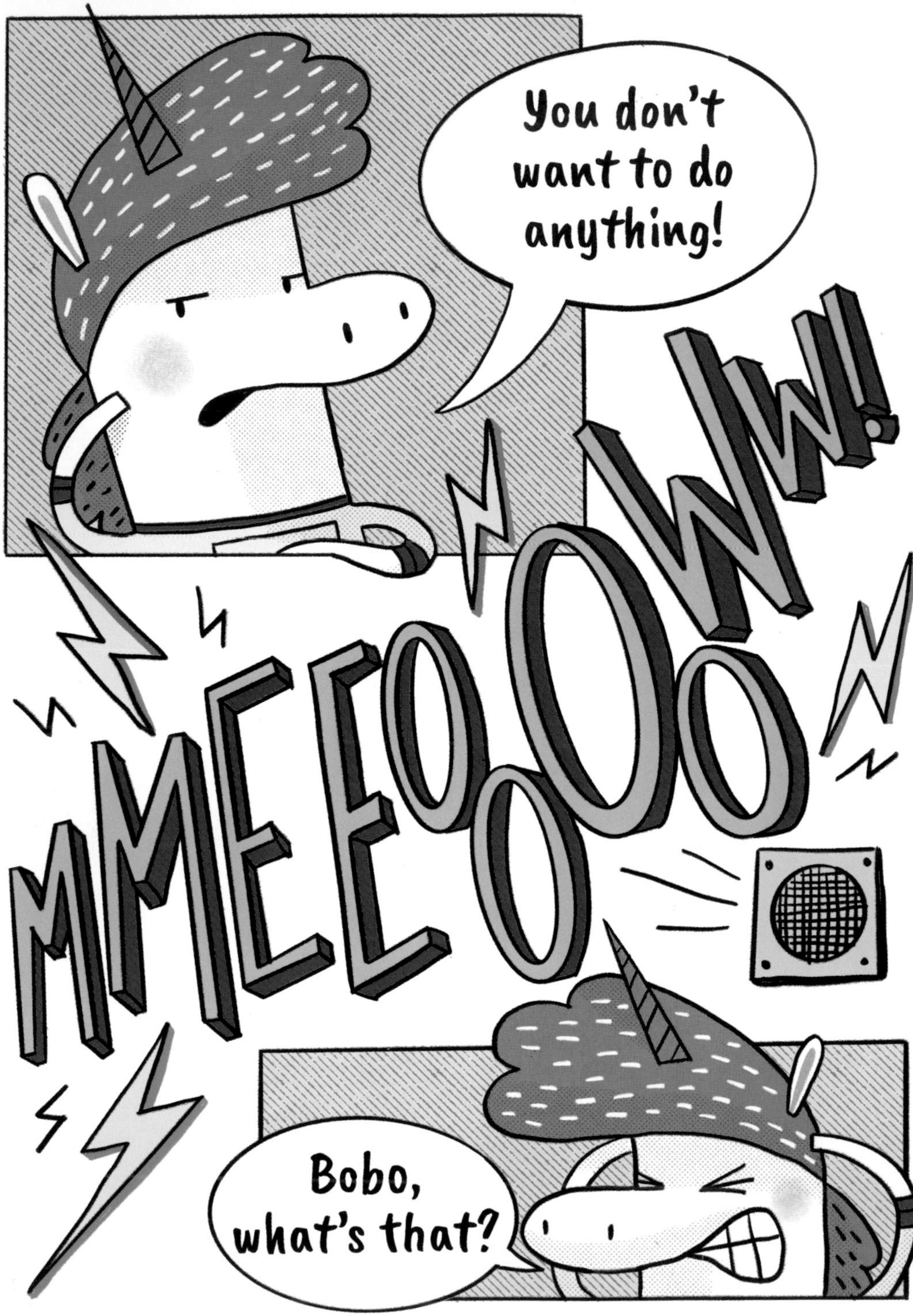
You don't want to do anything!
MMEEOOOOOWW!
Bobo, what's that?

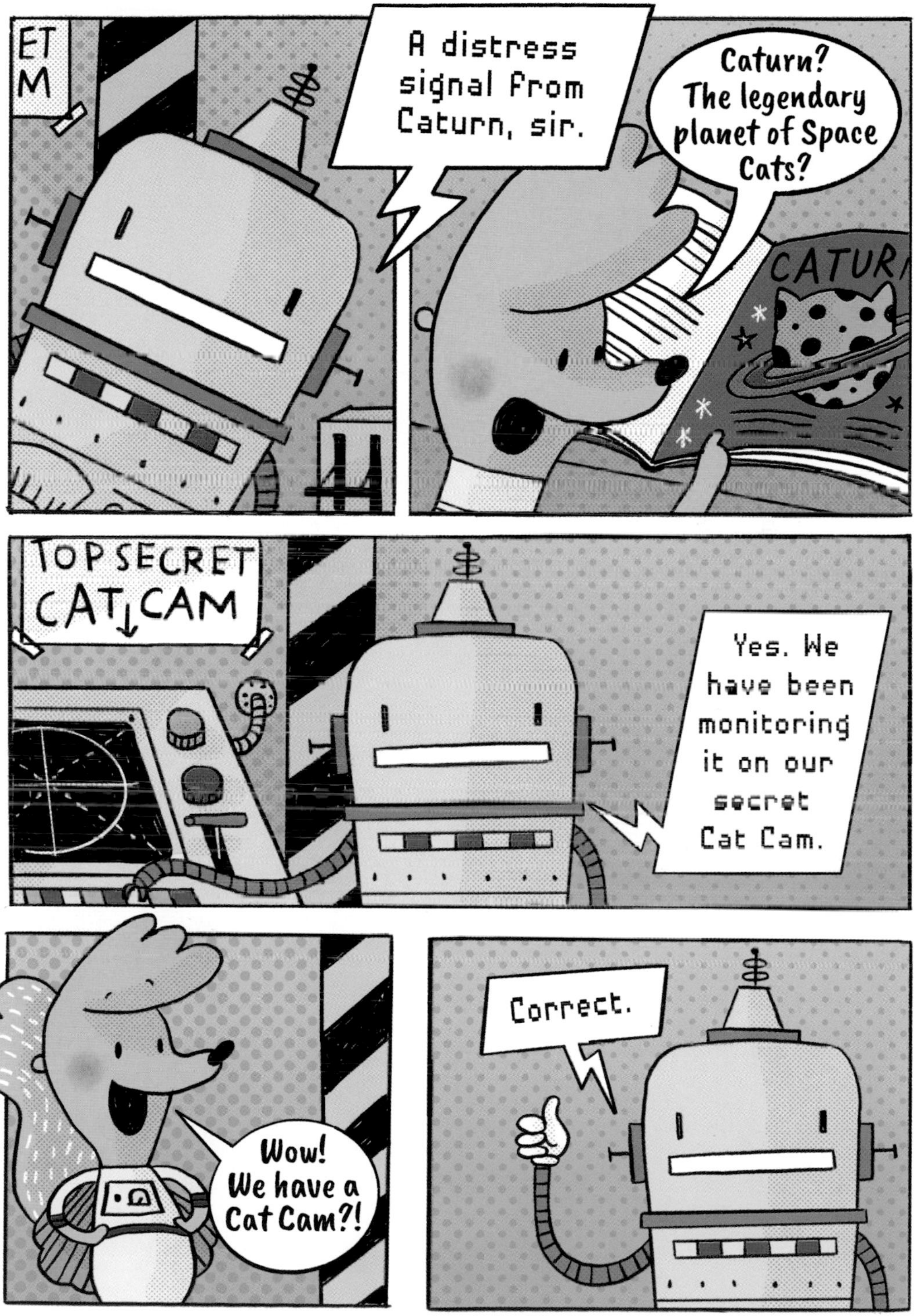
ET M
A distress signal from Caturn, sir.
Caturn? The legendary planet of Space Cats?
CATURN
TOP SECRET CAT CAM
Yes. We have been monitoring it on our secret Cat Cam.
Wow! We have a Cat Cam?!
Correct.

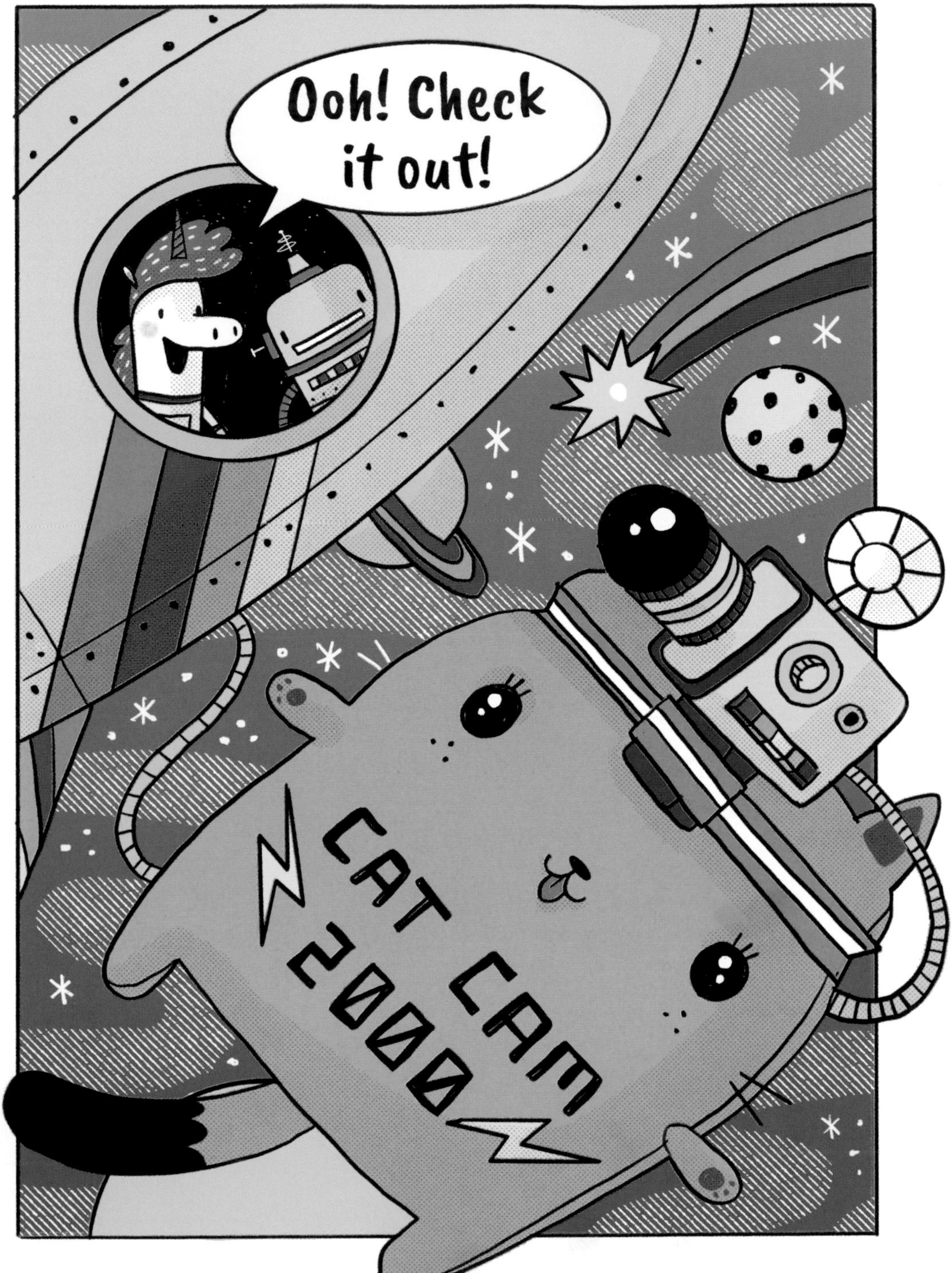
Ooh! Check it out!
CAT CAM 2000

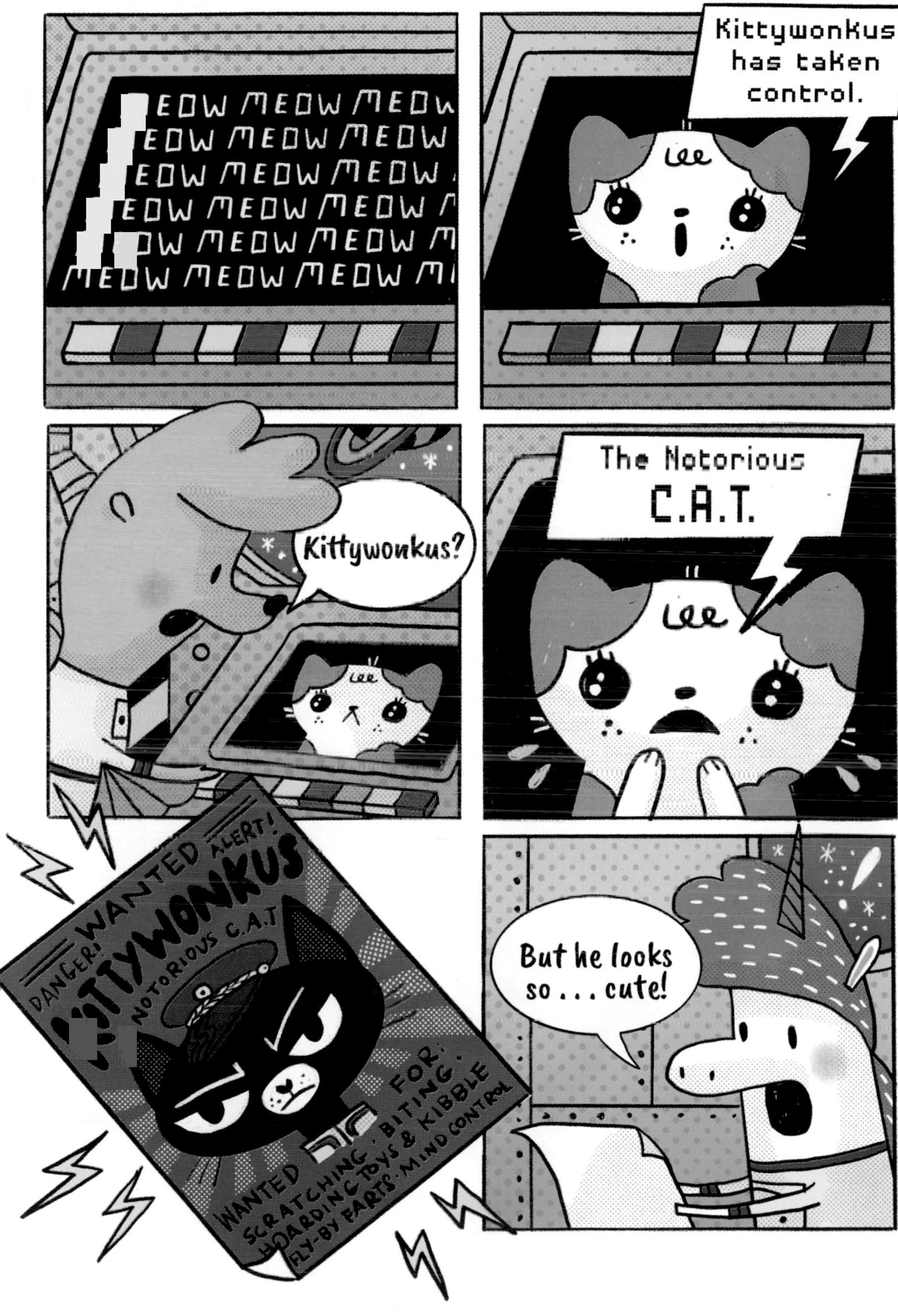
EOW MEOW MEOW
EOW MEOW MEOW
EOW MEOW MEOW
EOW MEOW MEOW
OW MEOW MEOW
MEOW MEOW MEOW
Kittywonkus has taken control.
Kittywonkus?
The Notorious C.A.T.
DANGER! WANTED ALERT!
ITTYWONKUS
NOTORIOUS C.A.T
WANTED FOR: SCRATCHING · BITING · HOARDING TOYS & KIBBLE · FLY-BY FARTS · MIND CONTROL
But he looks so . . . cute!

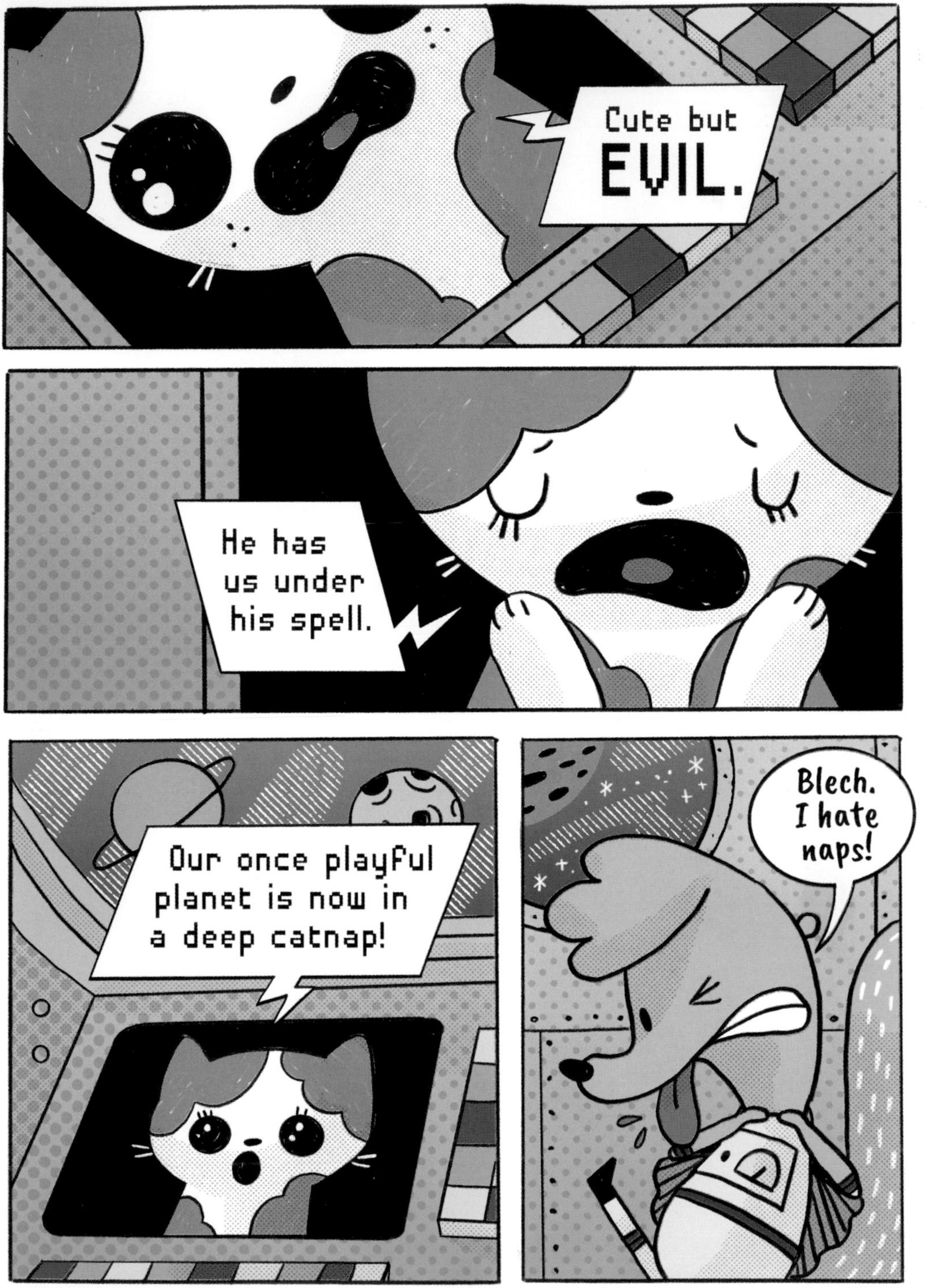
Cute but EVIL.
He has us under his spell.
Our once playful planet is now in a deep catnap!
Blech. I hate naps!

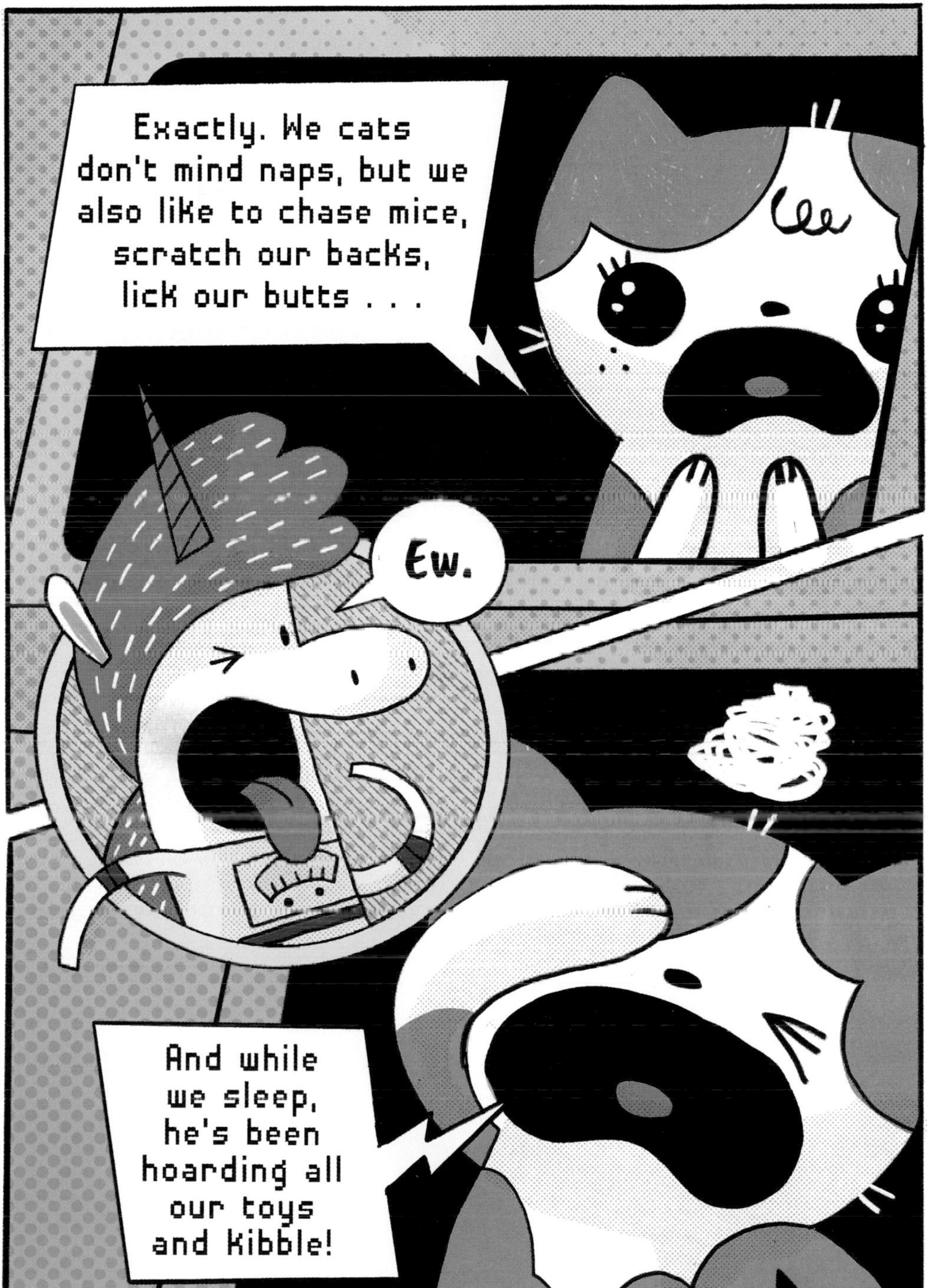
Exactly. We cats don't mind naps, but we also like to chase mice, scratch our backs, lick our butts . . .
Ew.
And while we sleep, he's been hoarding all our toys and kibble!

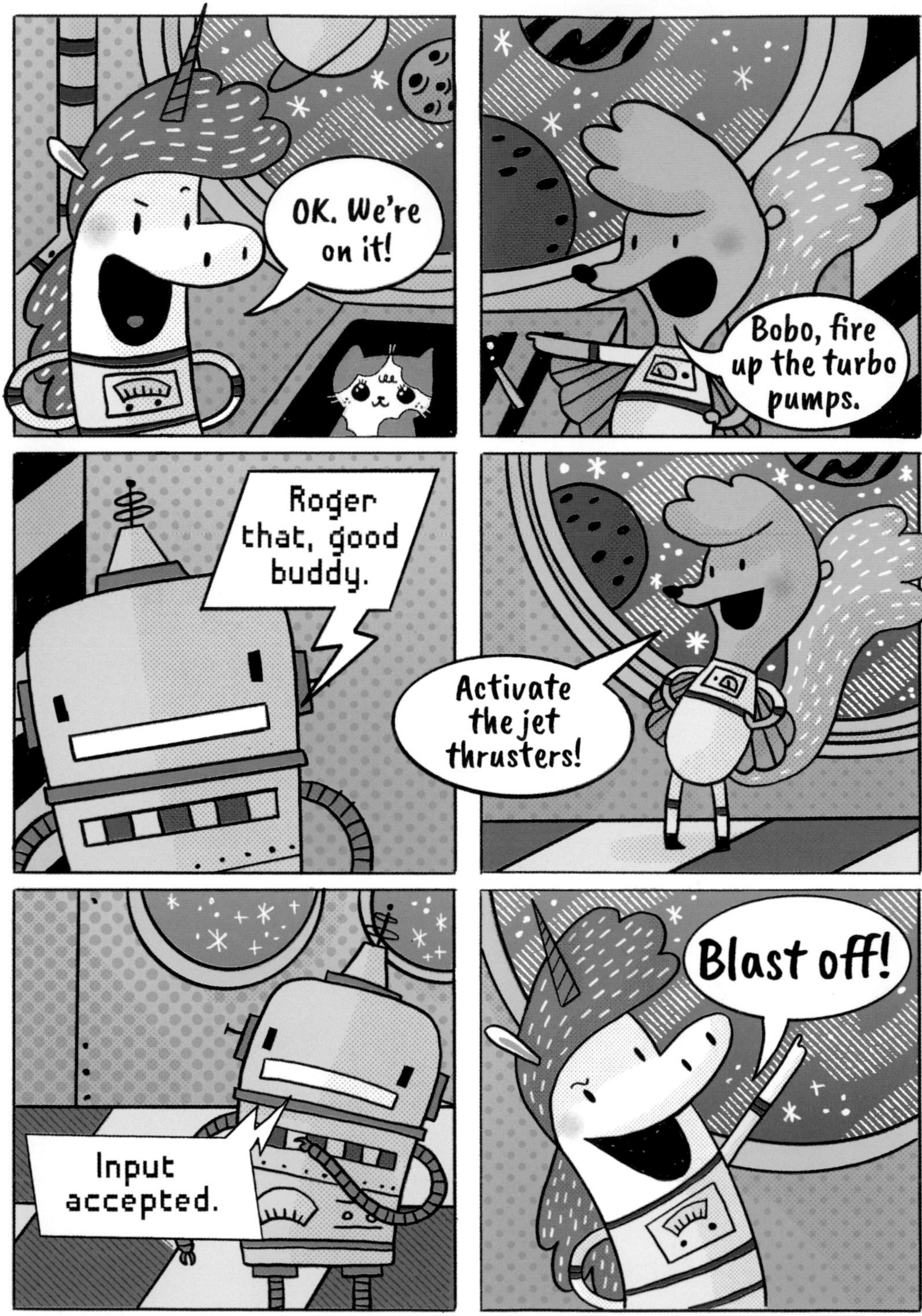
OK. We're on it!
Bobo, fire up the turbo pumps.
Roger that, good buddy.
Activate the jet thrusters!
Input accepted.
Blast off!

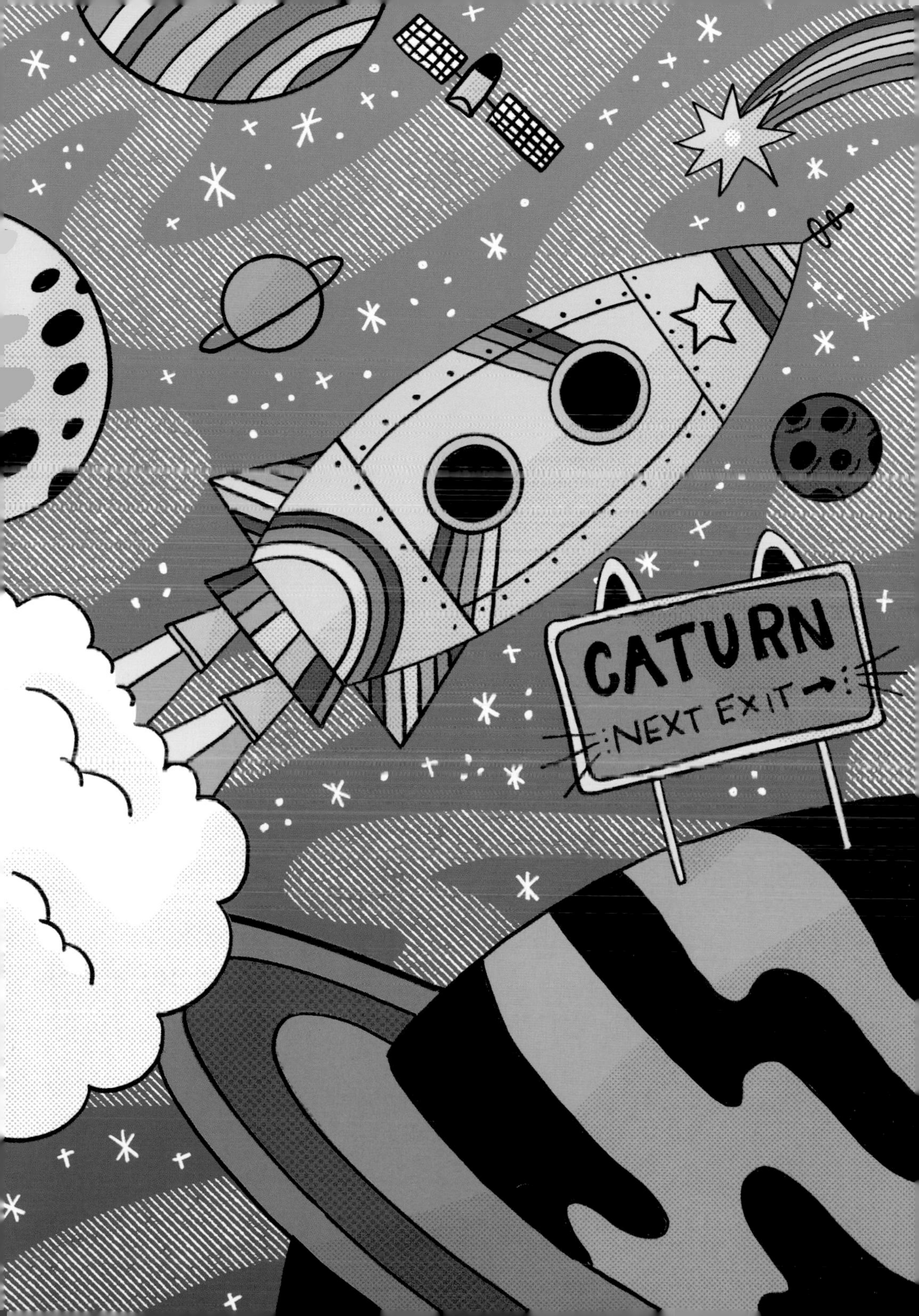
CATURN
NEXT EXIT →

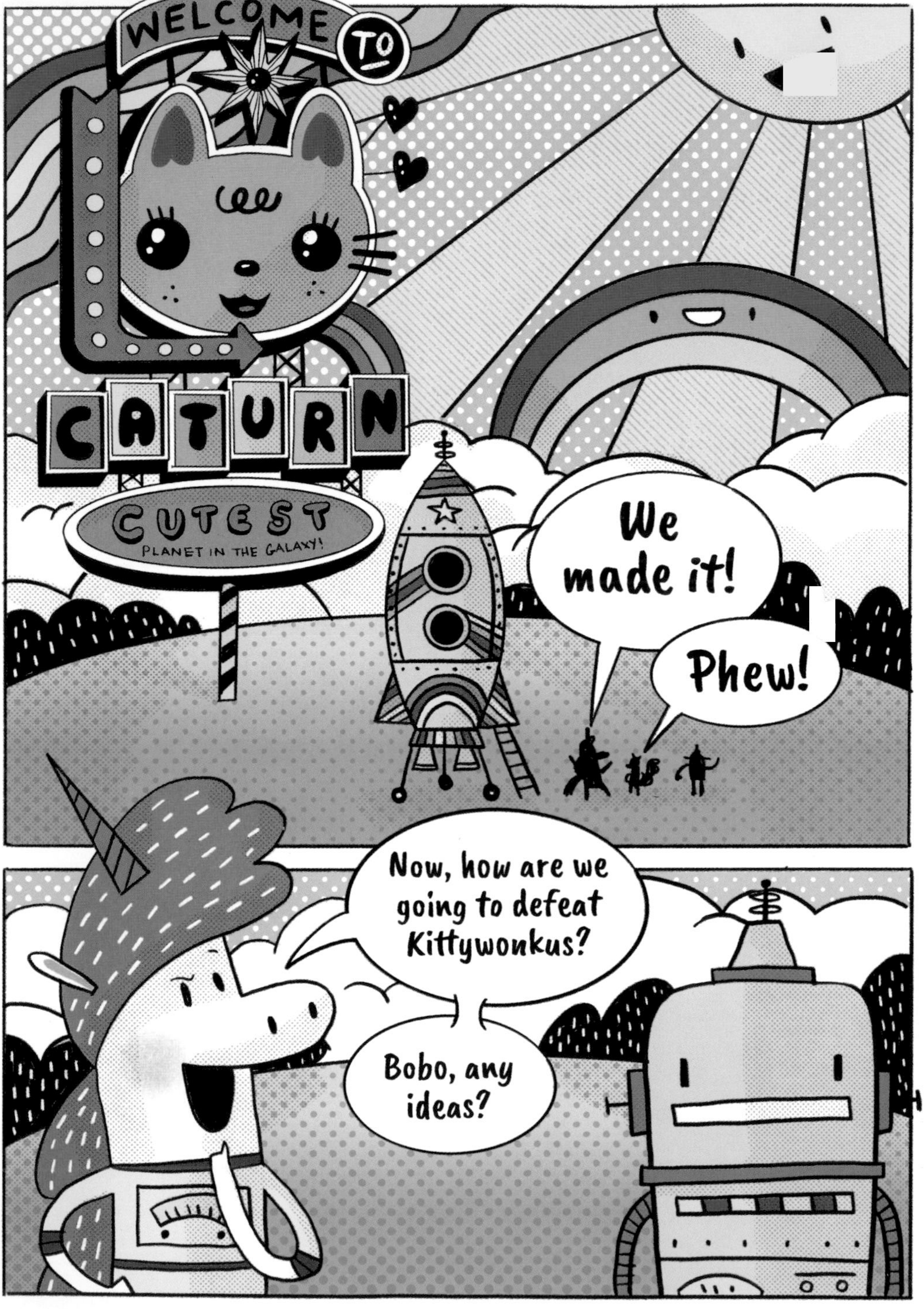
WELCOME TO
CATURN
CUTEST
PLANET IN THE GALAXY!
We made it!
Phew!
Now, how are we going to defeat Kittywonkus?
Bobo, any ideas?

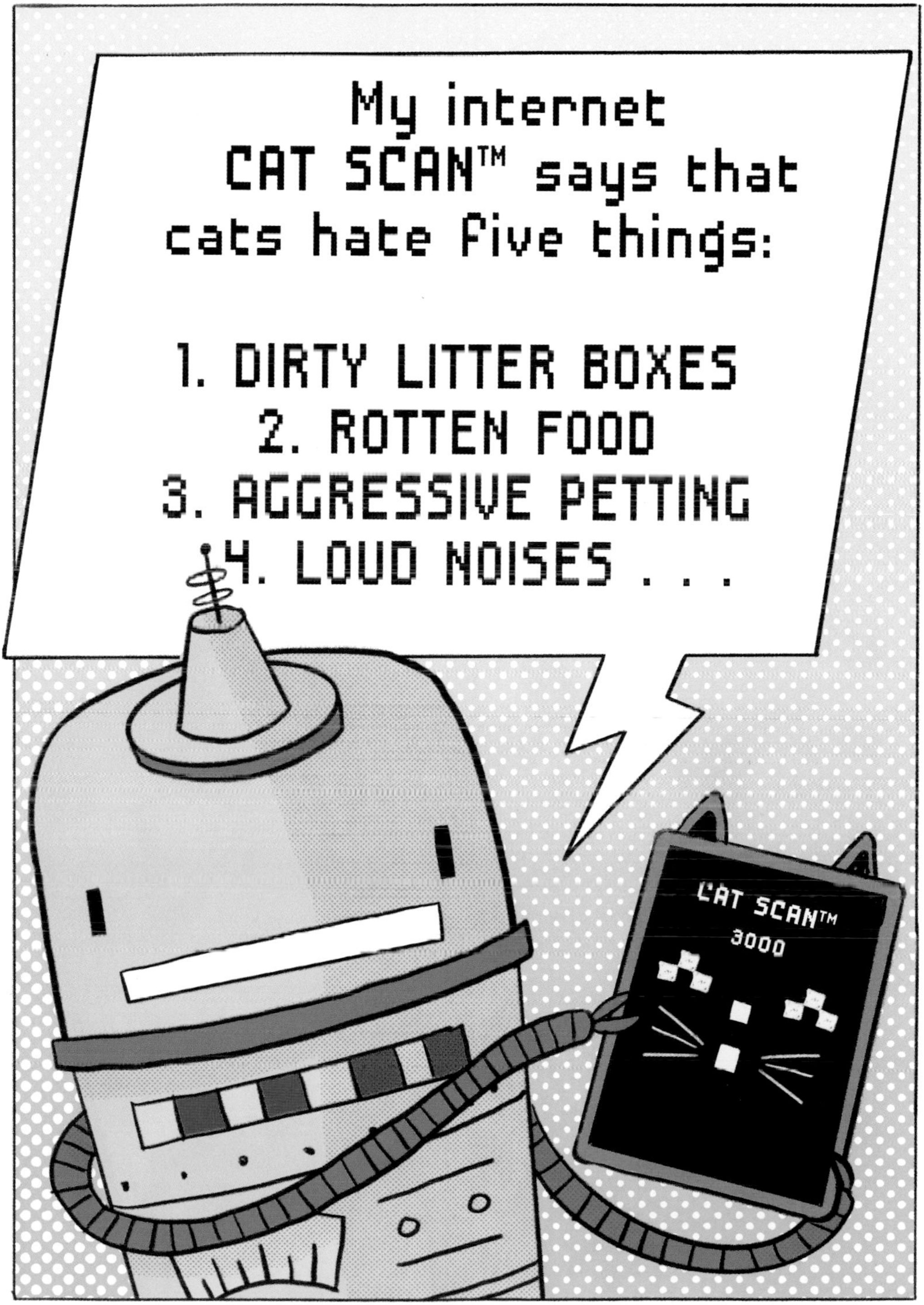
My internet CAT SCAN™ says that cats hate five things:
1. DIRTY LITTER BOXES
2. ROTTEN FOOD
3. AGGRESSIVE PETTING
4. LOUD NOISES . . .
CAT SCAN™ 3000

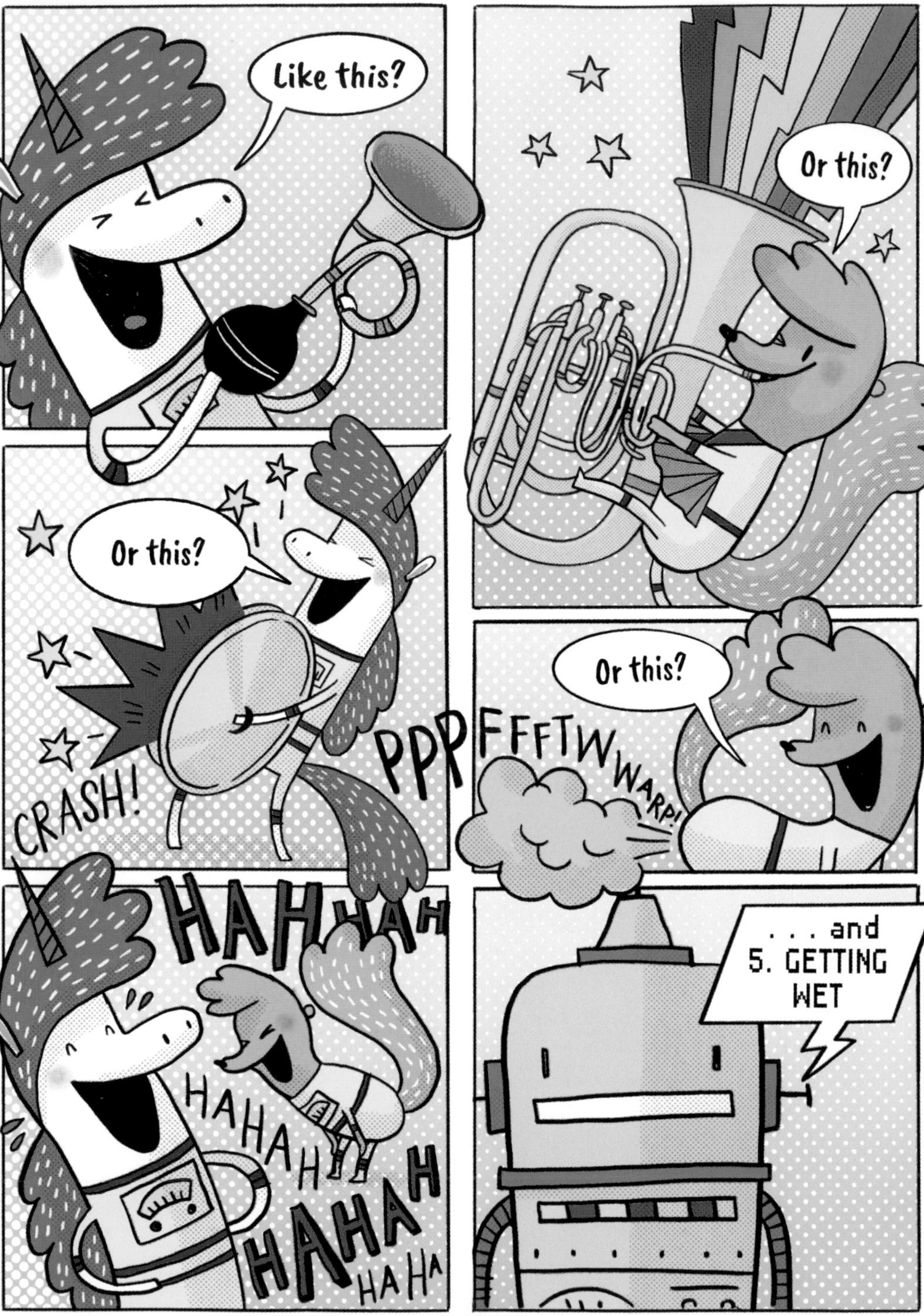
Like this?
Or this?
Or this?
CRASH!
Or this?
PPPFFFTWWARP!
HAHHAH
HAHAHH
HAHAH
HAHA
... and 5. GETTING WET

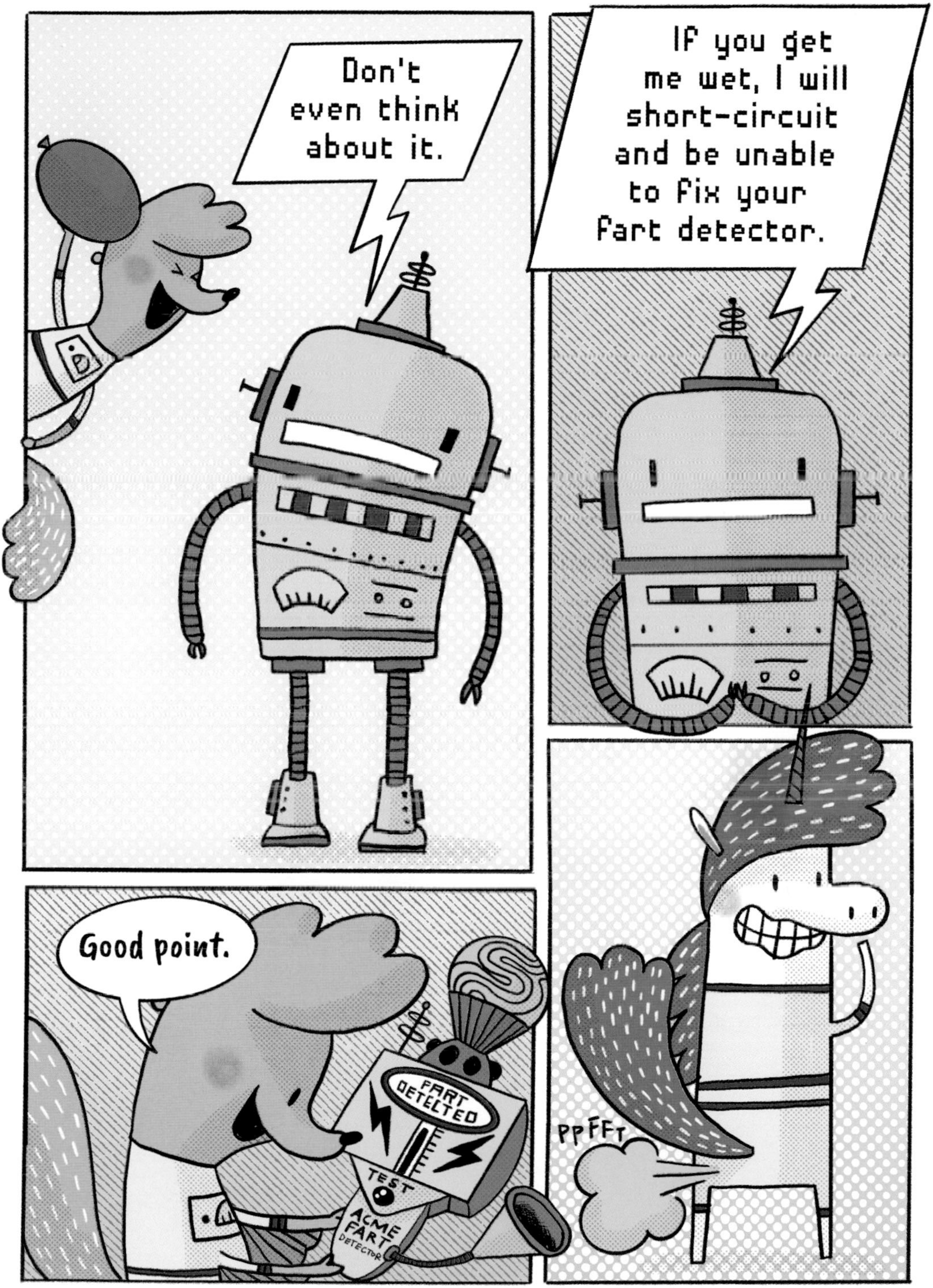
Don't even think about it.
If you get me wet, I will short-circuit and be unable to fix your fart detector.
Good point.
FART DETECTED
TEST
ACME FART DETECTOR
PPFFT

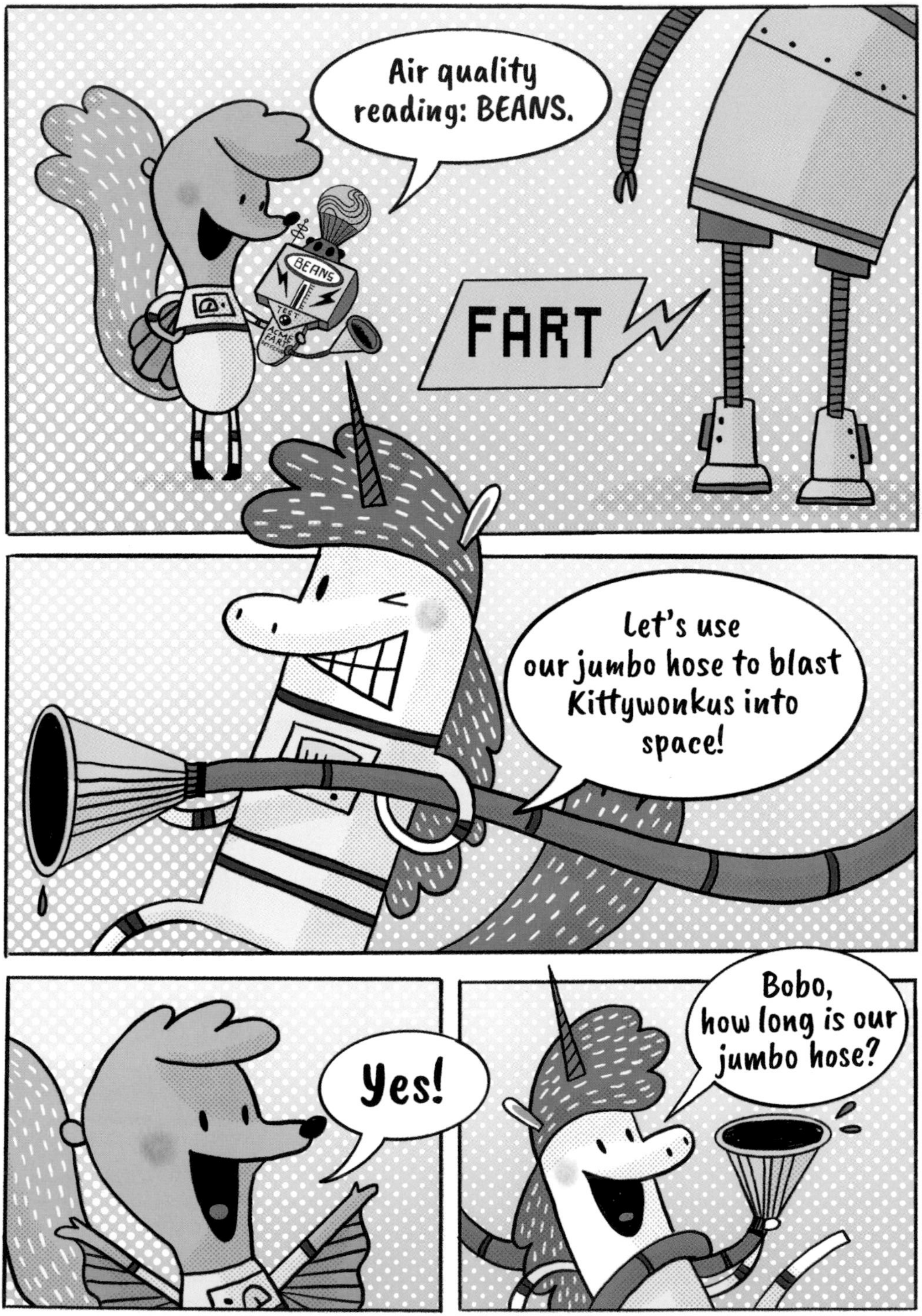
Air quality reading: BEANS.
BEANS
TEST
ACME FART
FART
Let's use our jumbo hose to blast Kittywonkus into space!
Yes!
Bobo, how long is our jumbo hose?

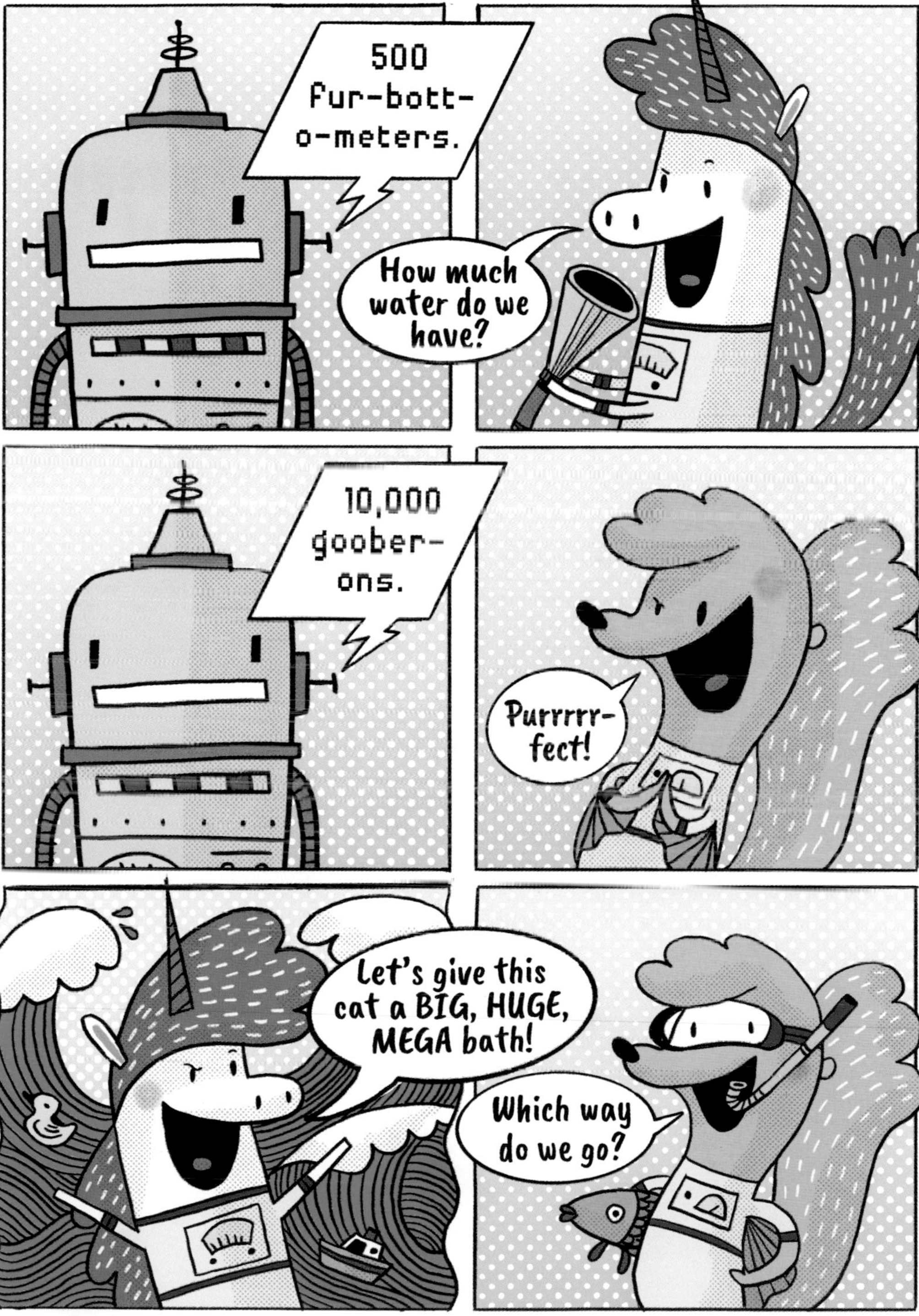
500 fur-bott-o-meters.
How much water do we have?
10,000 goober-ons.
Purrrrr-fect!
Let's give this cat a BIG, HUGE, MEGA bath!
Which way do we go?

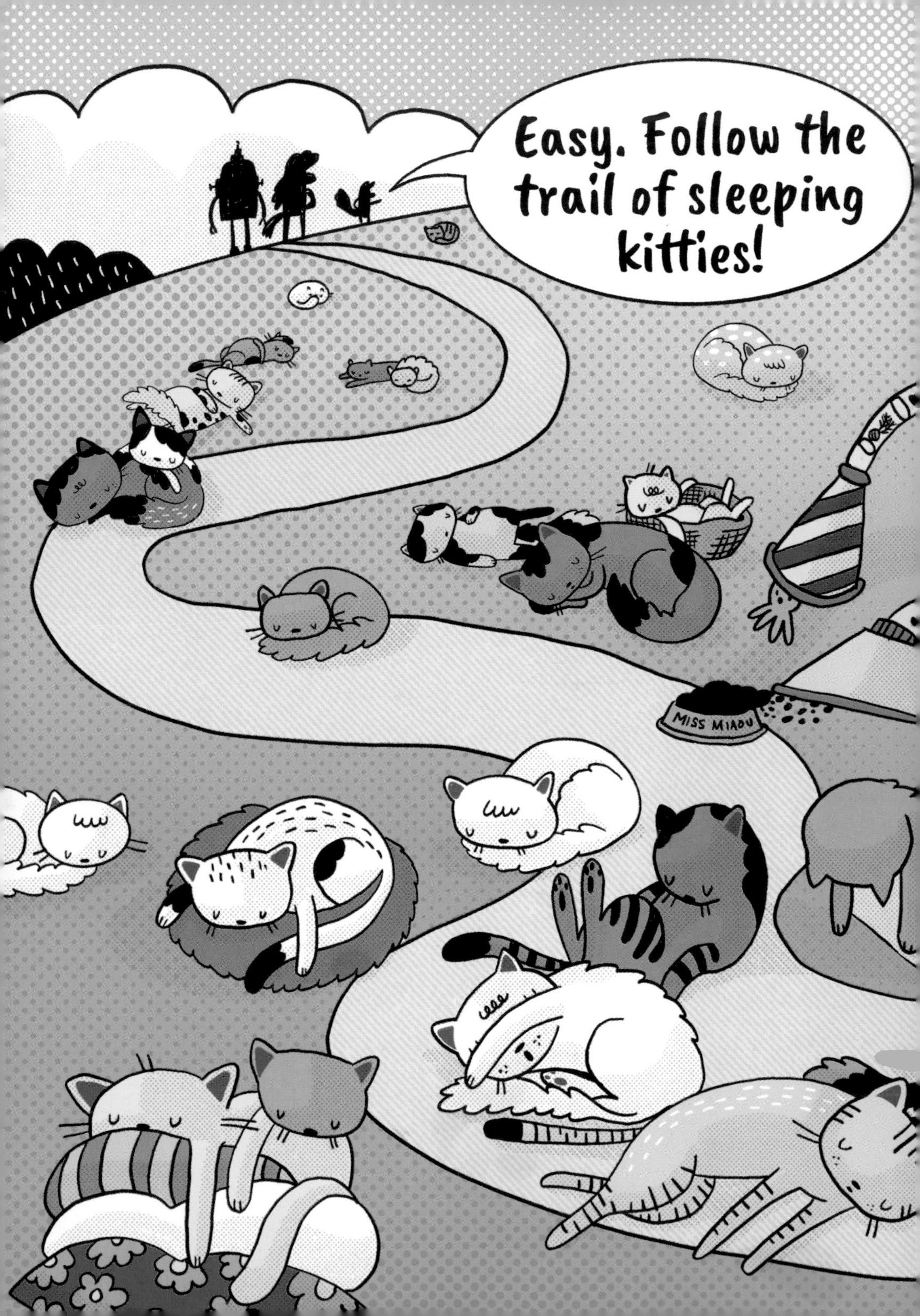
Easy. Follow the trail of sleeping kitties!
MISS MIAOU

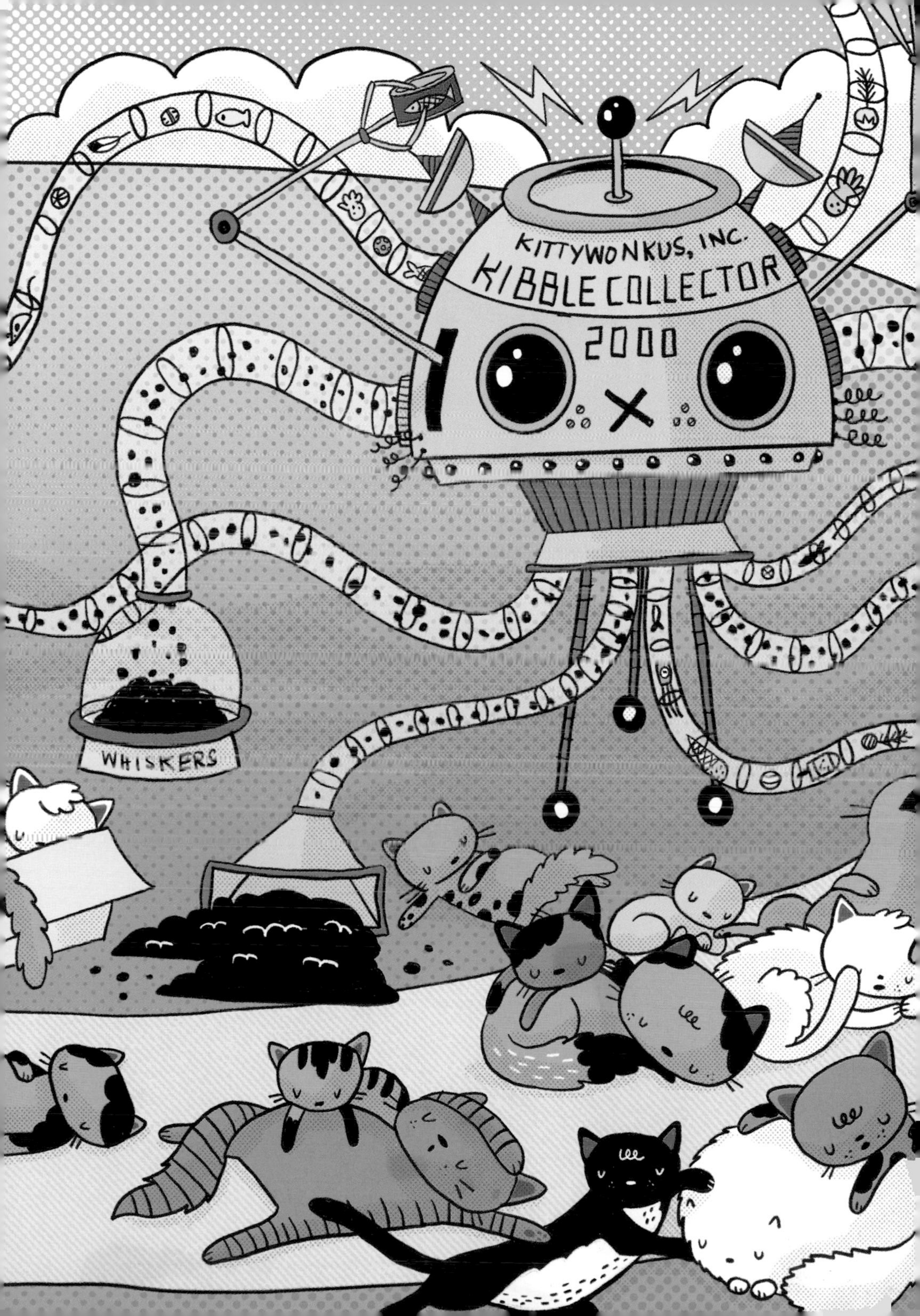
KITTYWONKUS, INC.
KIBBLE COLLECTOR
2000
WHISKERS

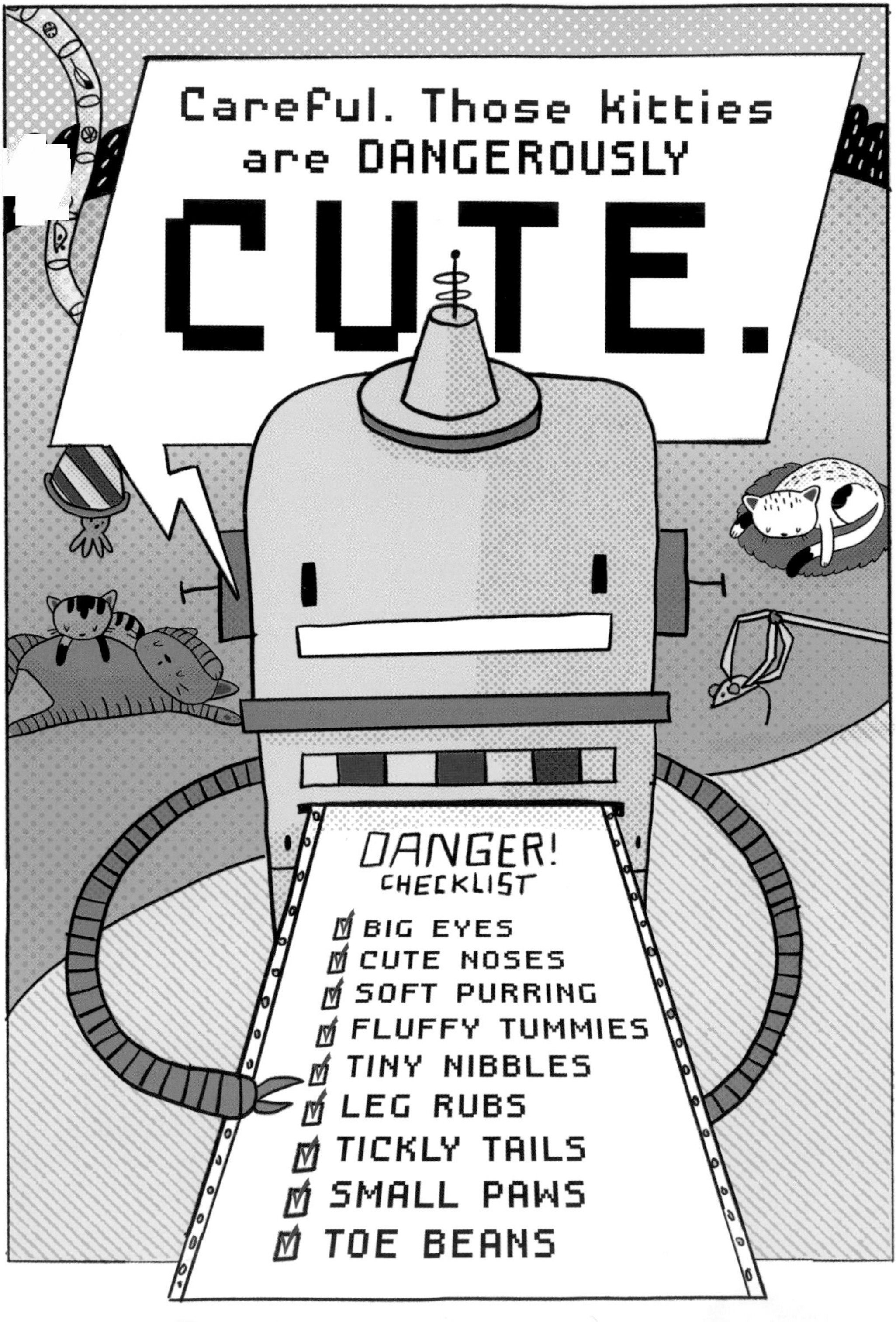
Careful. Those kitties are DANGEROUSLY CUTE.
DANGER! CHECKLIST
BIG EYES
CUTE NOSES
SOFT PURRING
FLUFFY TUMMIES
TINY NIBBLES
LEG RUBS
TICKLY TAILS
SMALL PAWS
TOE BEANS

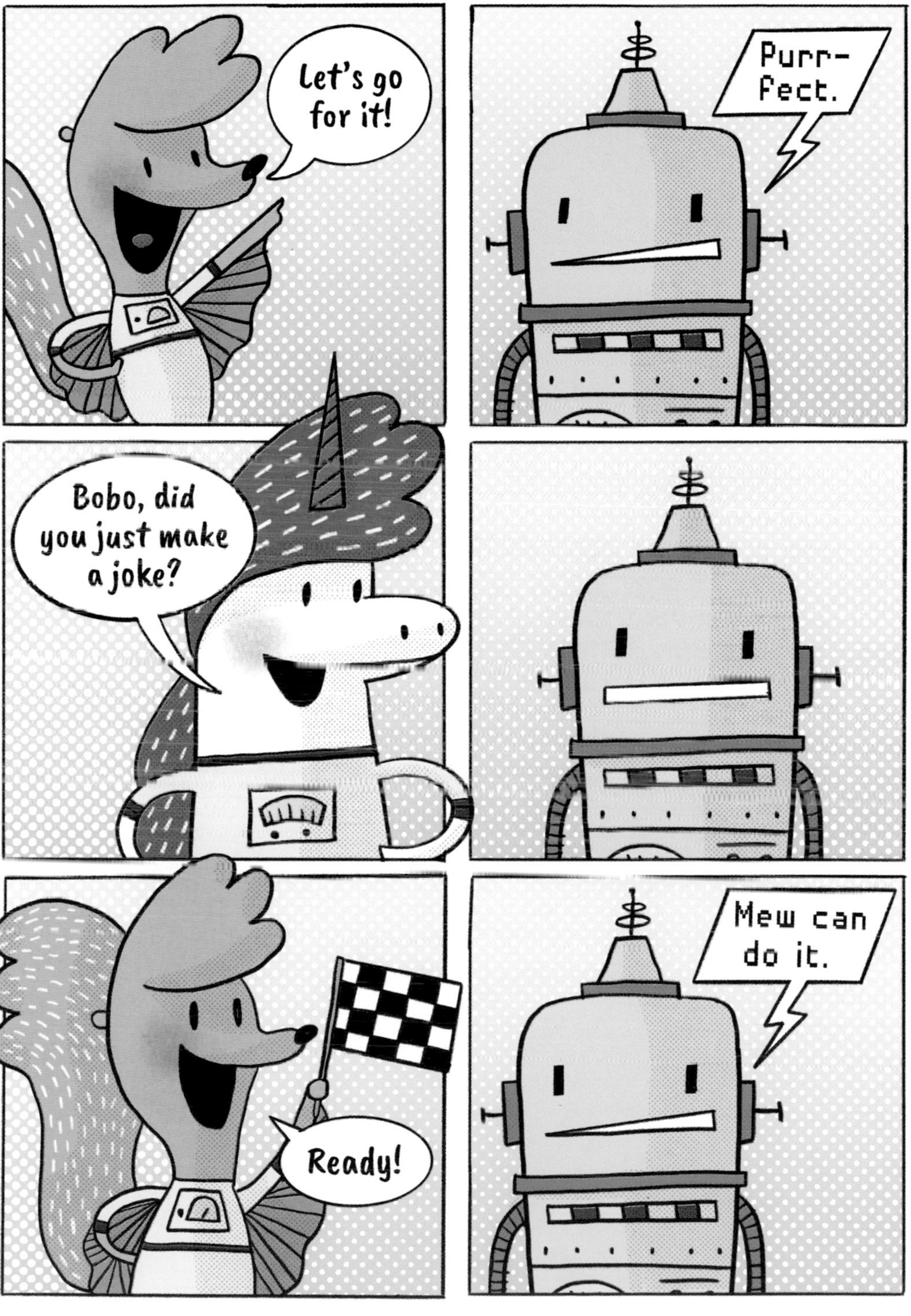
Let's go for it!
Purr-fect.
Bobo, did you just make a joke?
Ready!
Mew can do it.

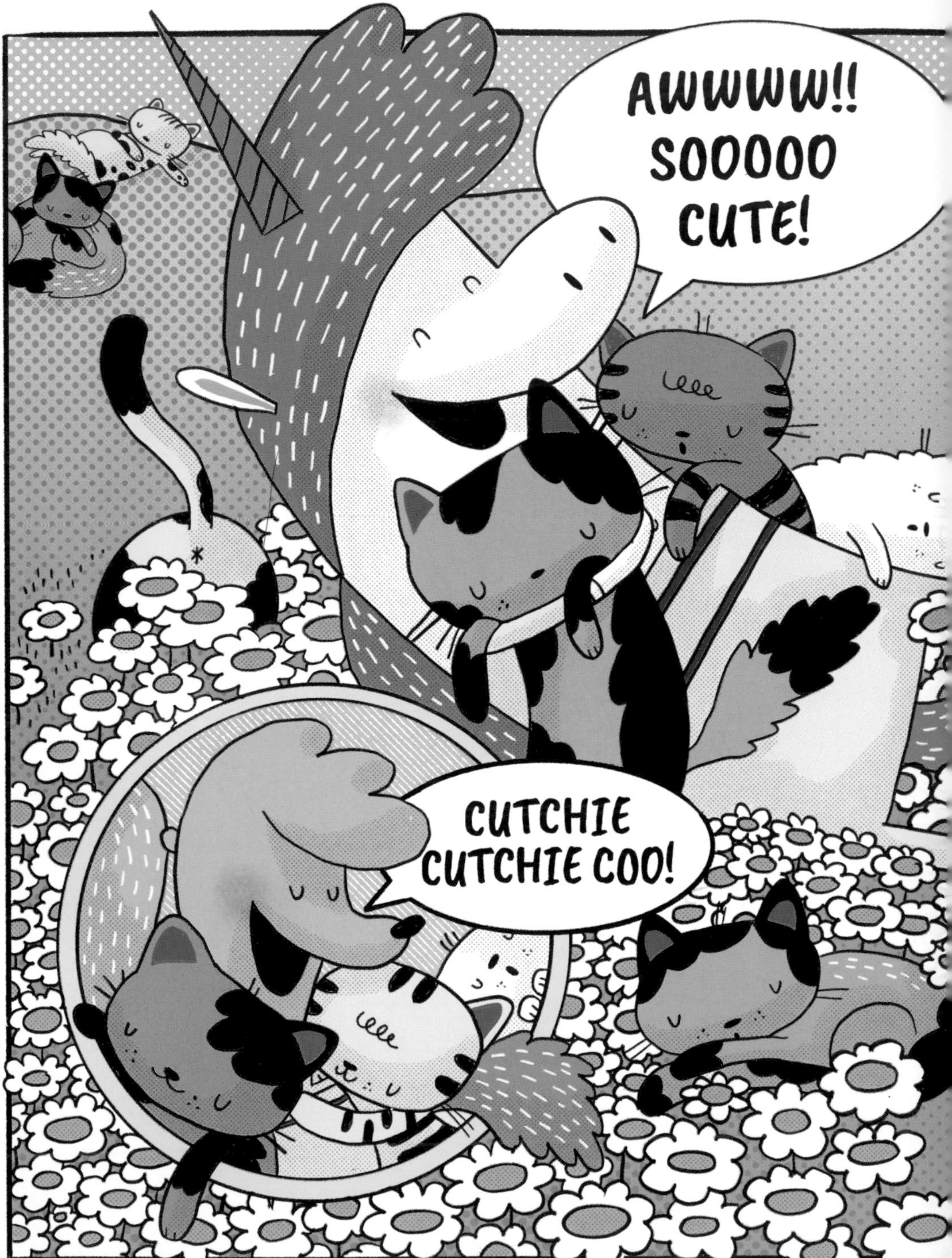
AWWWW!! SOOOOO CUTE!
CUTCHIE CUTCHIE COO!

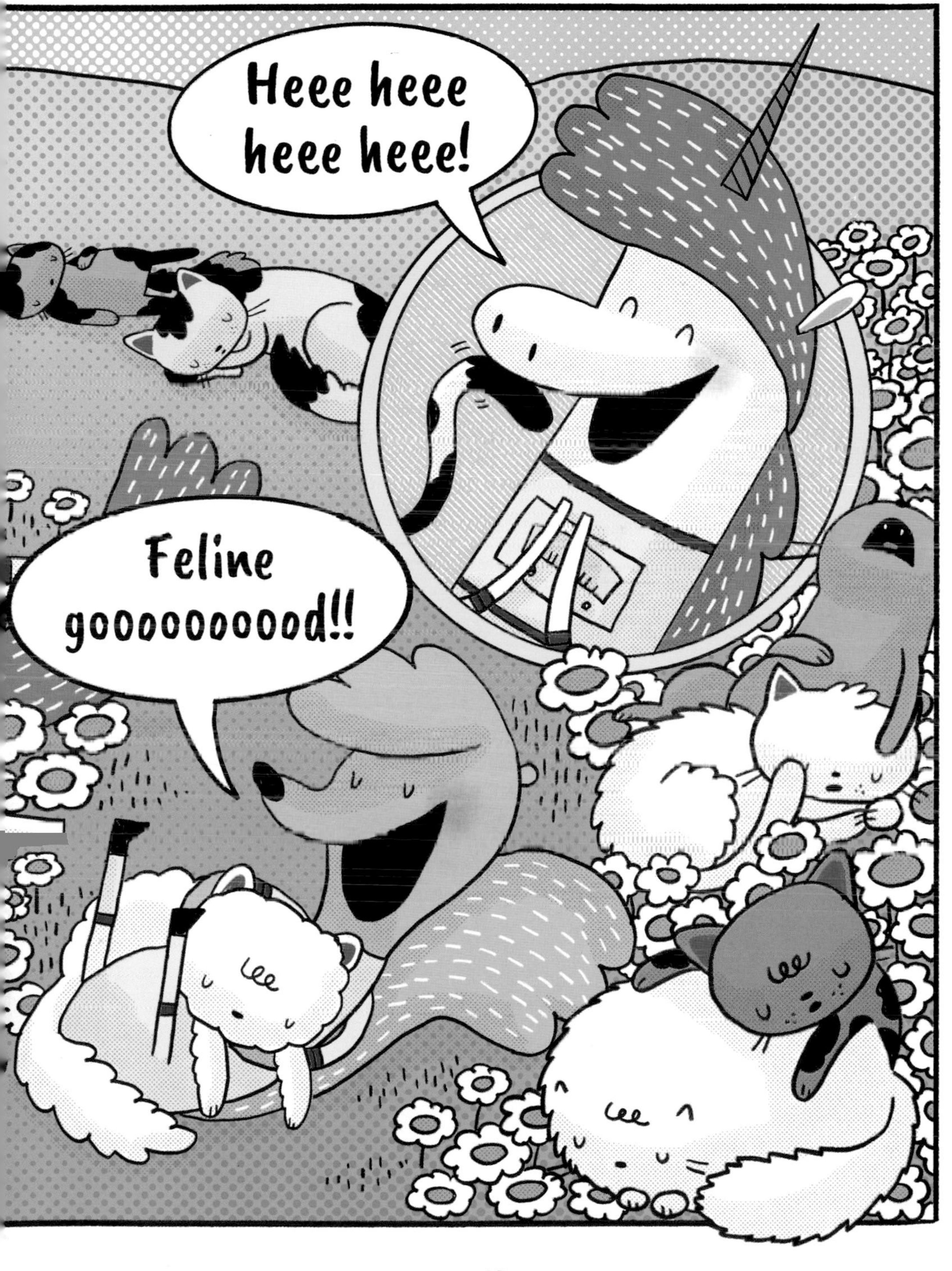
Heee heee heee heee!
Feline gooooooooood!!

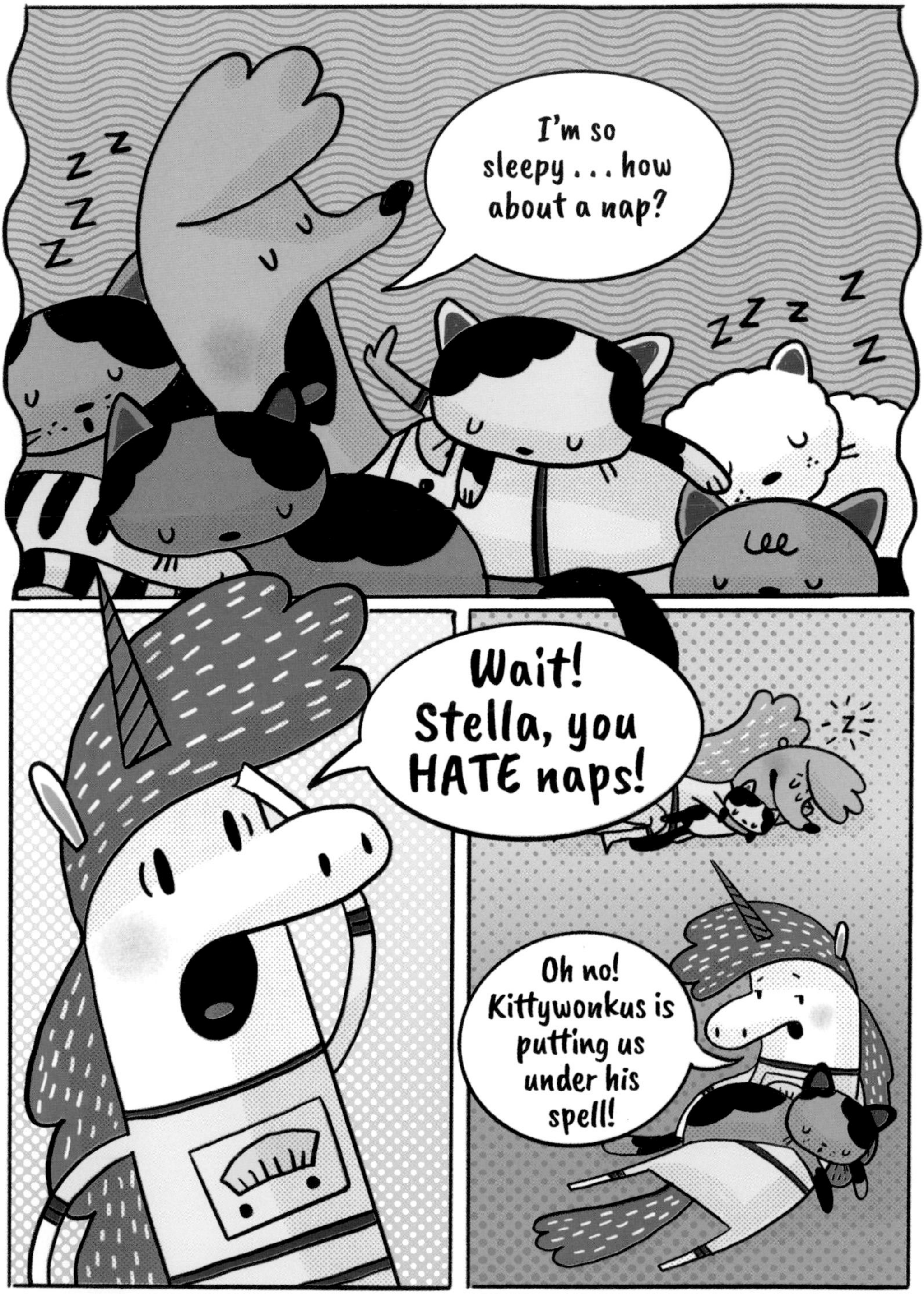
I'm so sleepy . . . how about a nap?
ZZZZ
ZZZZZ
Wait! Stella, you HATE naps!
Z
Oh no! Kittywonkus is putting us under his spell!

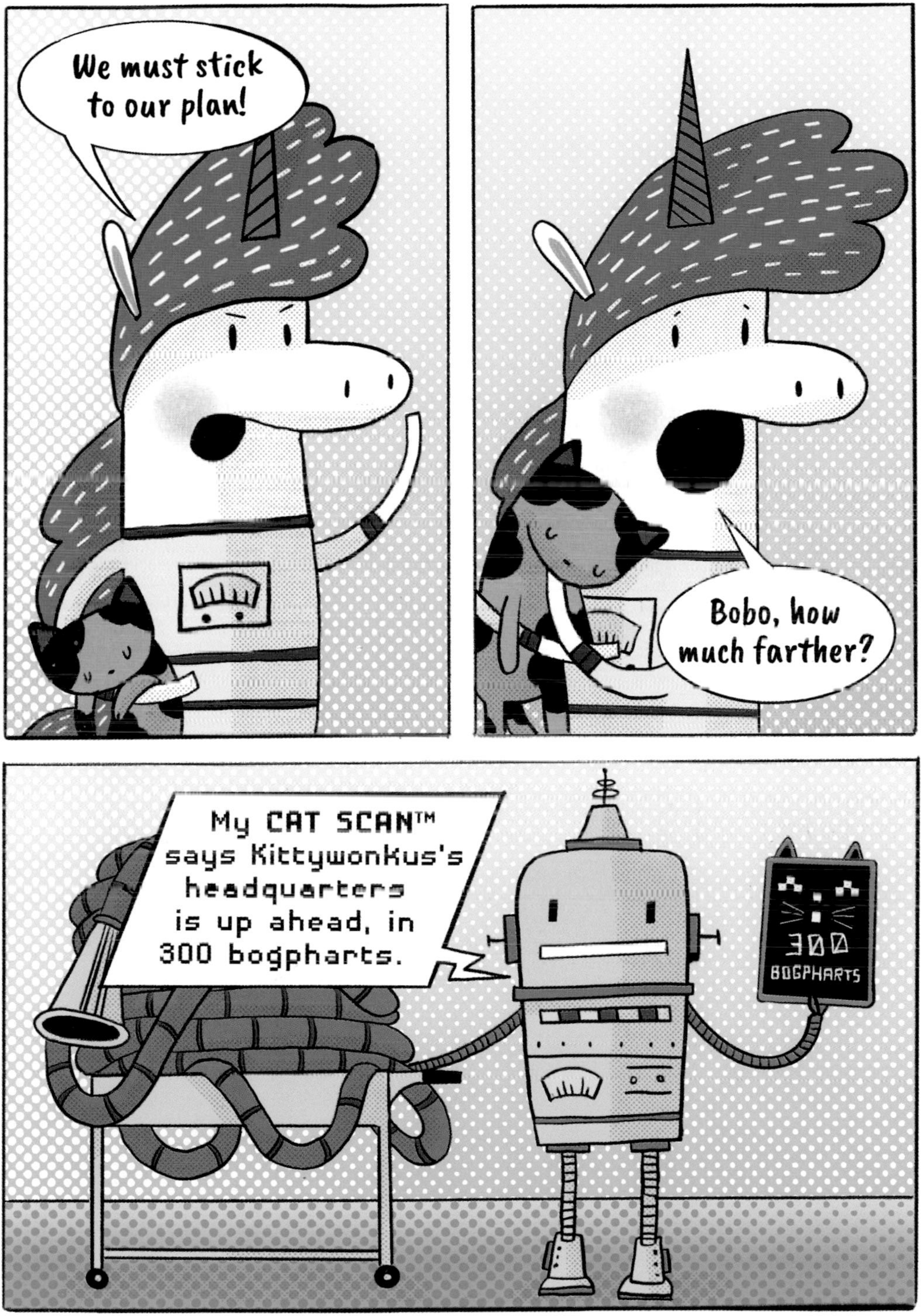
We must stick to our plan!
Bobo, how much farther?
My CAT SCAN™ says Kittywonkus's headquarters is up ahead, in 300 bogpharts.
300 BOGPHARTS

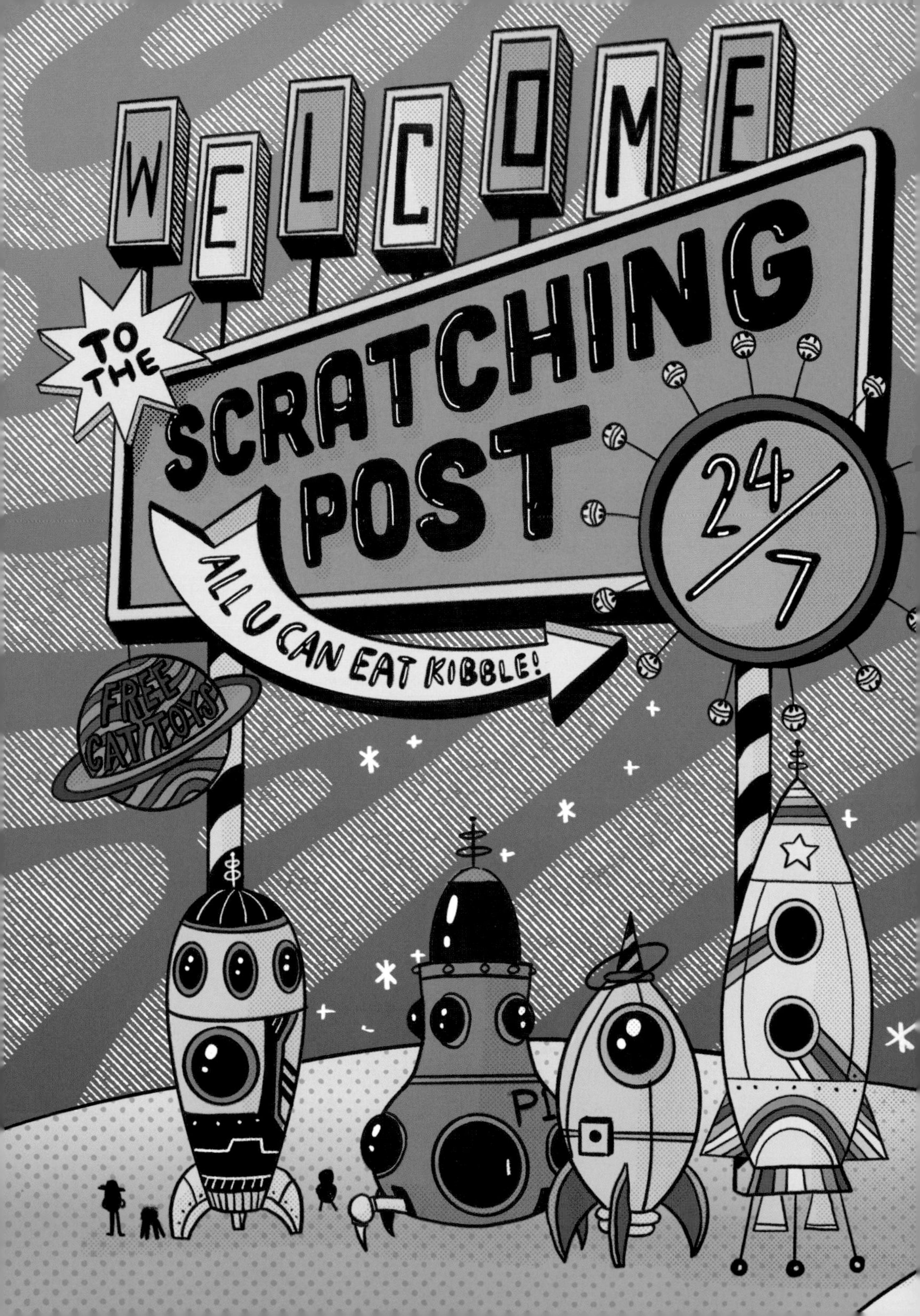
WELCOME
TO THE
SCRATCHING POST
24/7
ALL U CAN EAT KIBBLE!
FREE CAT TOYS

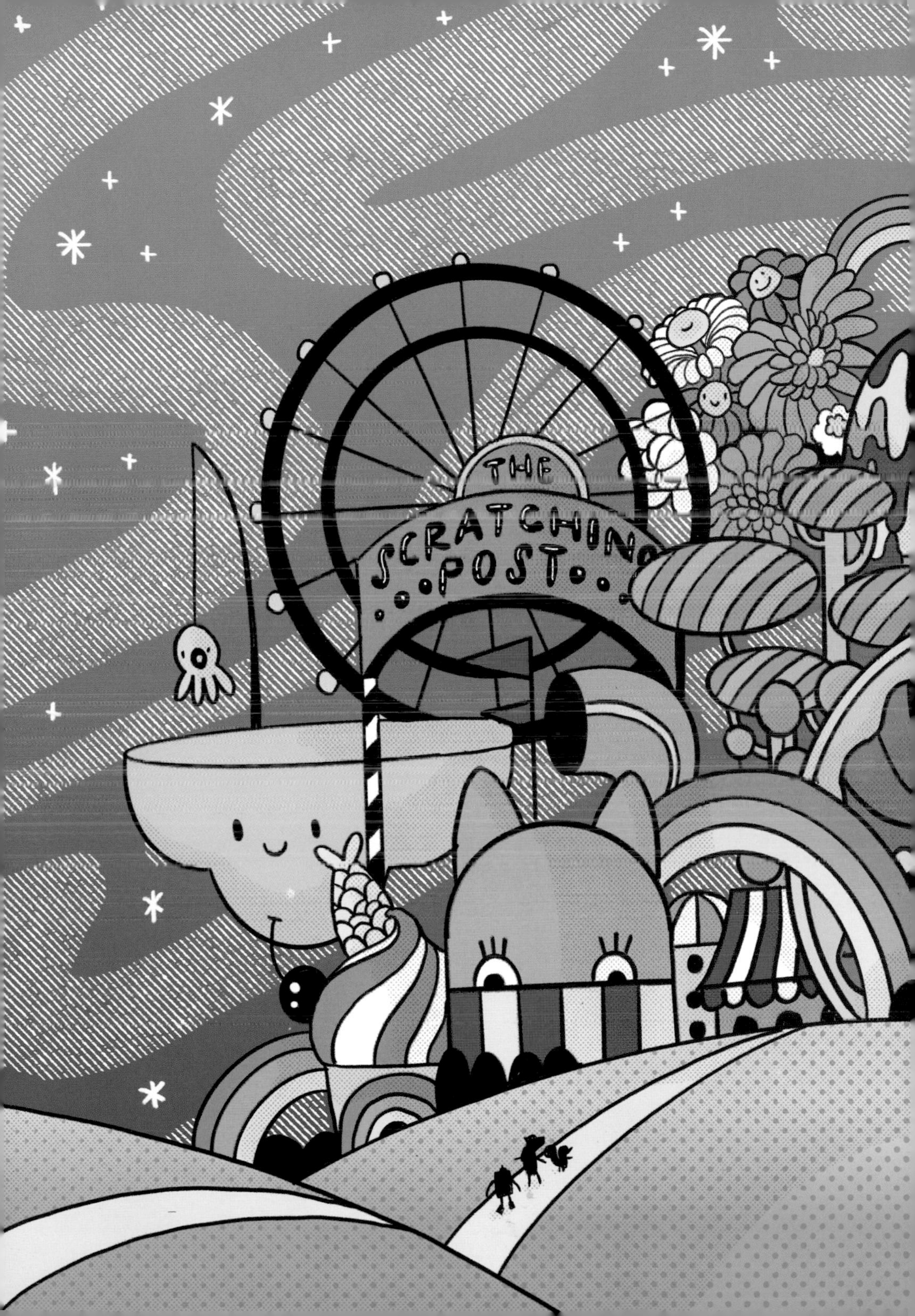
THE
SCRATCHING
POST

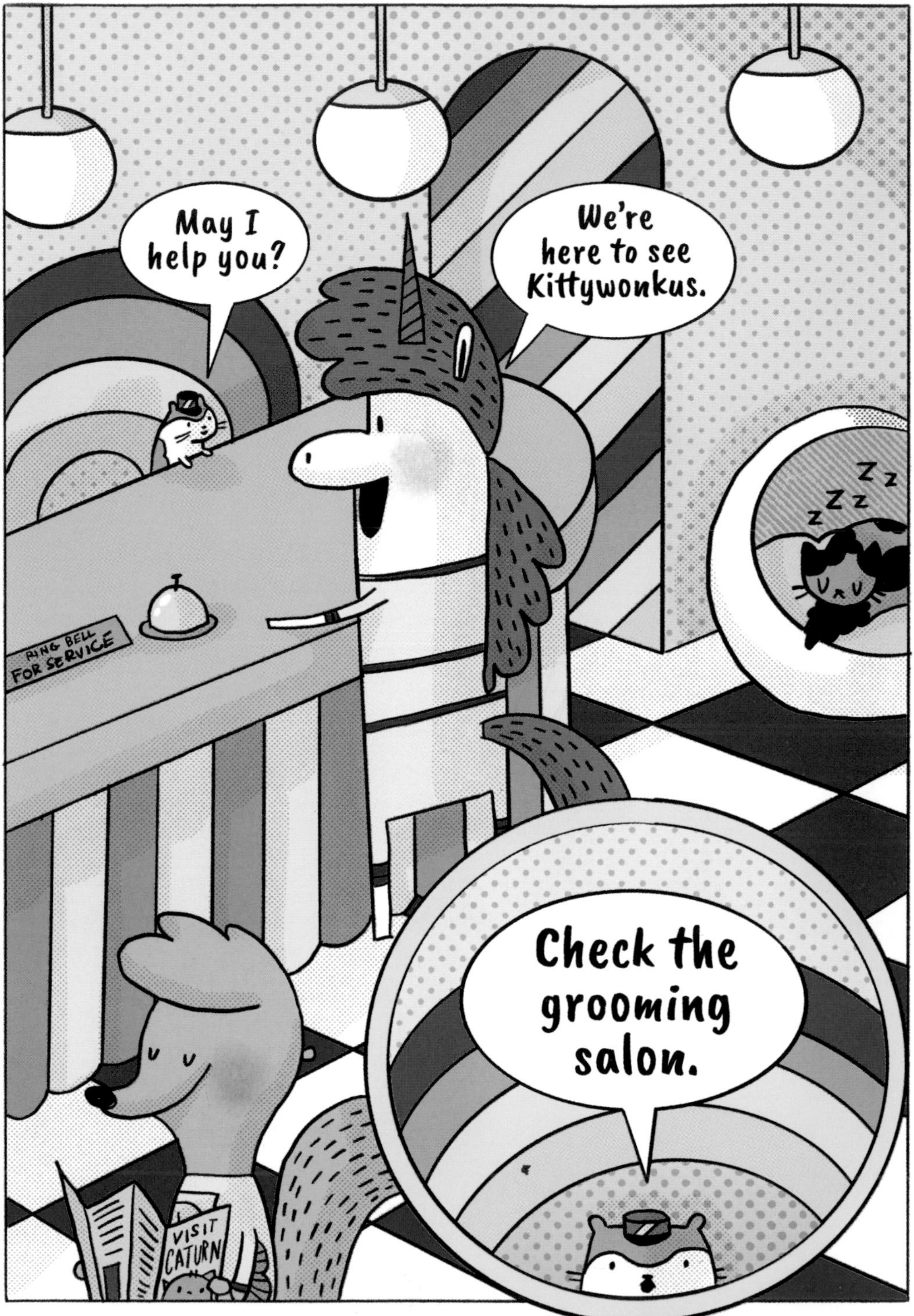
May I help you?
We're here to see Kittywonkus.
RING BELL FOR SERVICE
Check the grooming salon.
VISIT CATURN

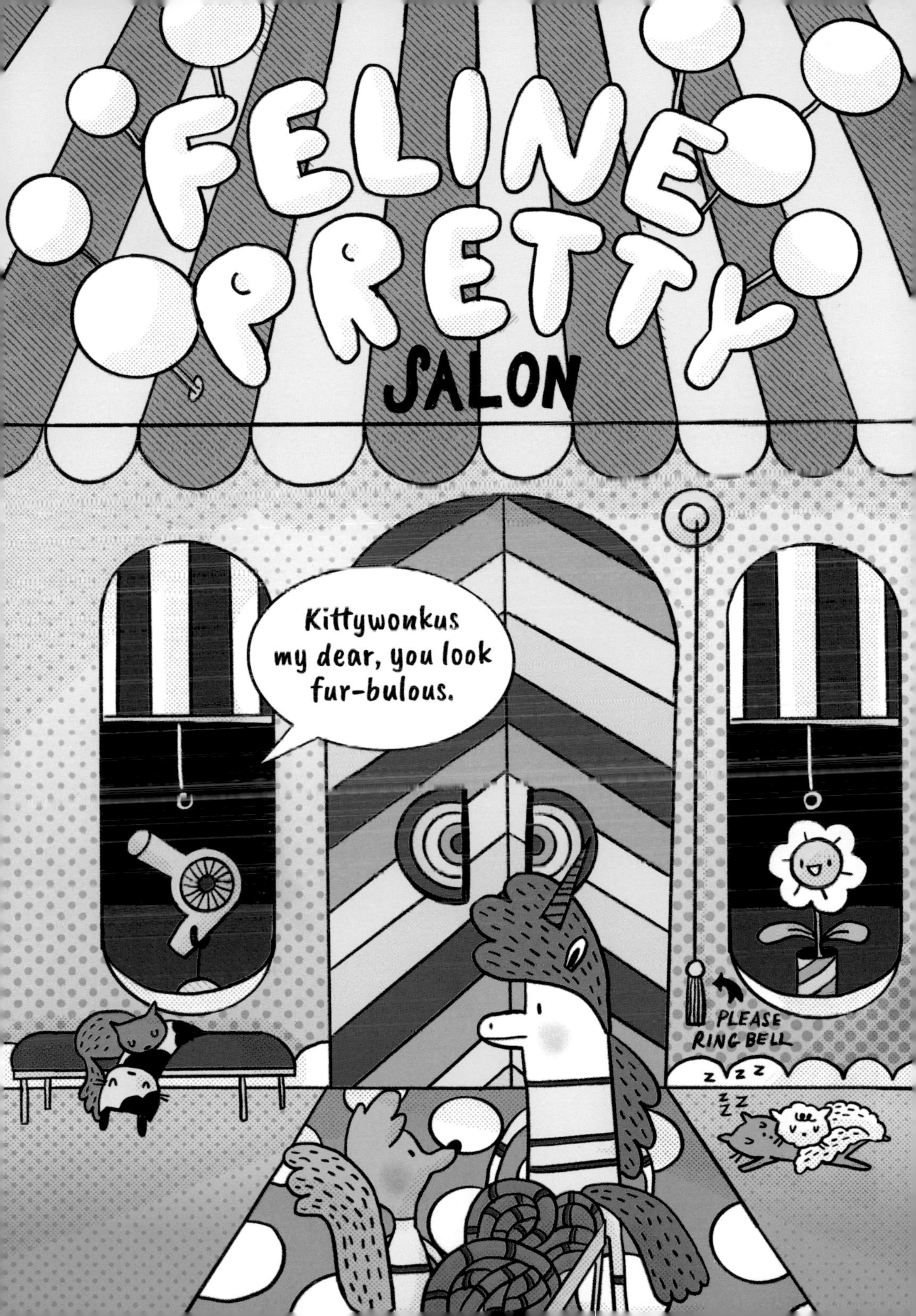
FELINE PRETTY
SALON
Kittywonkus my dear, you look fur-bulous.
PLEASE RING BELL
Z Z Z
Z Z Z

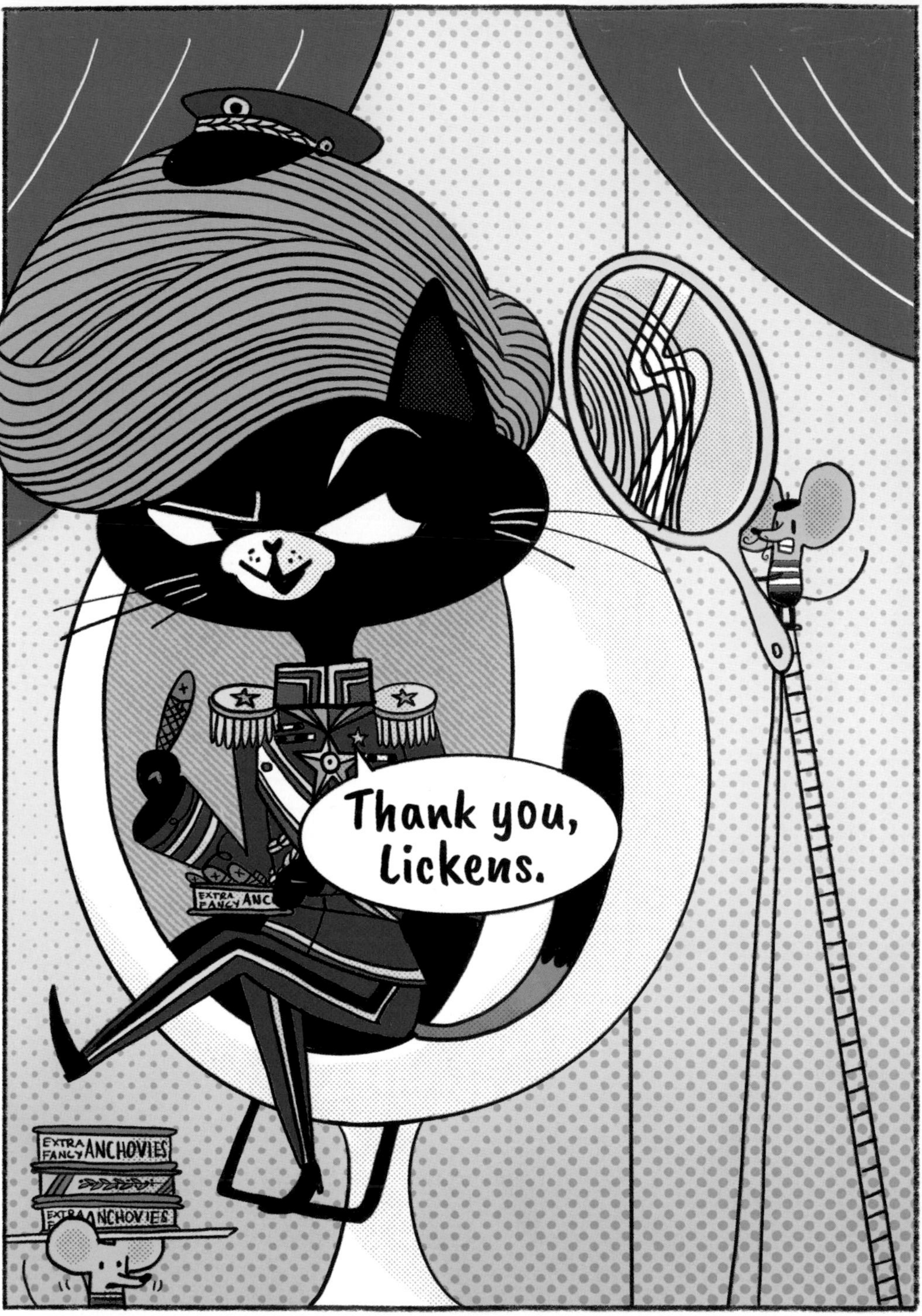
Thank you, Lickens.
EXTRA FANCY ANC
EXTRA FANCY ANCHOVIES
ANCHOVIES

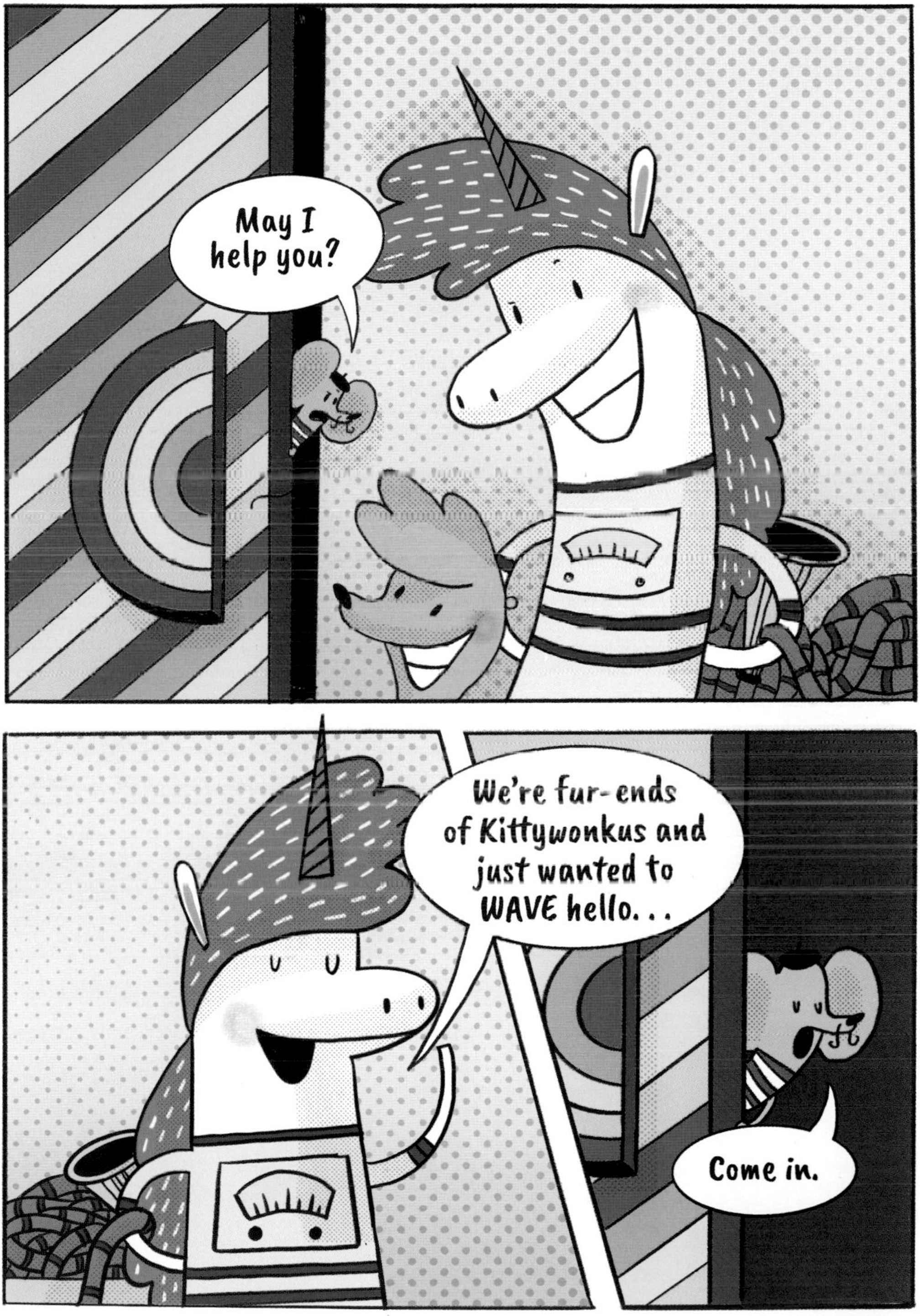
May I help you?
We're fur-ends of Kittywonkus and just wanted to WAVE hello. . .
Come in.

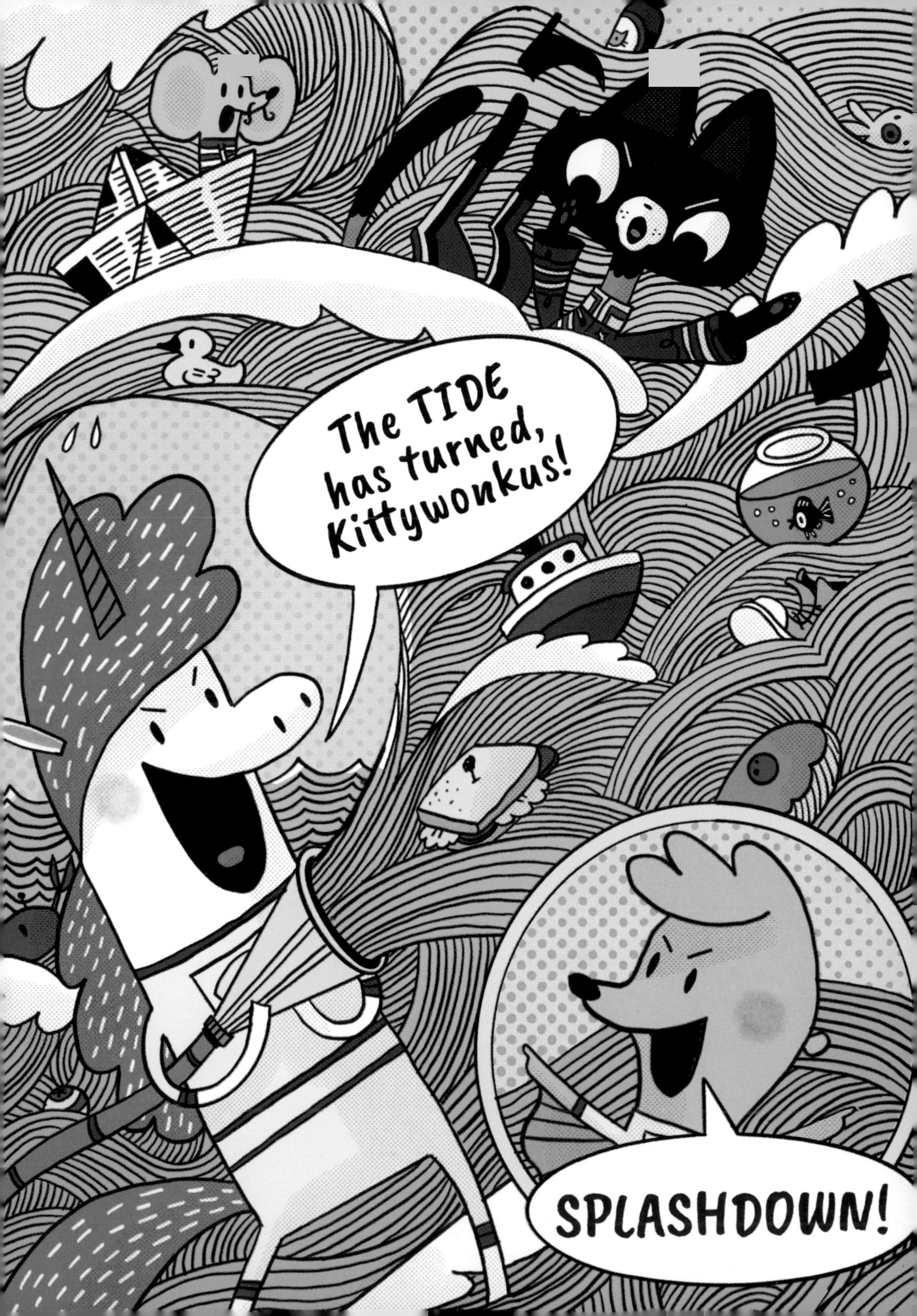
The TIDE has turned, Kittywonkus!
SPLASHDOWN!

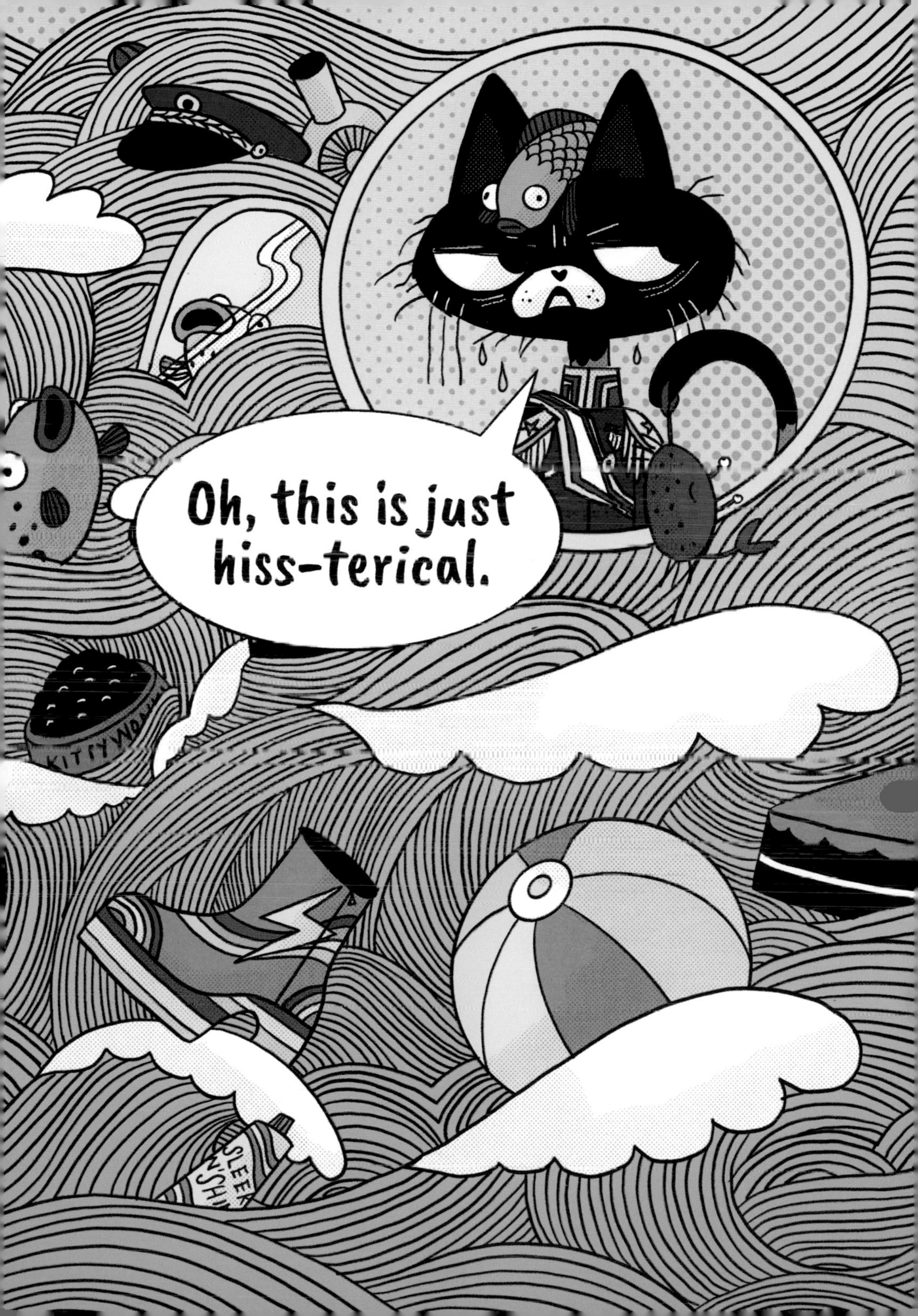
Oh, this is just hiss-terical.

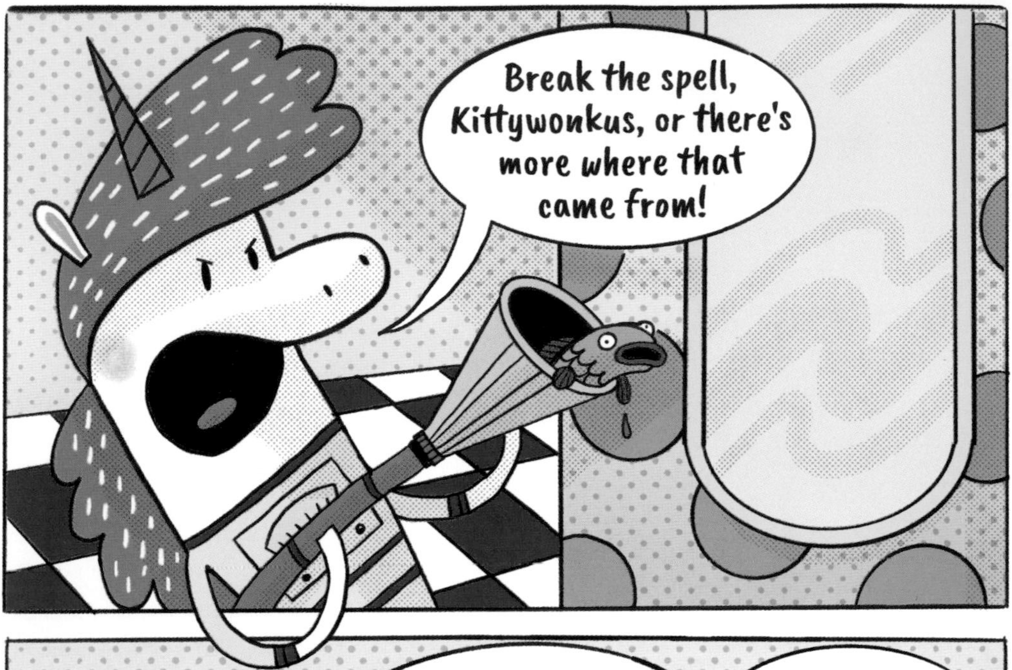
Break the spell, Kittywonkus, or there's more where that came from!

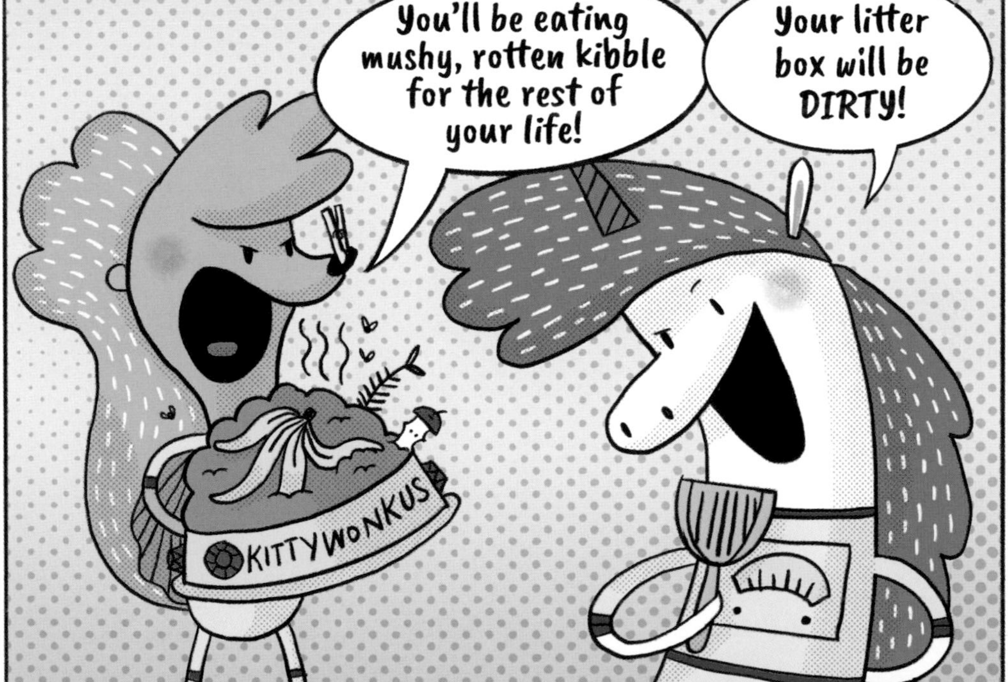
You'll be eating mushy, rotten kibble for the rest of your life!
Your litter box will be DIRTY!
KITTYWONKUS

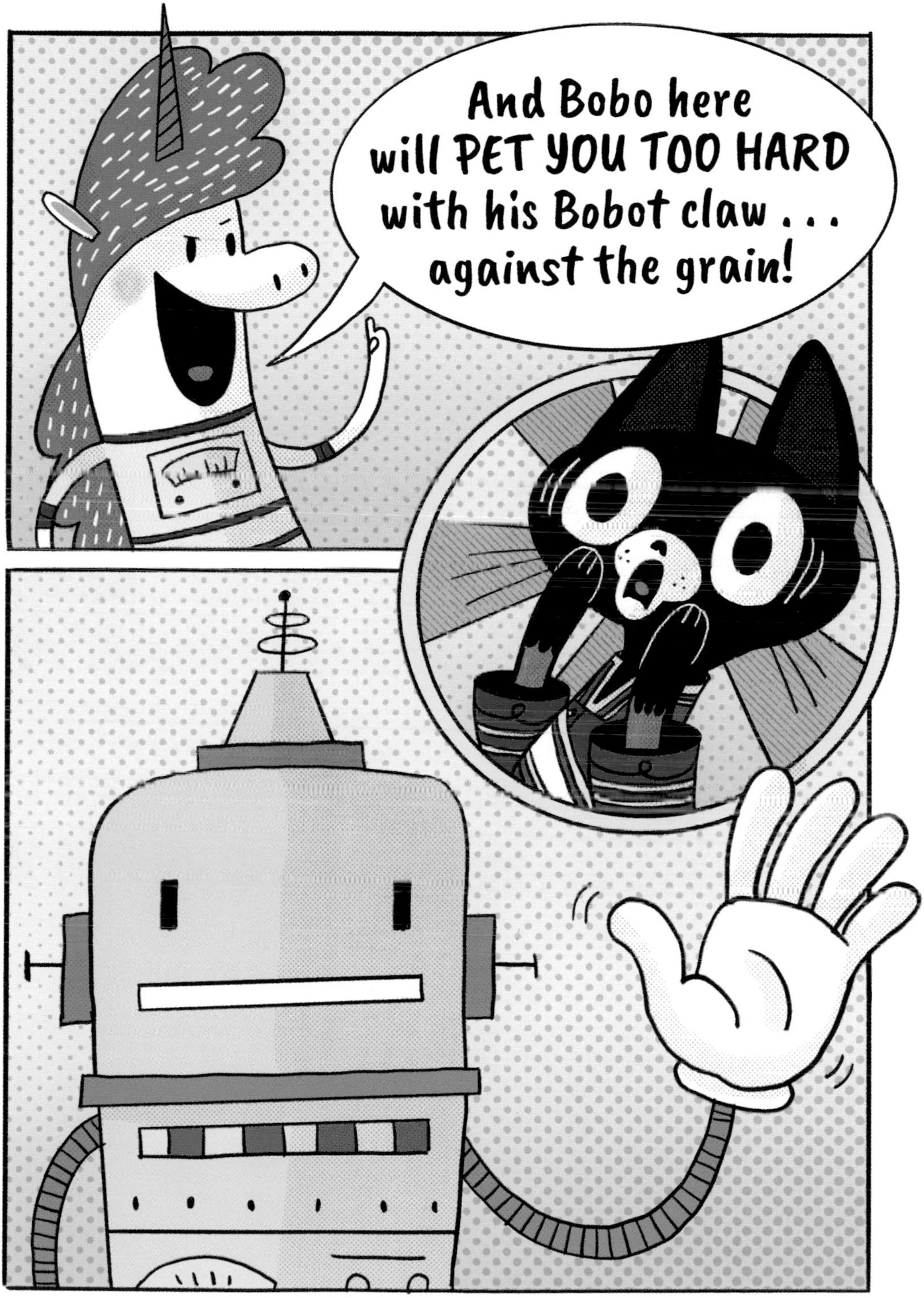
And Bobo here will PET YOU TOO HARD with his Bobot claw . . . against the grain!

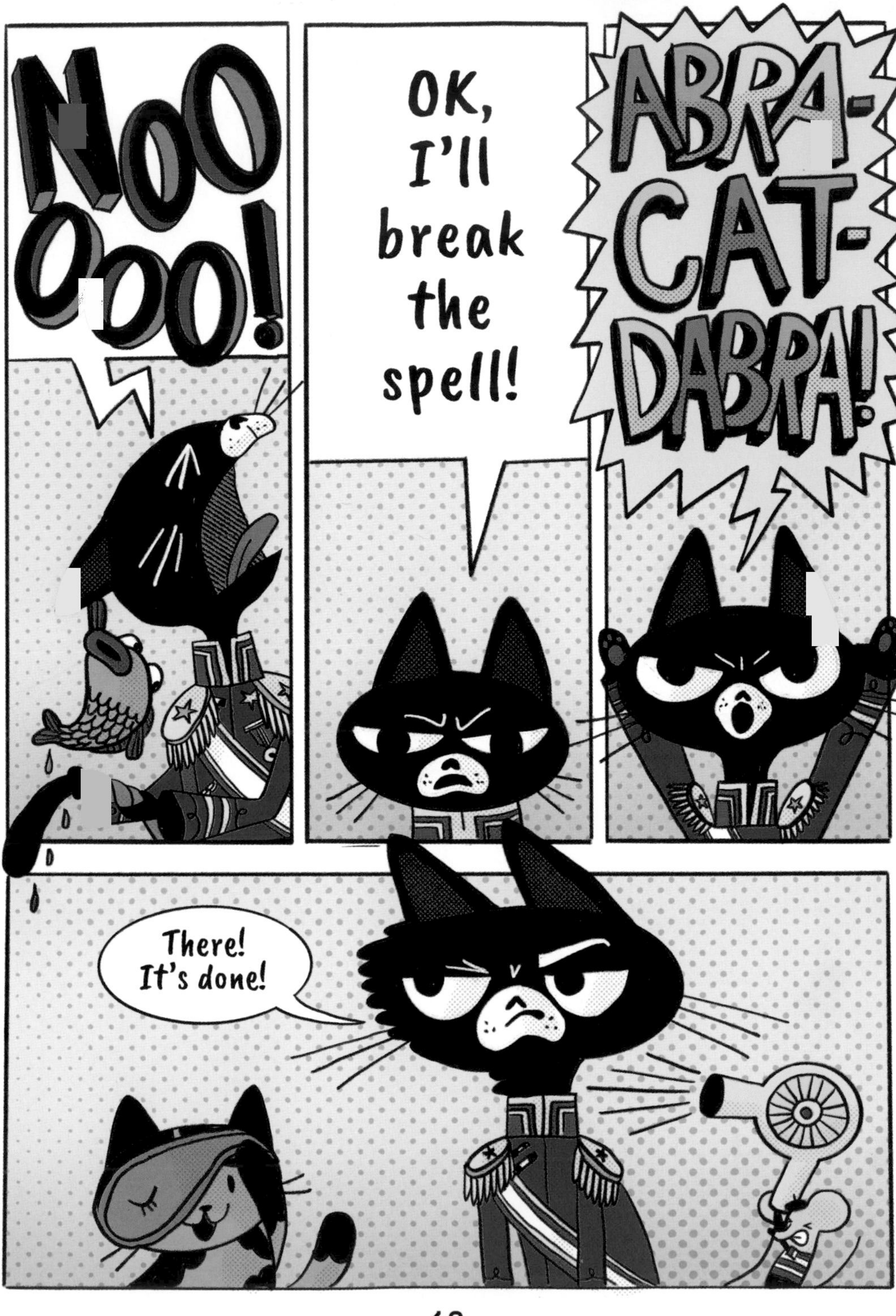
NOOOOOO!
OK, I'll break the spell!
ABRA-CAT-DABRA!
There! It's done!

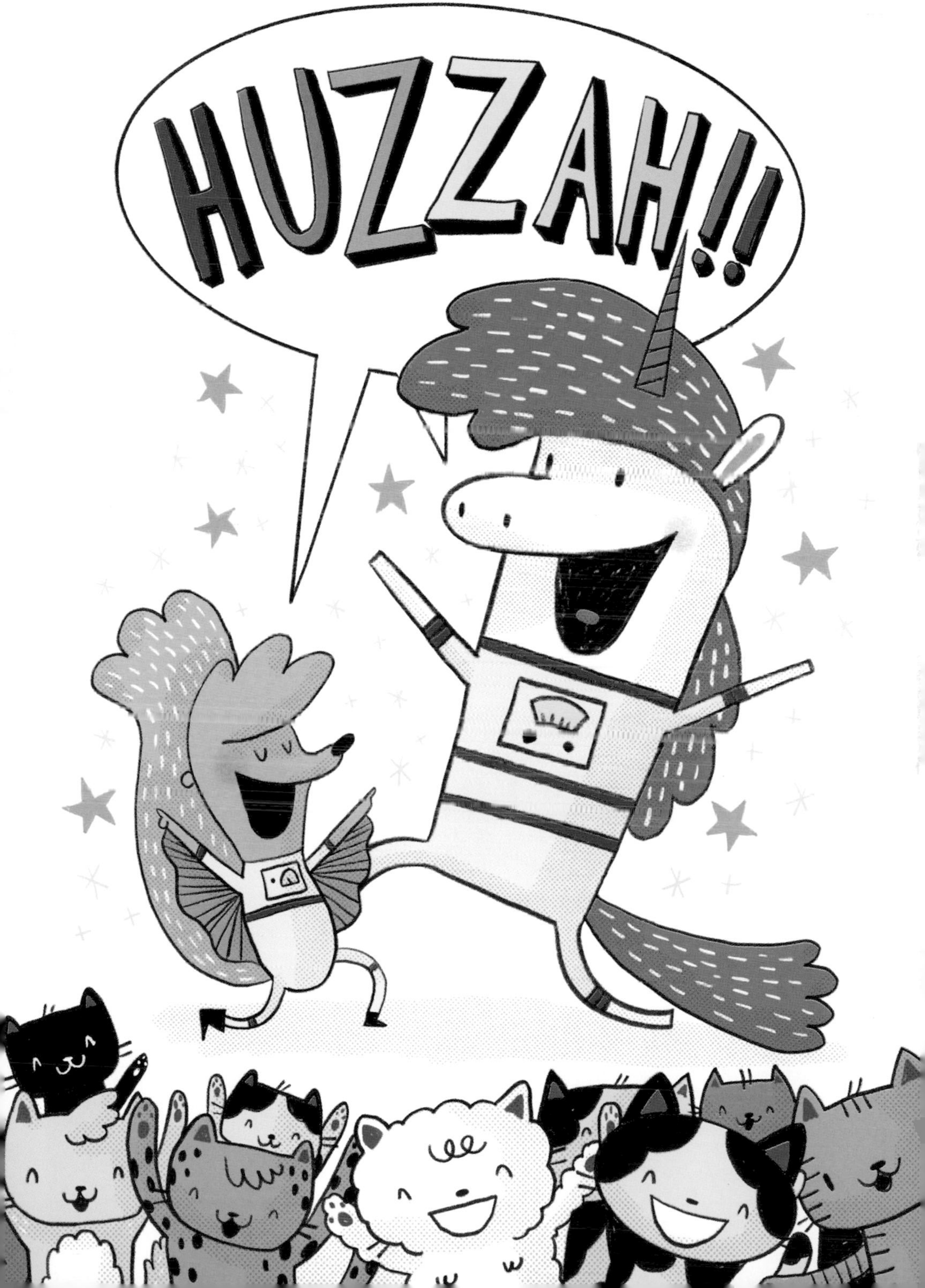
HUZZAH!!

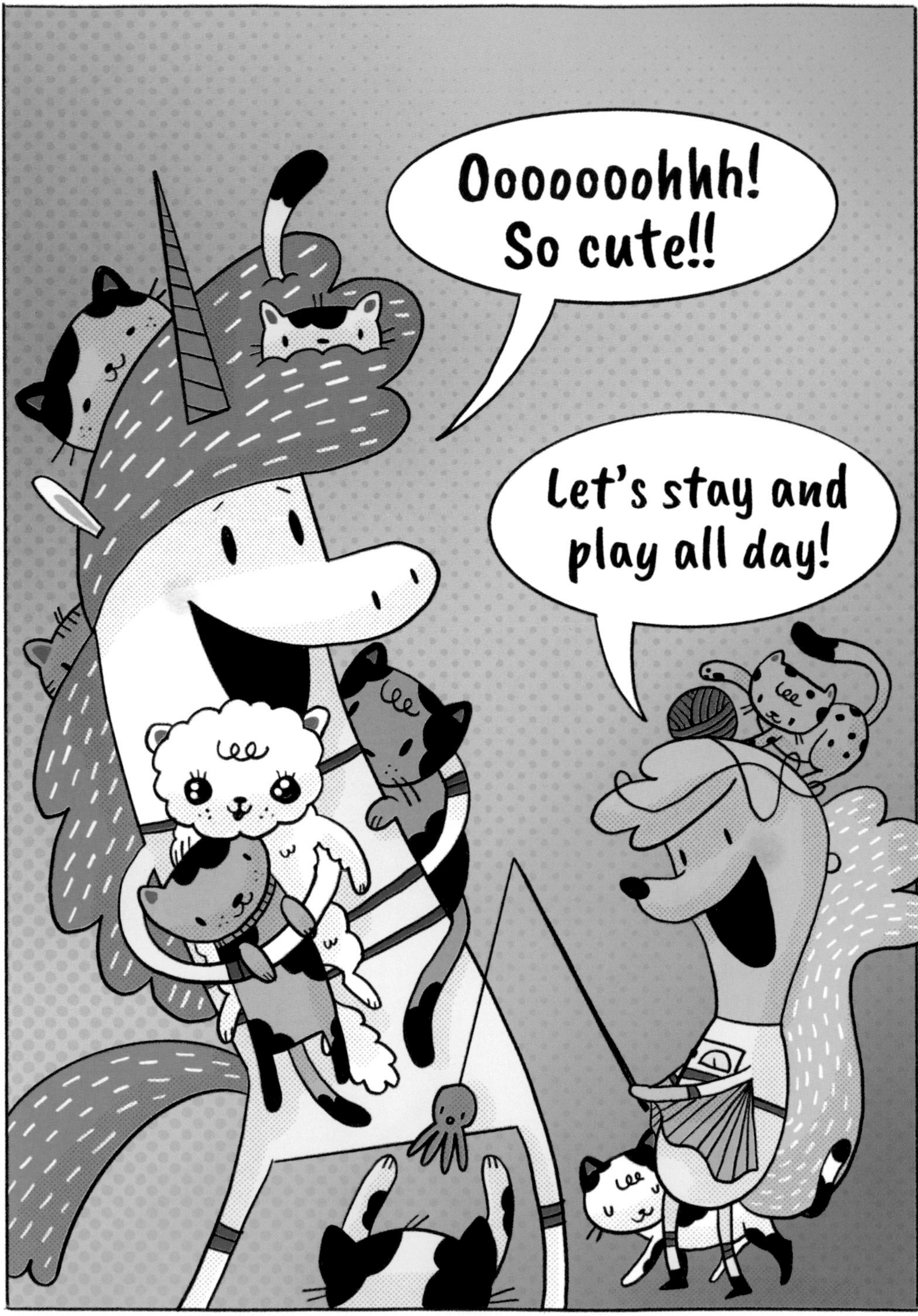
Ooooooohhh! So cute!!
Let's stay and play all day!

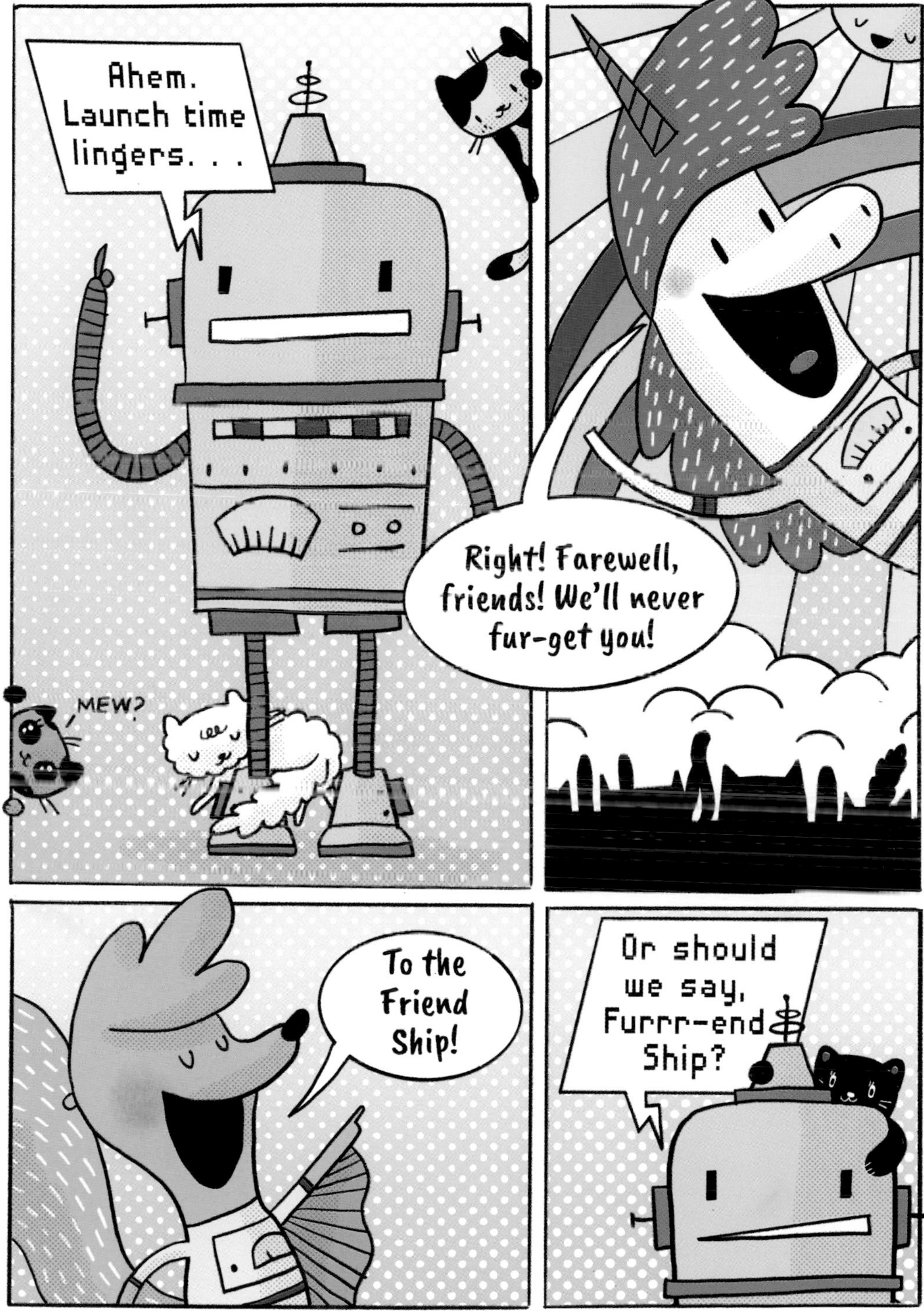

Ahem. Launch time lingers. . .
MEW?
Right! Farewell, friends! We'll never fur-get you!
To the Friend Ship!
Or should we say, Furrr-end Ship?

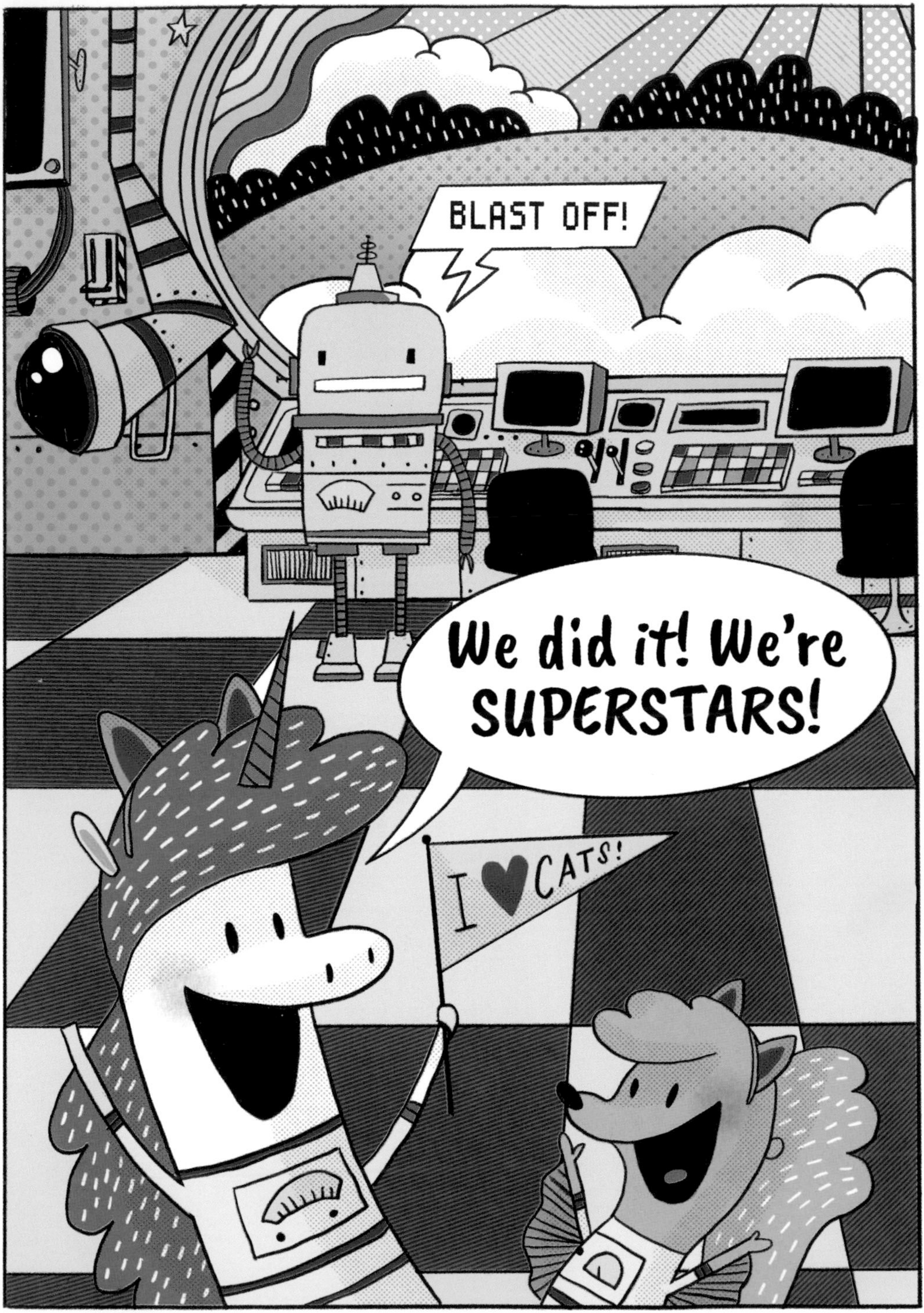
BLAST OFF!
We did it! We're SUPERSTARS!
I ♥ CATS!

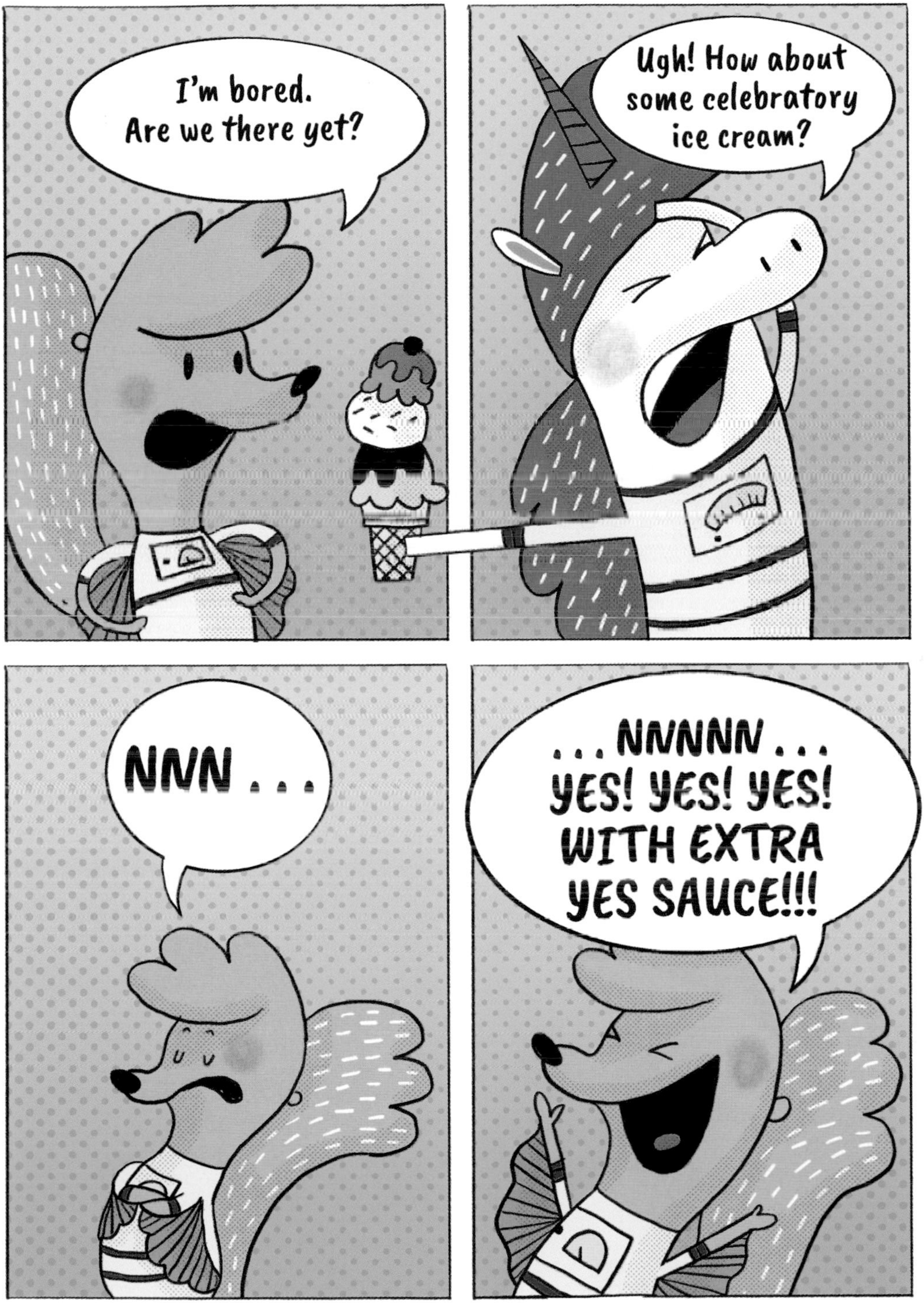
I'm bored.
Are we there yet?
Ugh! How about some celebratory ice cream?
NNN . . .
. . . NNNNN . . .
YES! YES! YES!
WITH EXTRA
YES SAUCE!!!

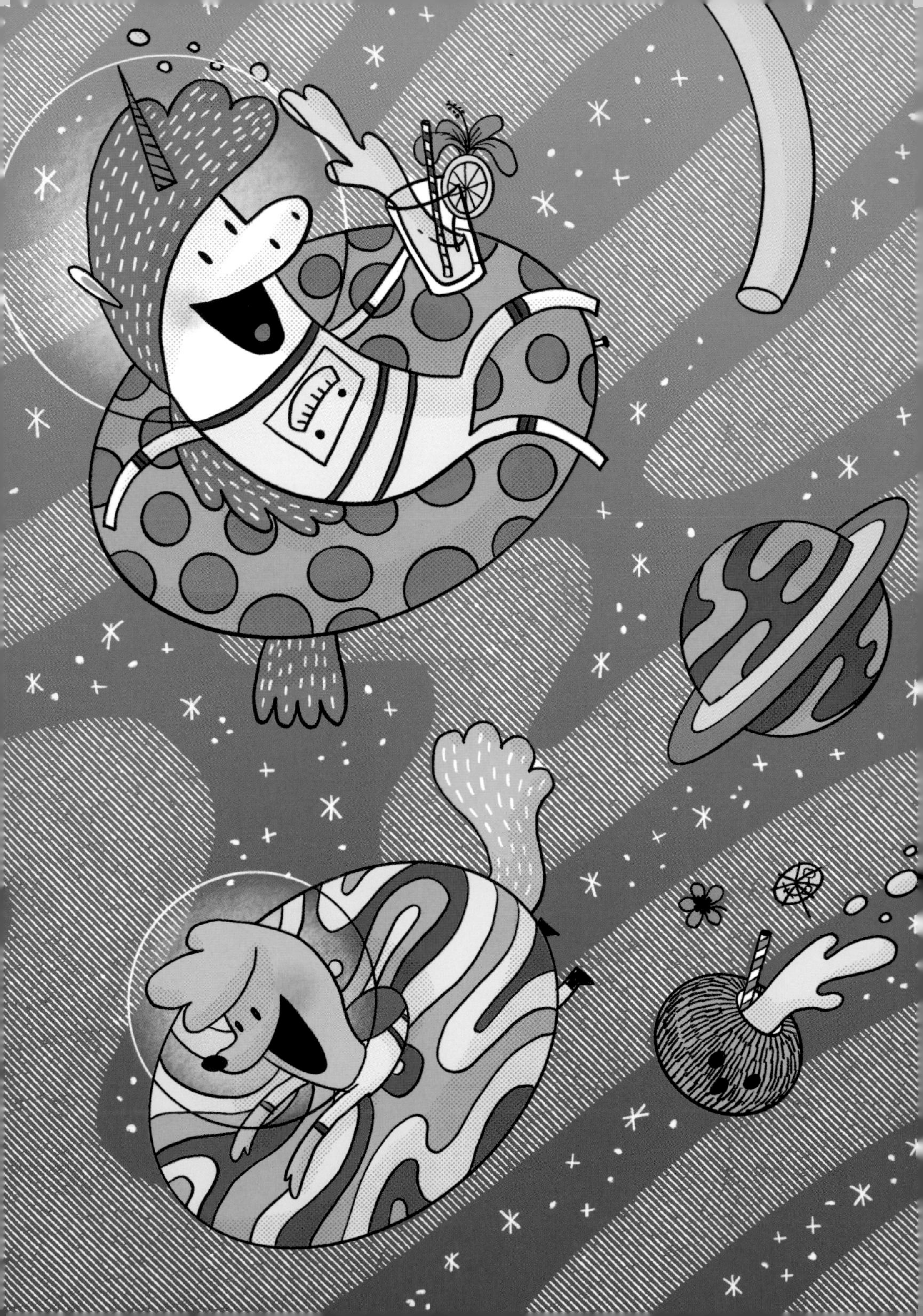

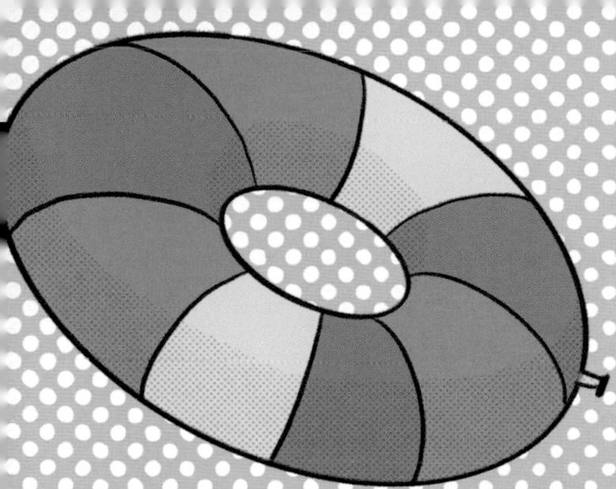

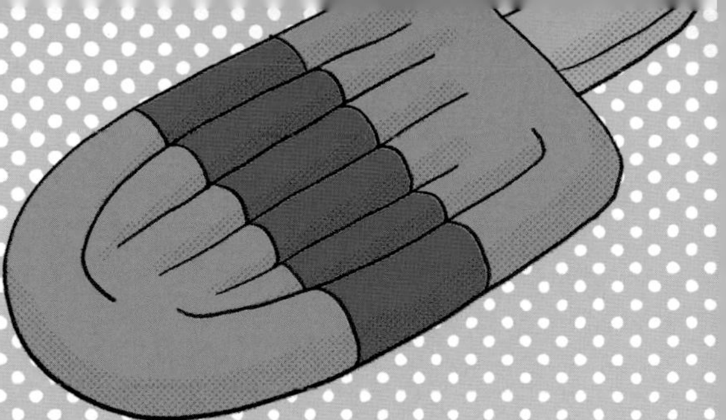

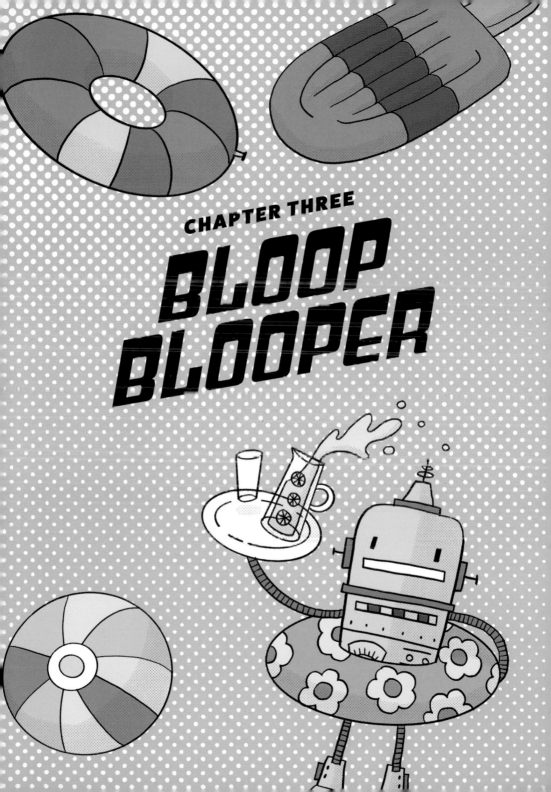

CHAPTER THREE

BLOOP BLOOPER

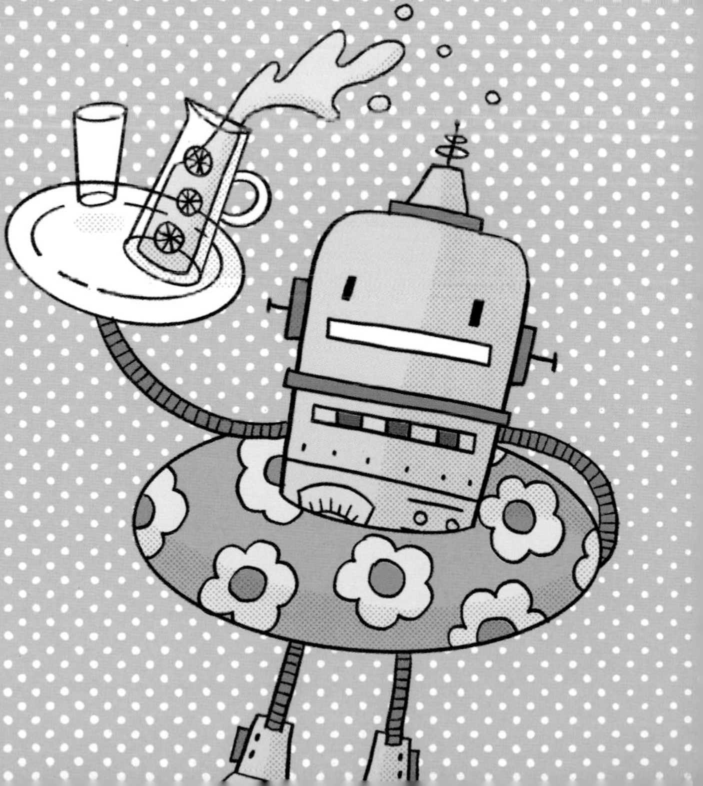

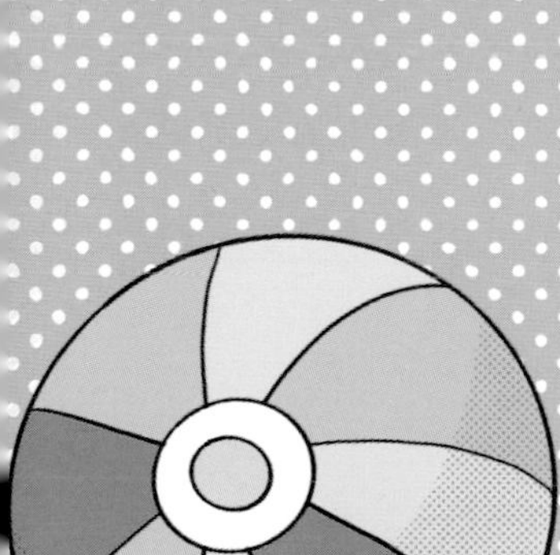

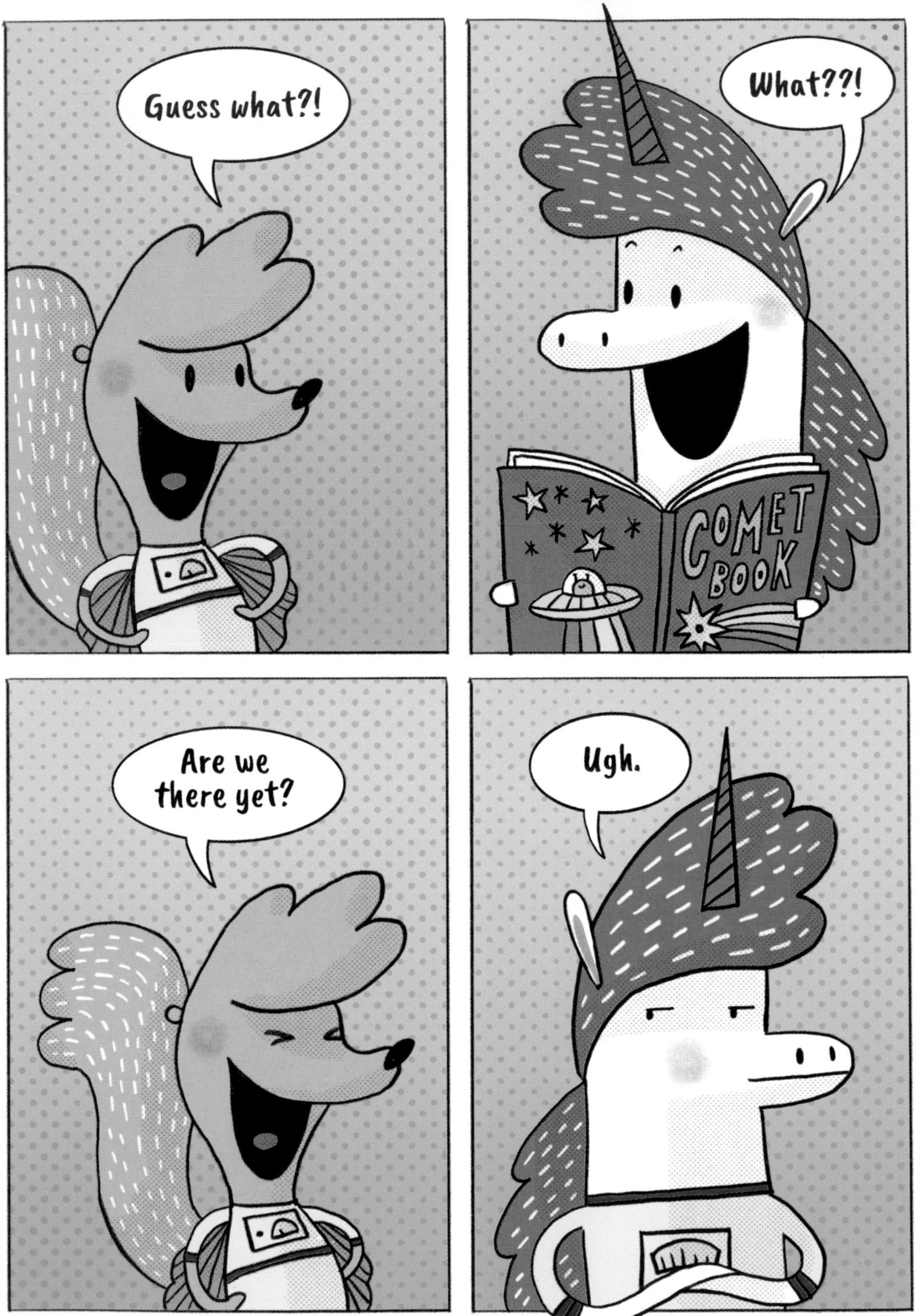
Guess what?!
What??!
COMET BOOK
Are we there yet?
Ugh.

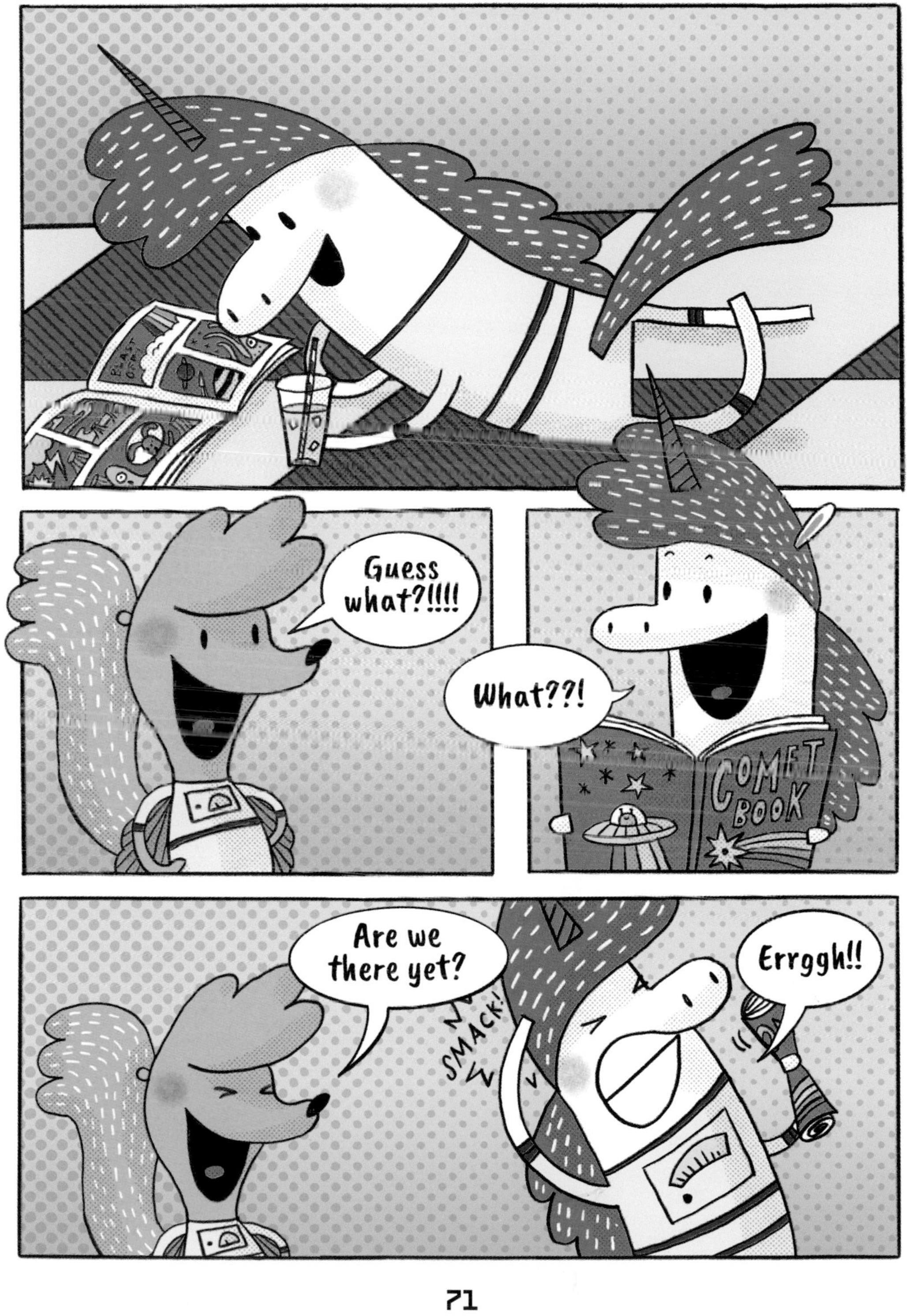
Guess what?!!!!!
What??!
COMET BOOK
Are we there yet?
SMACK!
Errggh!!

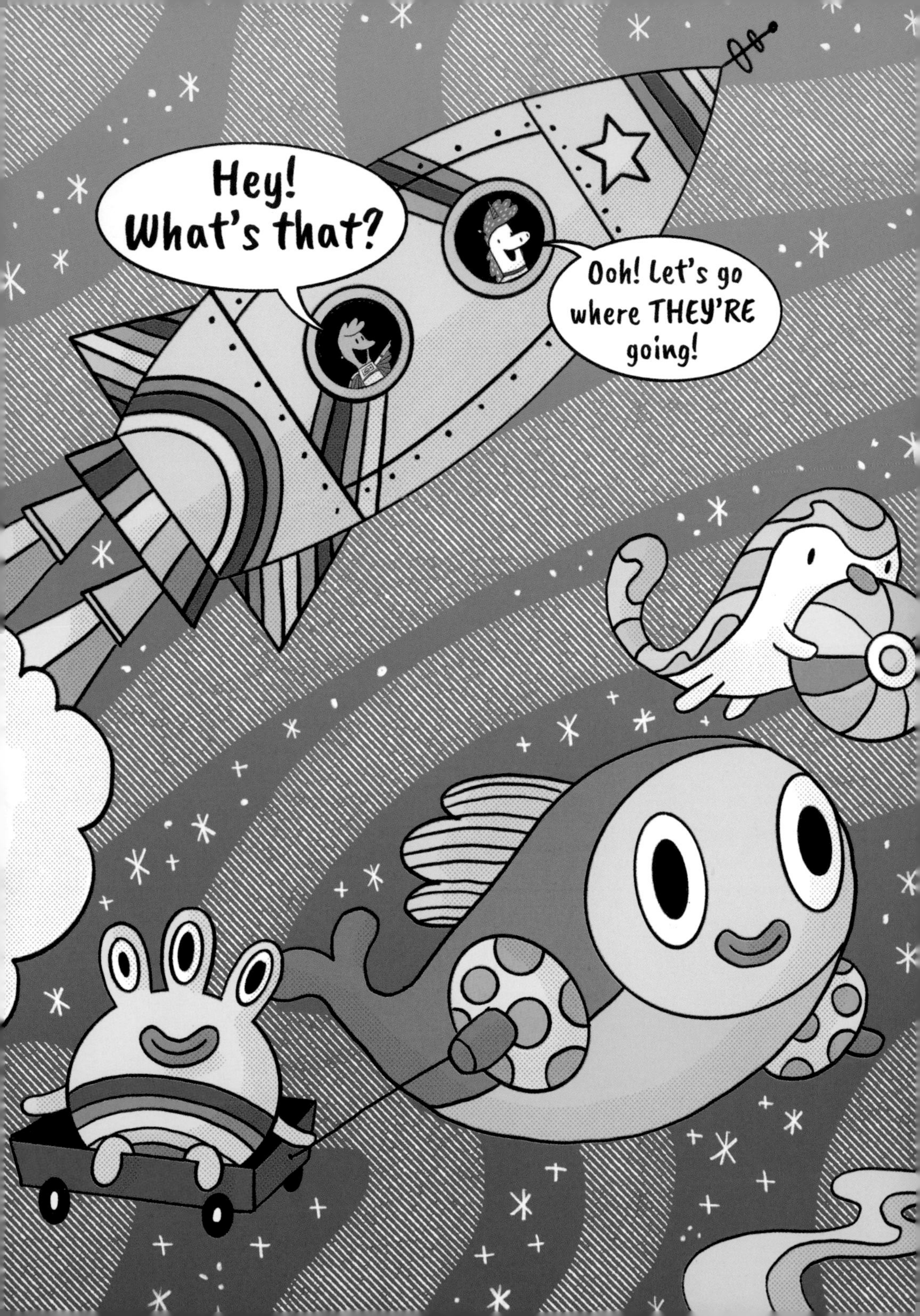
Hey! What's that?
Ooh! Let's go where THEY'RE going!

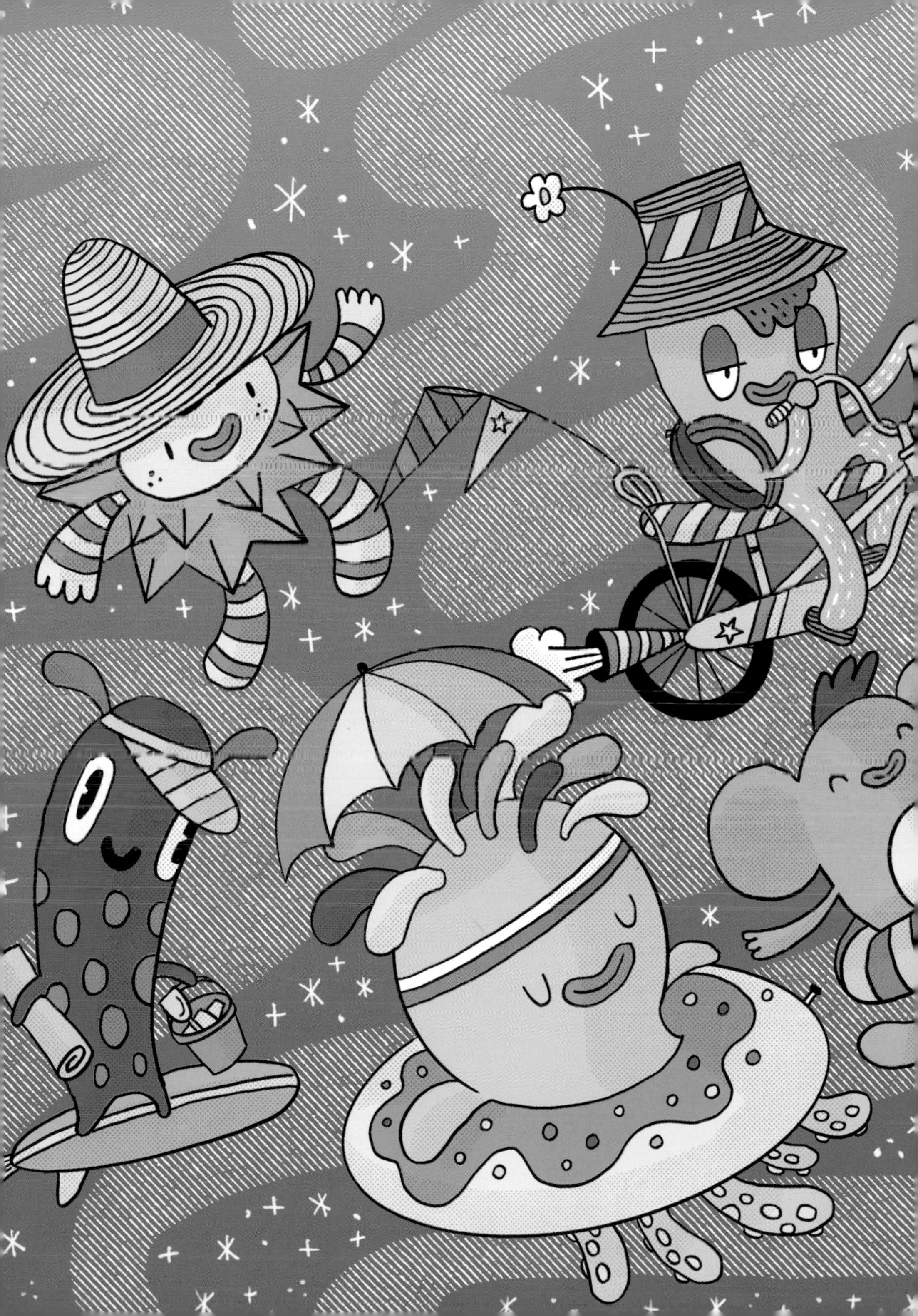

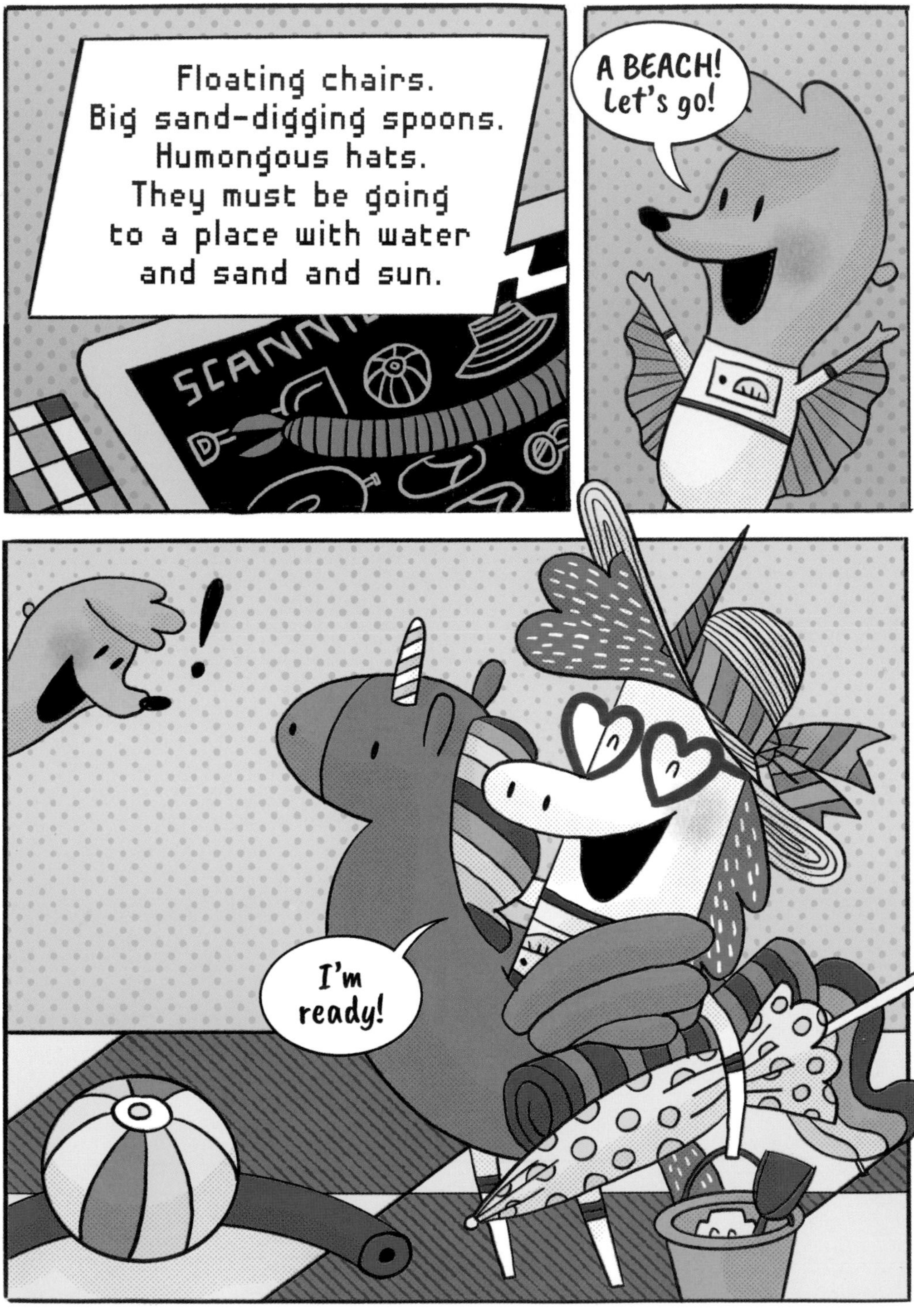

Floating chairs.
Big sand-digging spoons.
Humongous hats.
They must be going
to a place with water
and sand and sun.
A BEACH!
Let's go!
!
I'm
ready!

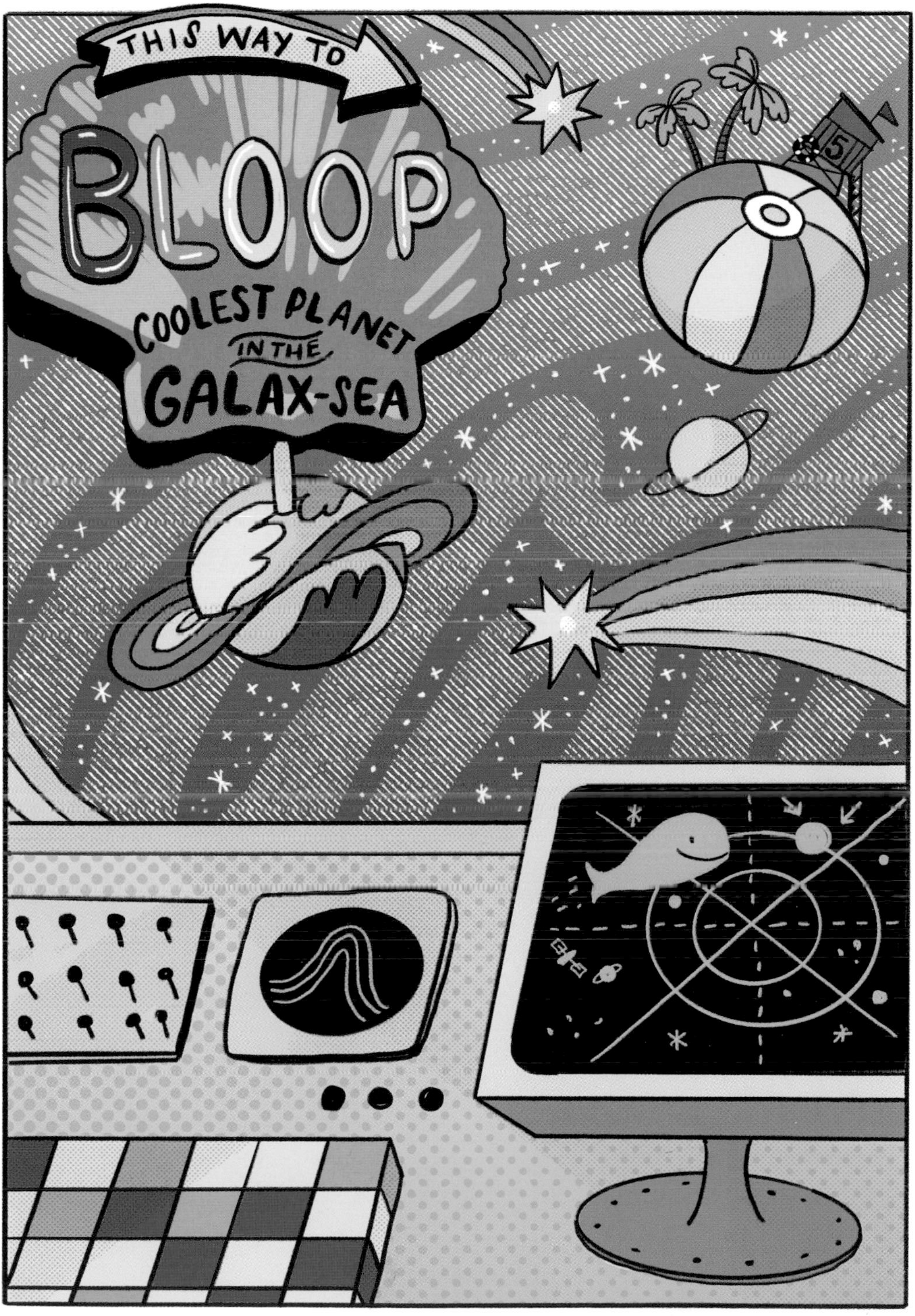
THIS WAY TO
BLOOP
COOLEST PLANET IN THE GALAX-SEA

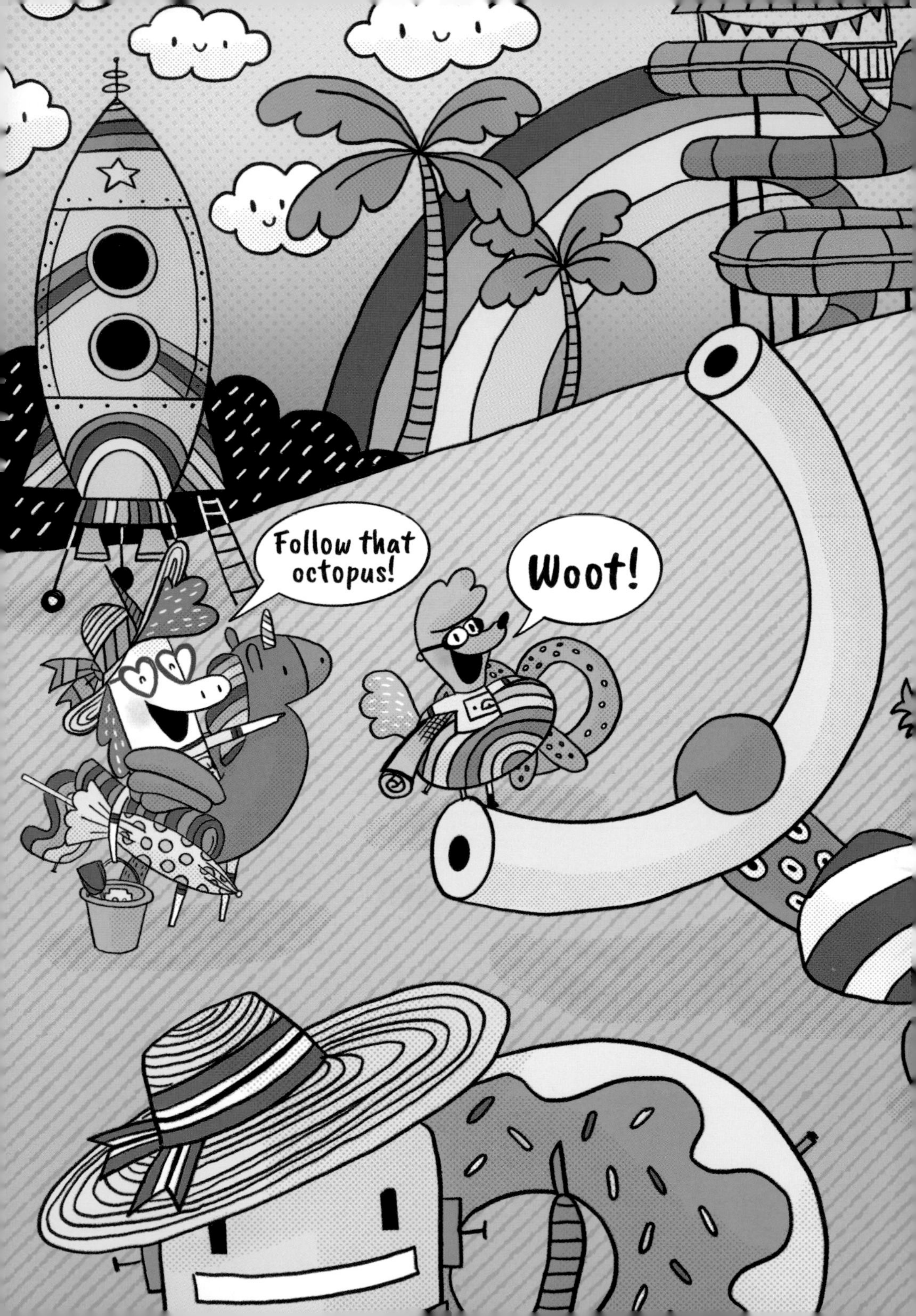
Follow that octopus!
Woot!

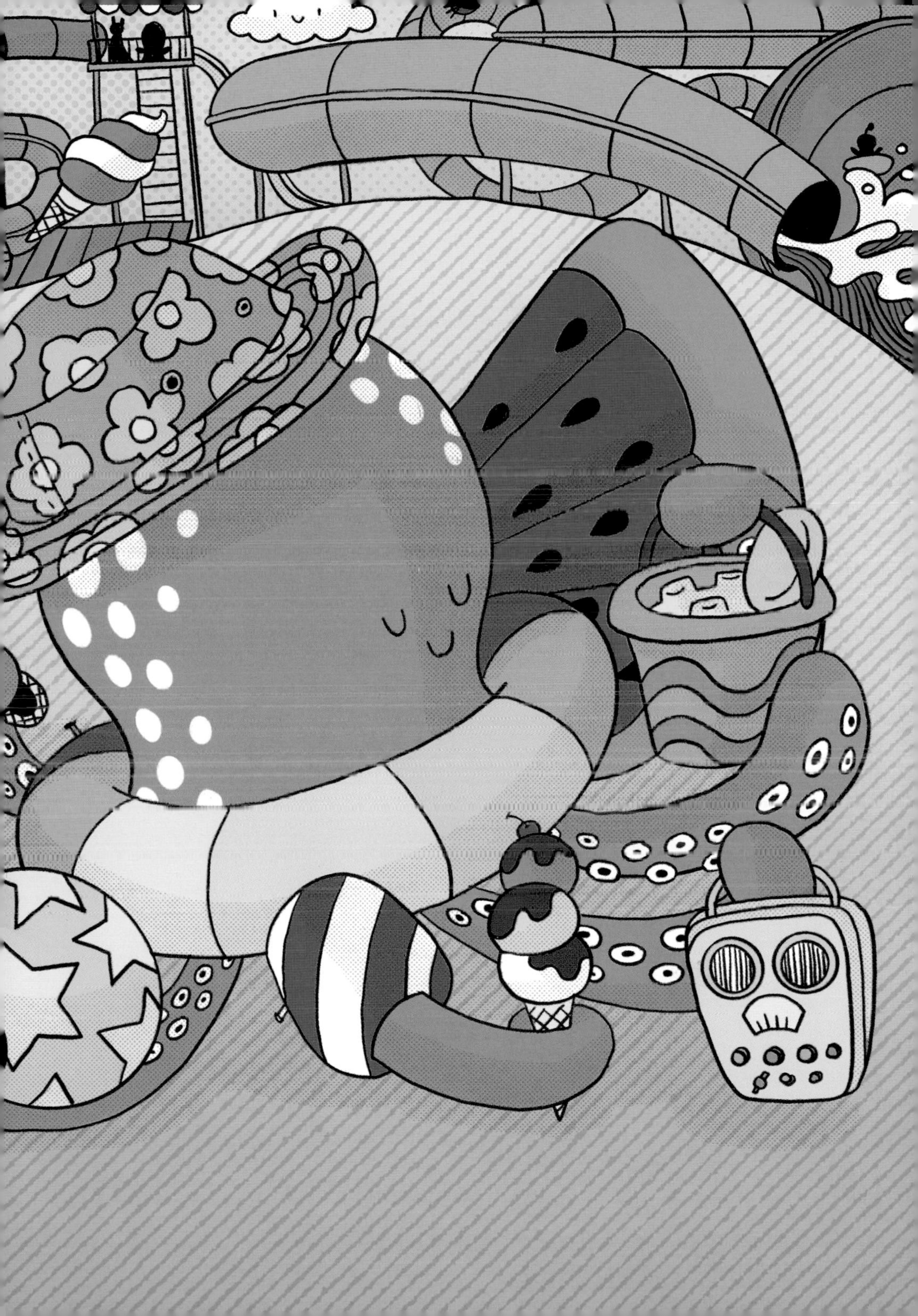

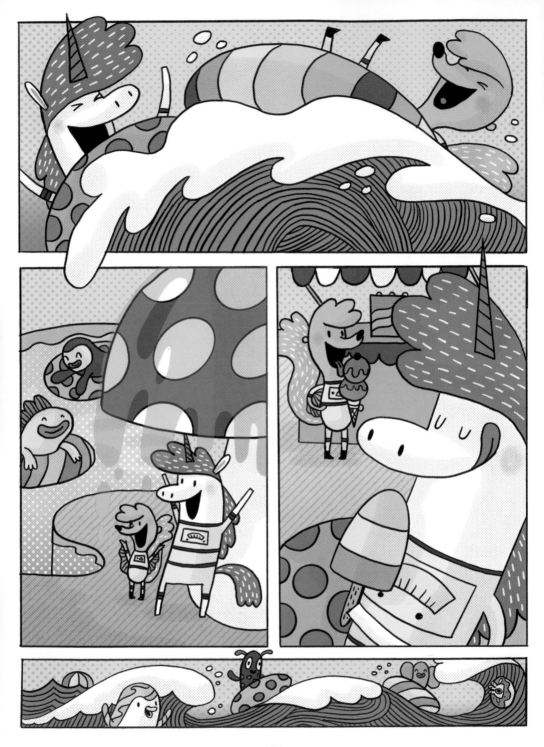

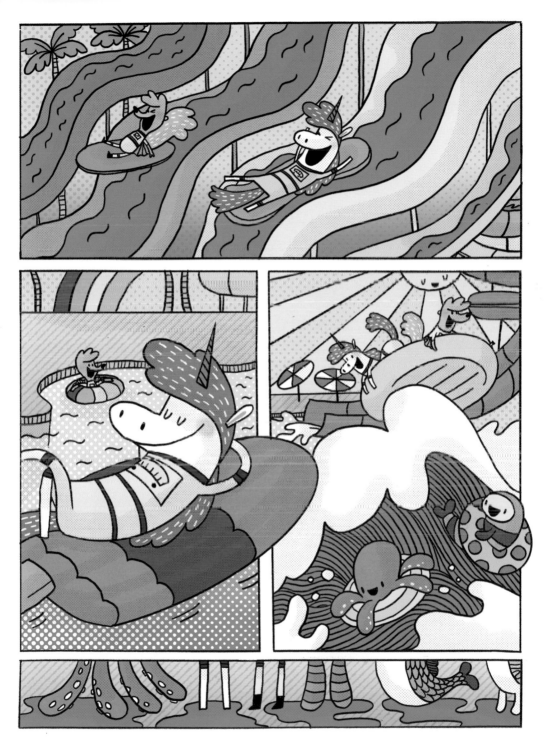

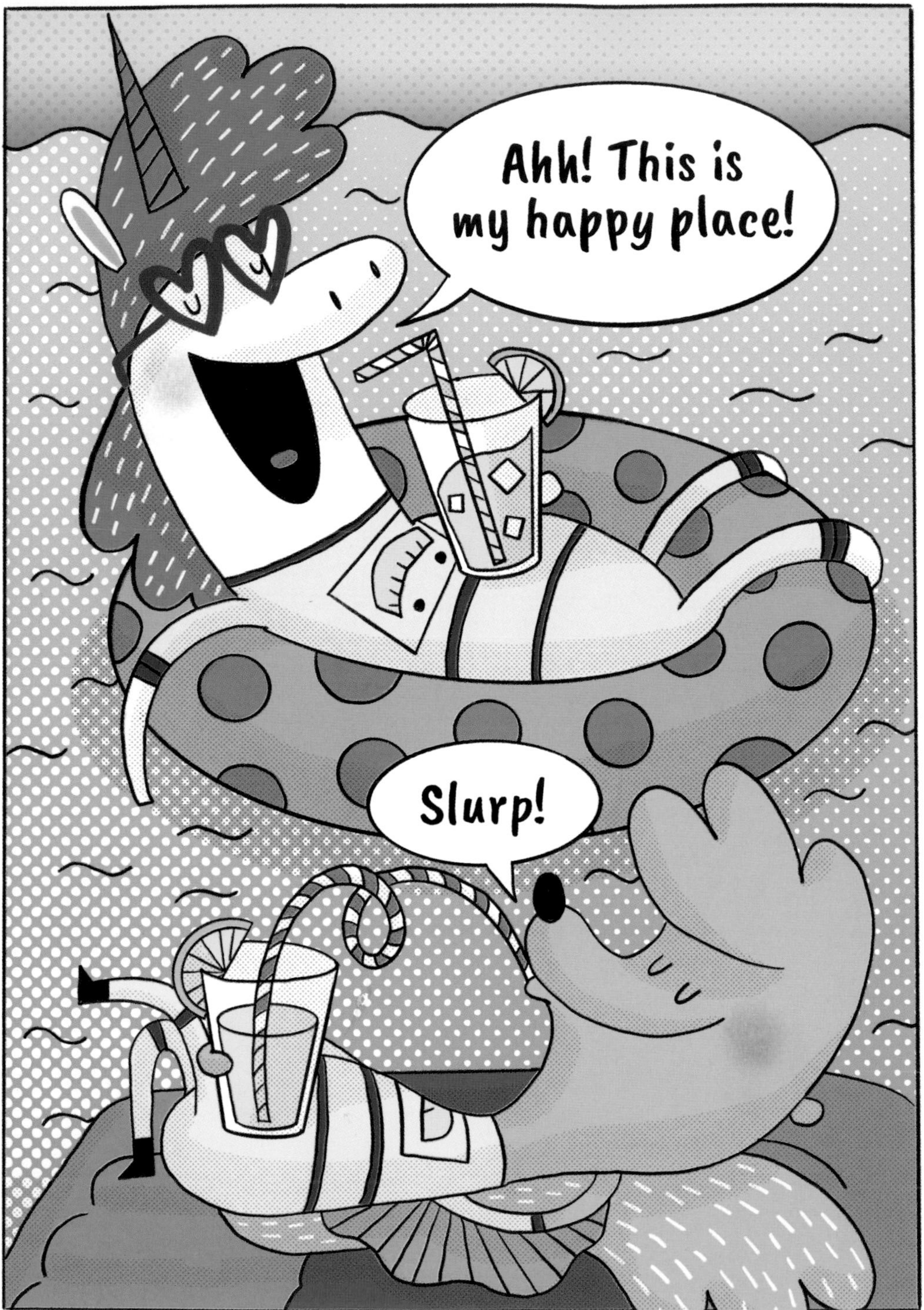
Ahh! This is my happy place!
Slurp!

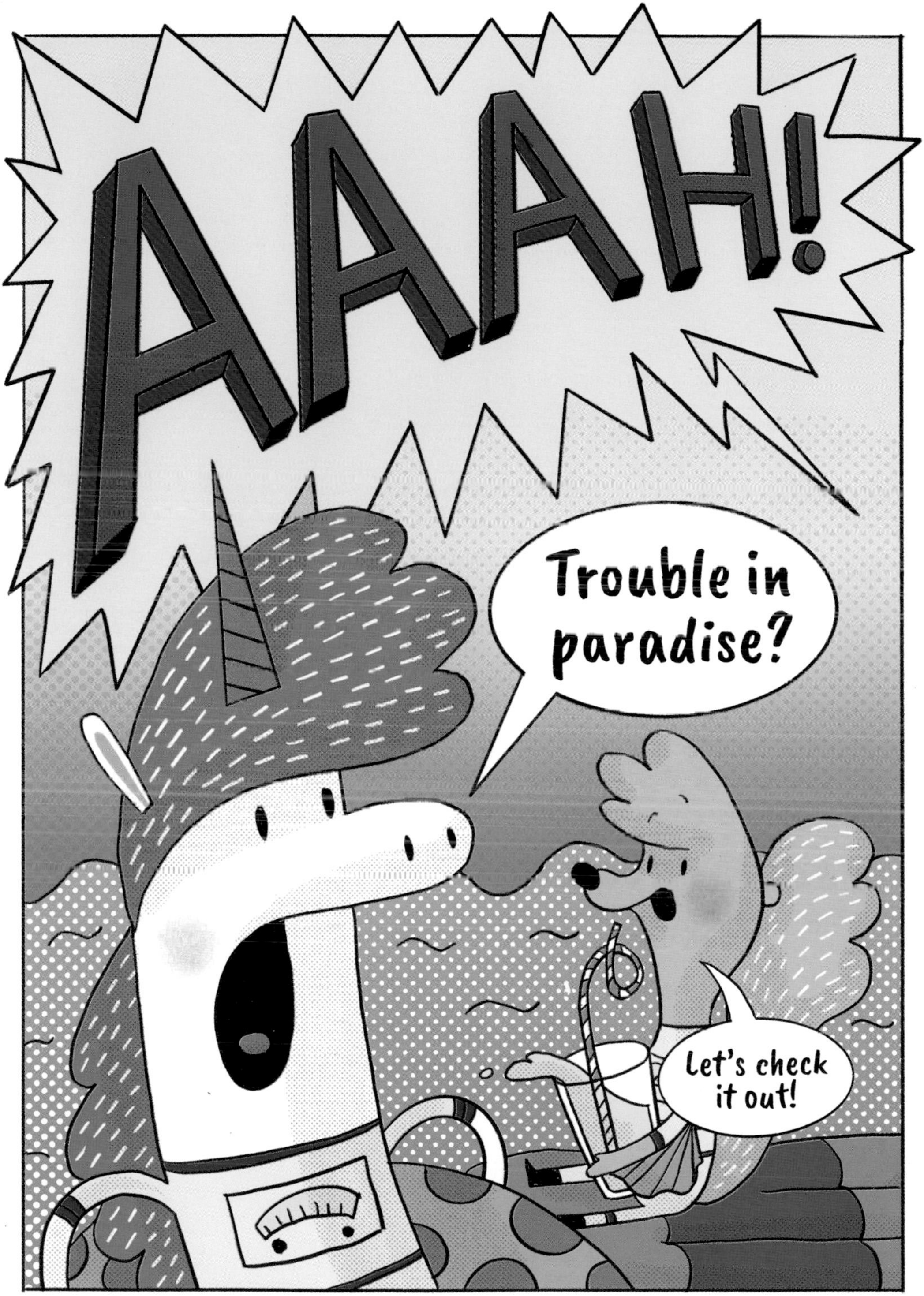
AAAH!
Trouble in paradise?
Let's check it out!

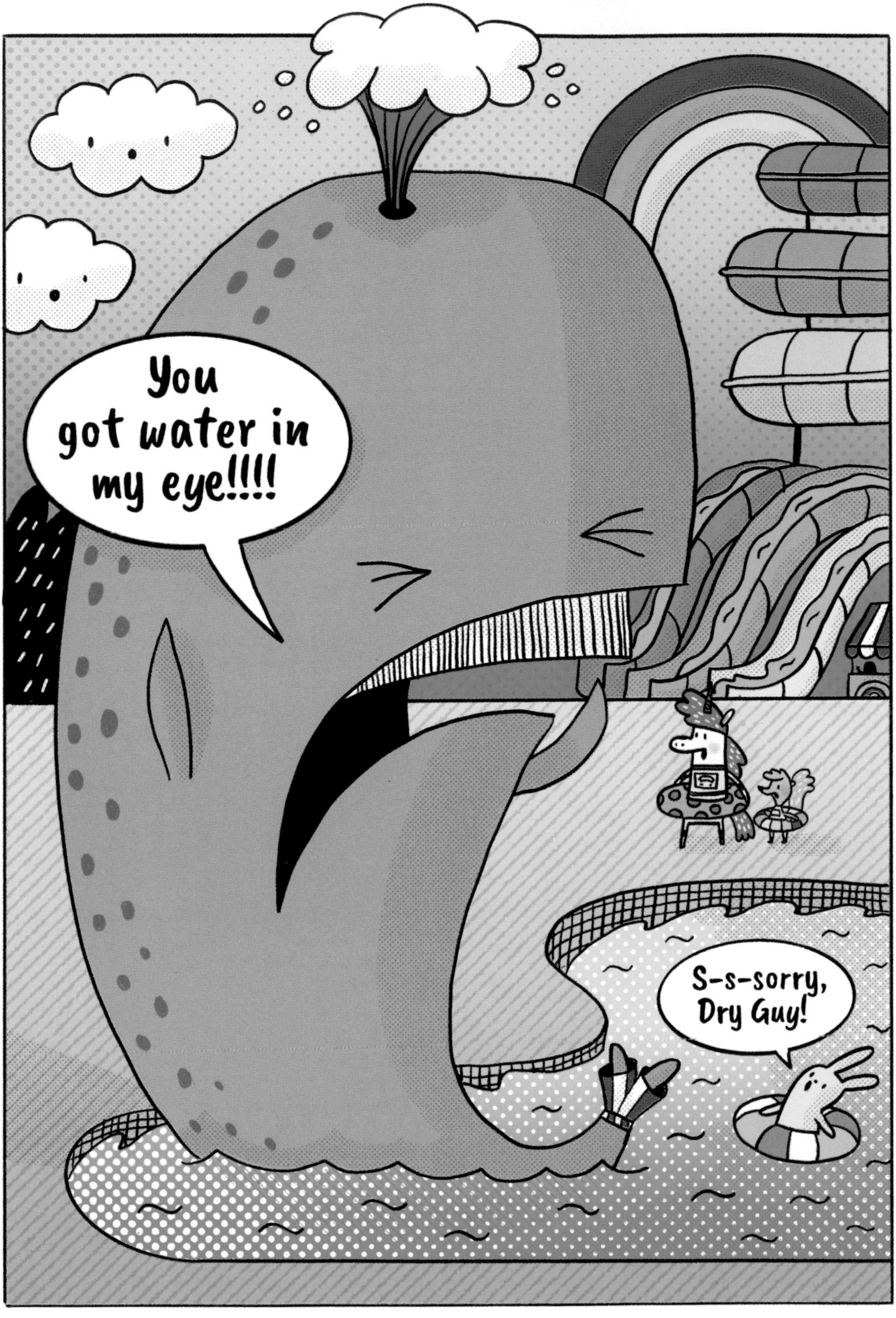
You got water in my eye!!!!
S-s-sorry, Dry Guy!

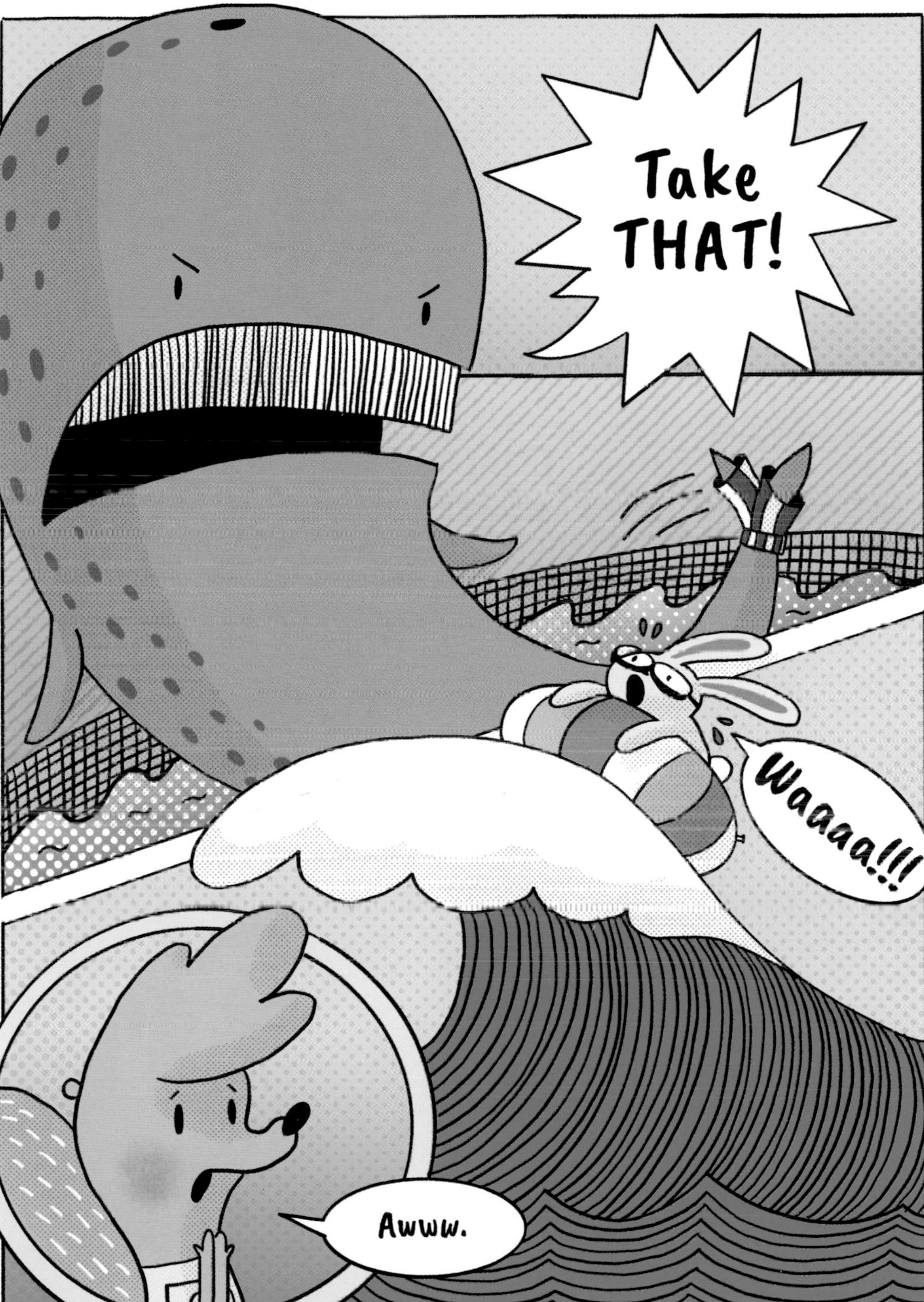
Take THAT!
Waaaaa!!!
Awww.

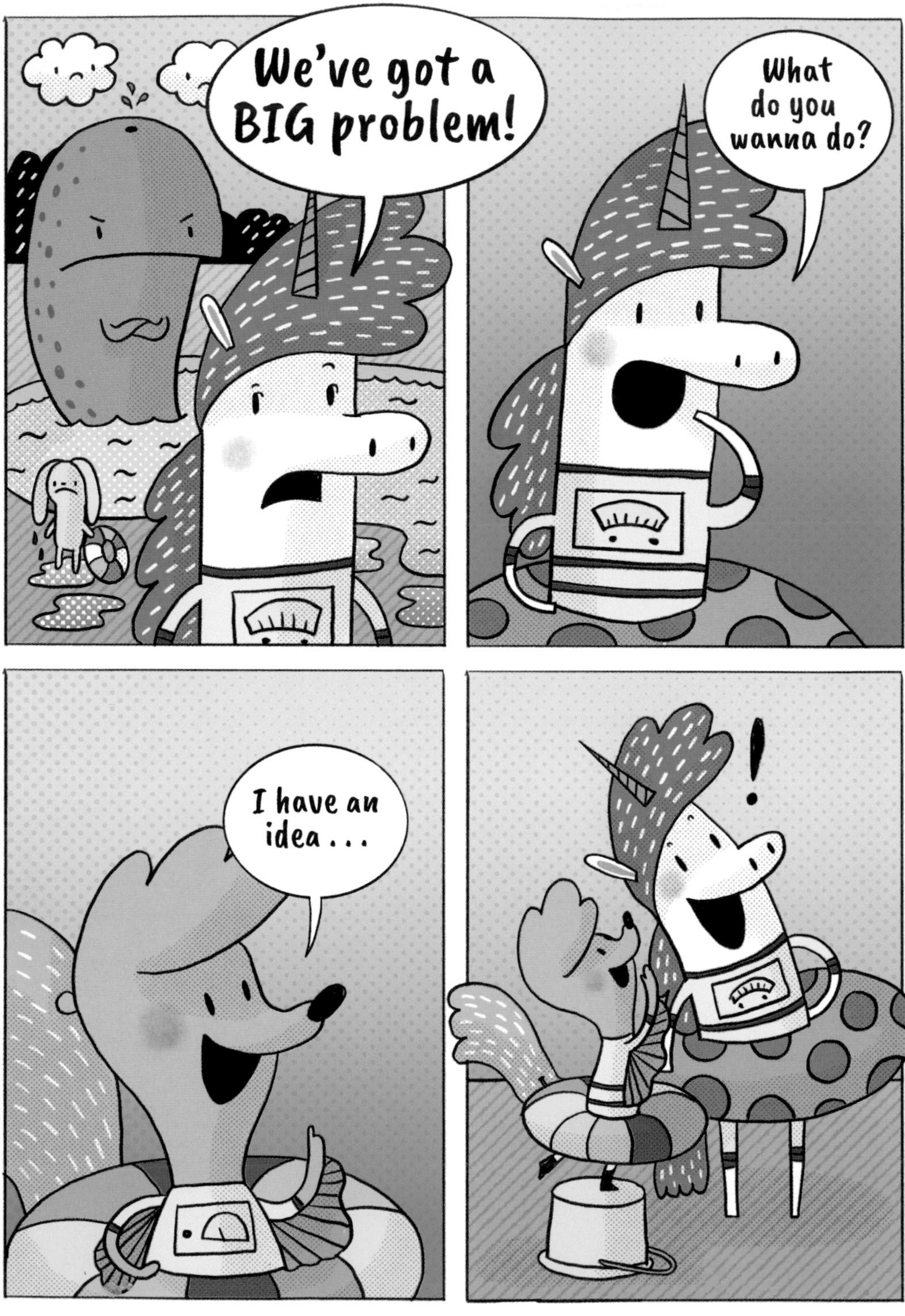
We've got a BIG problem!
What do you wanna do?
I have an idea . . .
!

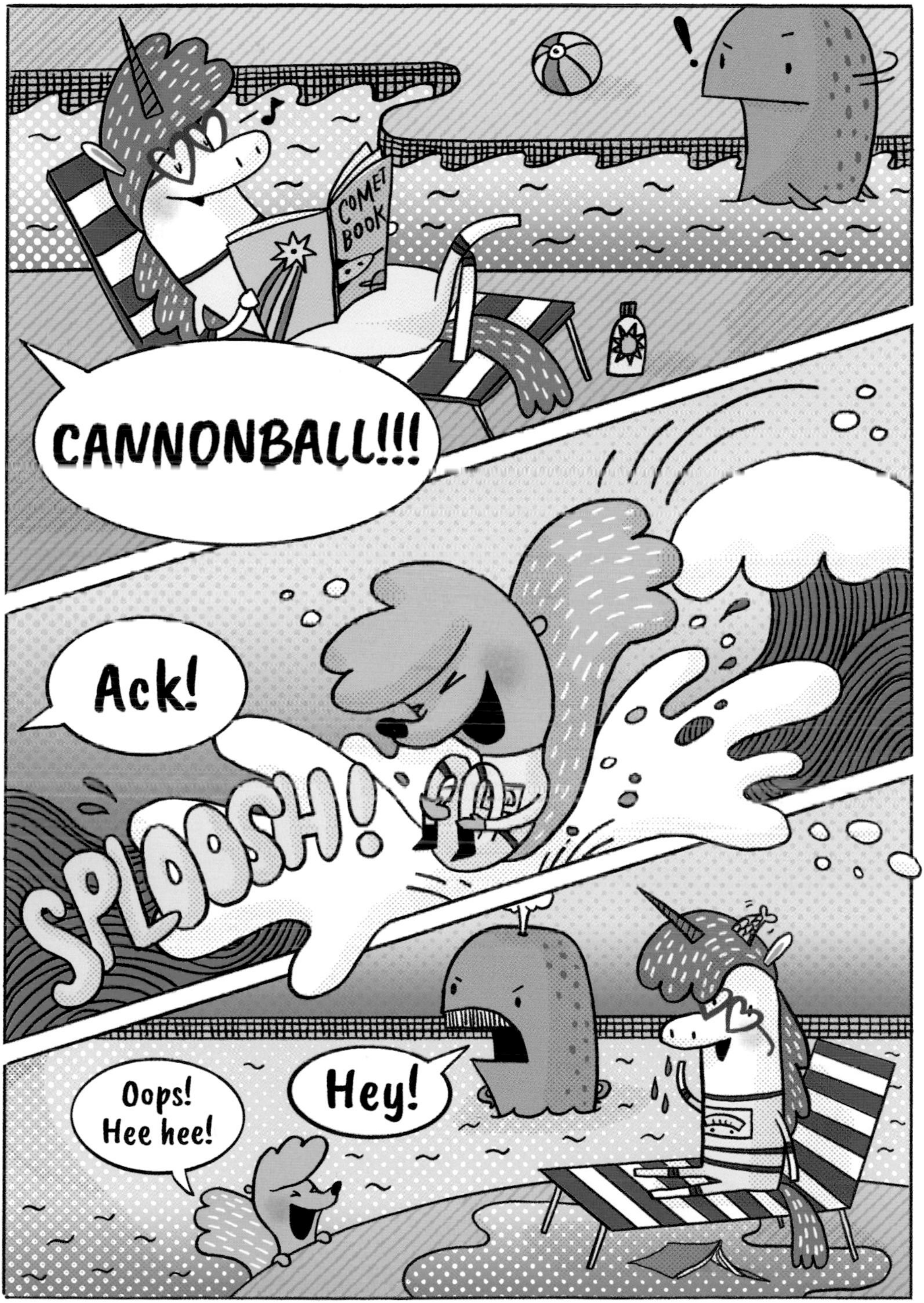
!
COMET BOOK
CANNONBALL!!!
Ack!
SPLOOSH!
Oops!
Hee hee!
Hey!

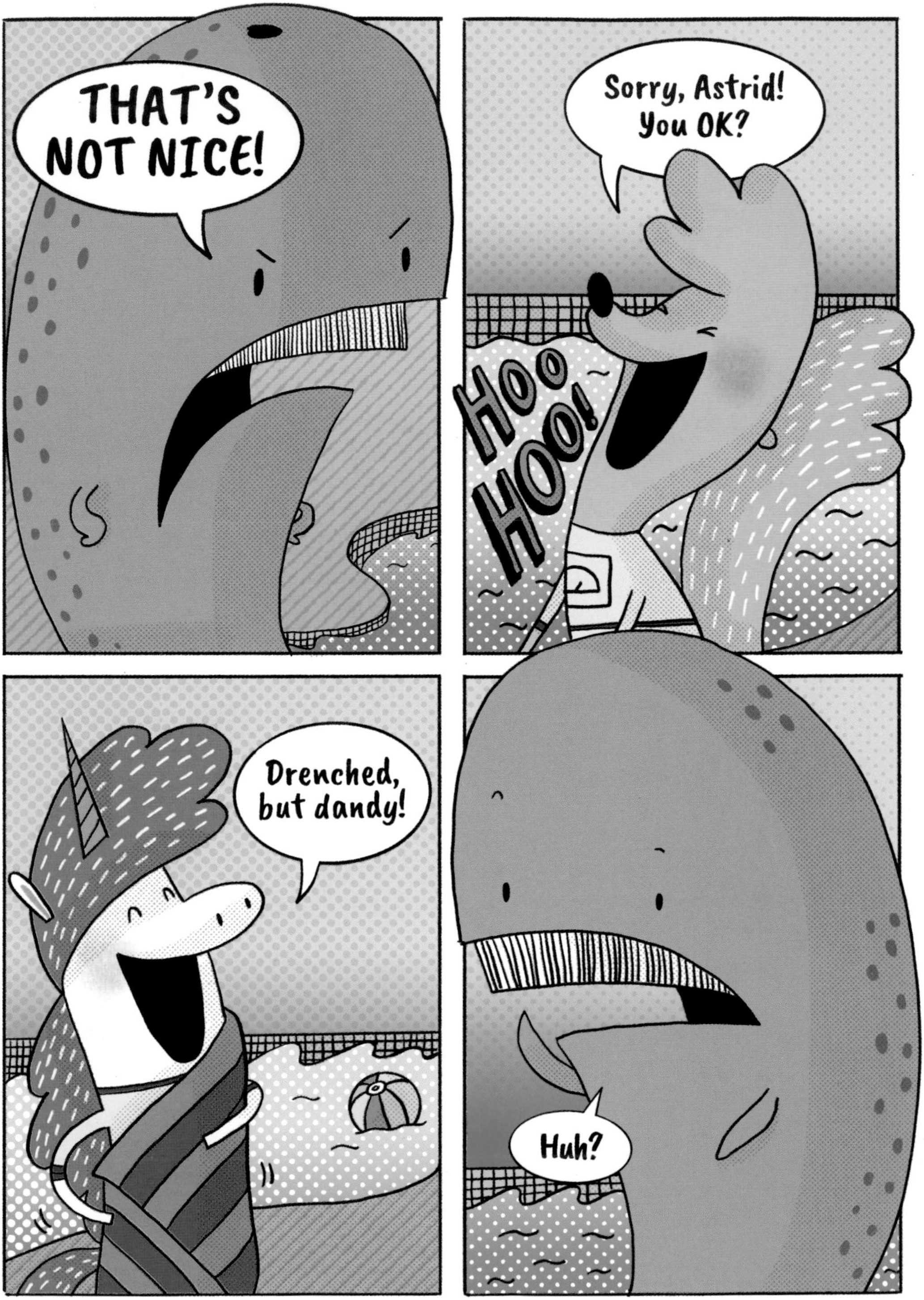
THAT'S NOT NICE!
Sorry, Astrid! You OK?
HOO HOO!
Drenched, but dandy!
Huh?

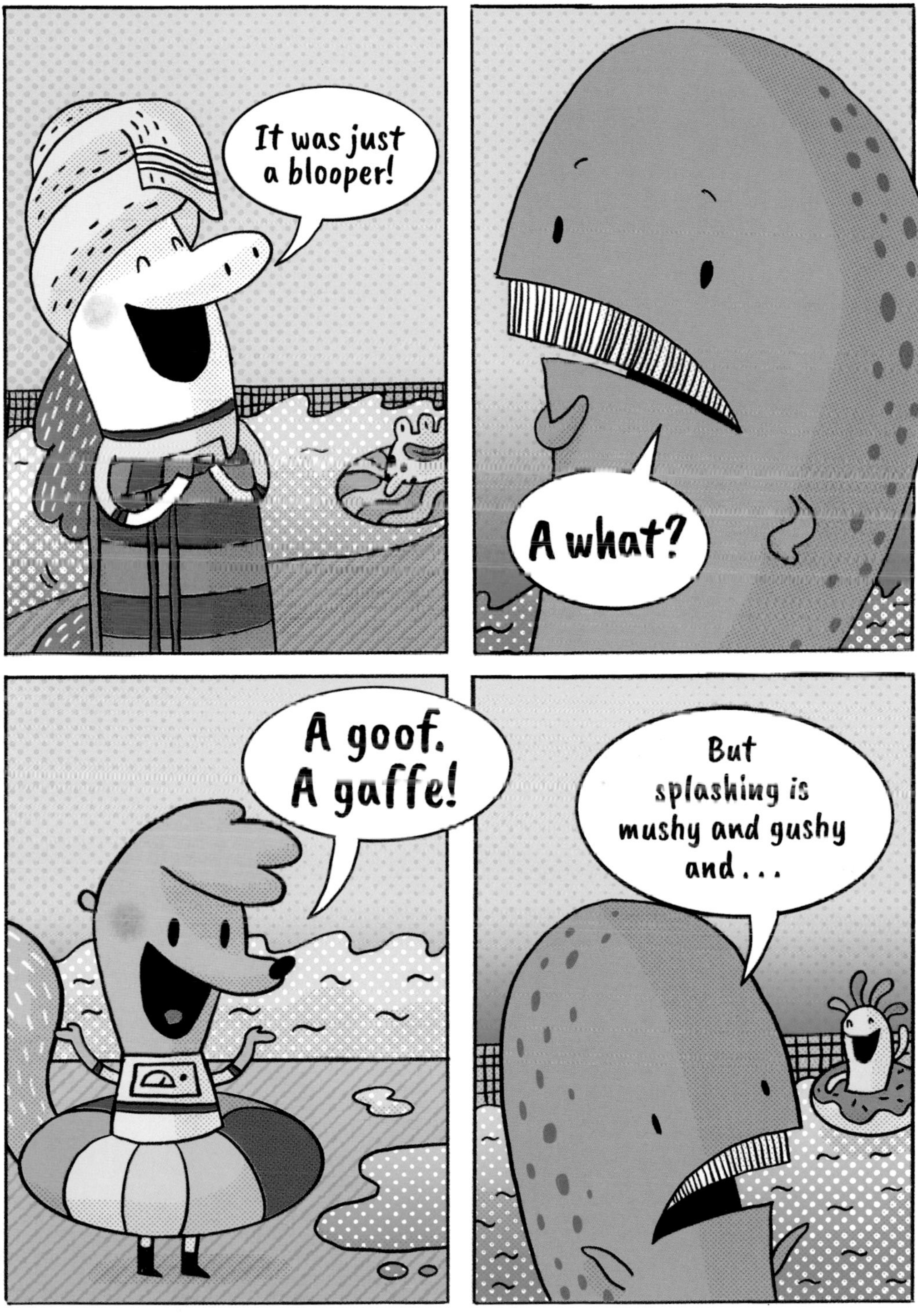
It was just a blooper!
A what?
A goof. A gaffe!
But splashing is mushy and gushy and . . .

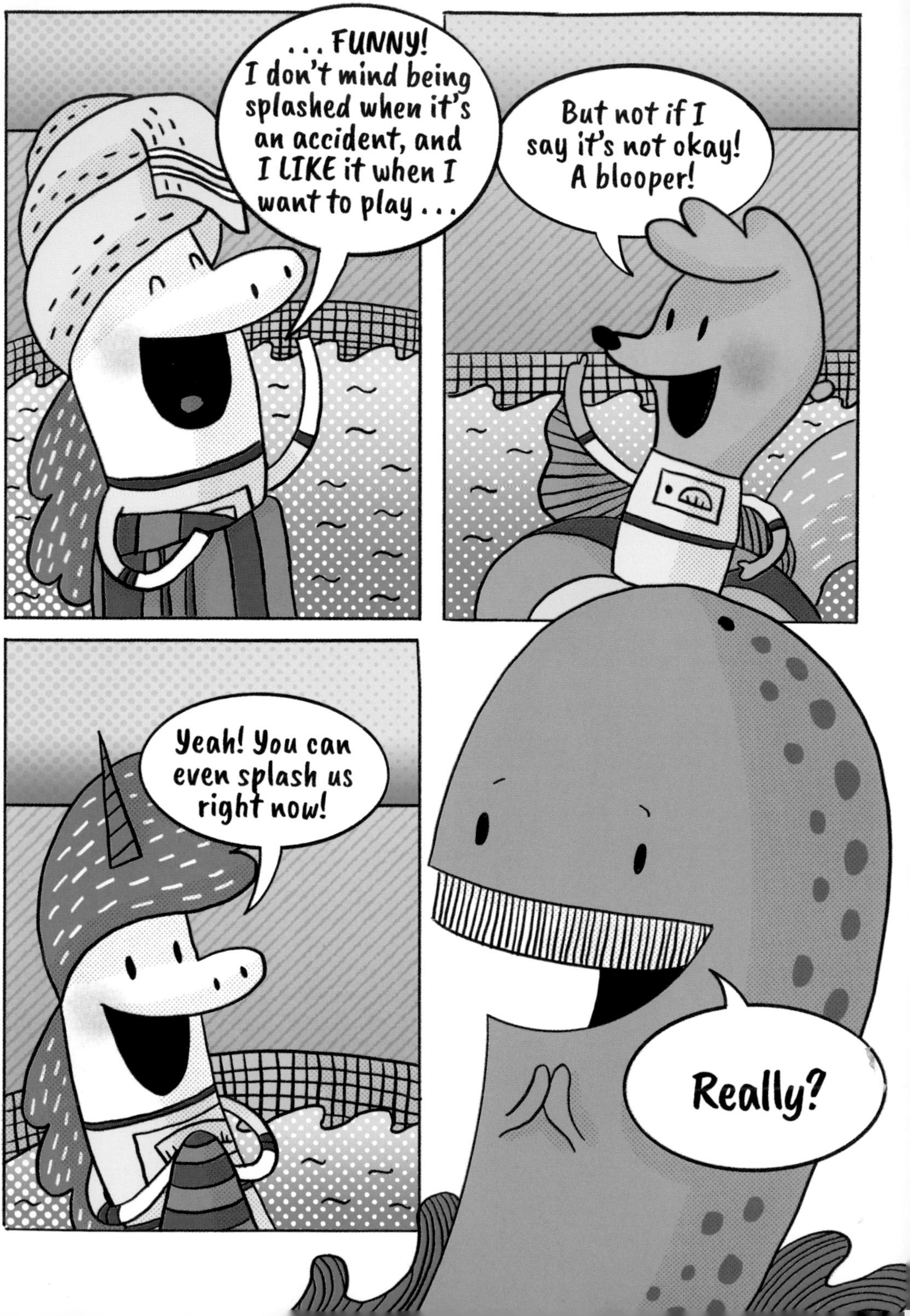
. . . FUNNY! I don't mind being splashed when it's an accident, and I LIKE it when I want to play . . .
But not if I say it's not okay! A blooper!
Yeah! You can even splash us right now!
Really?

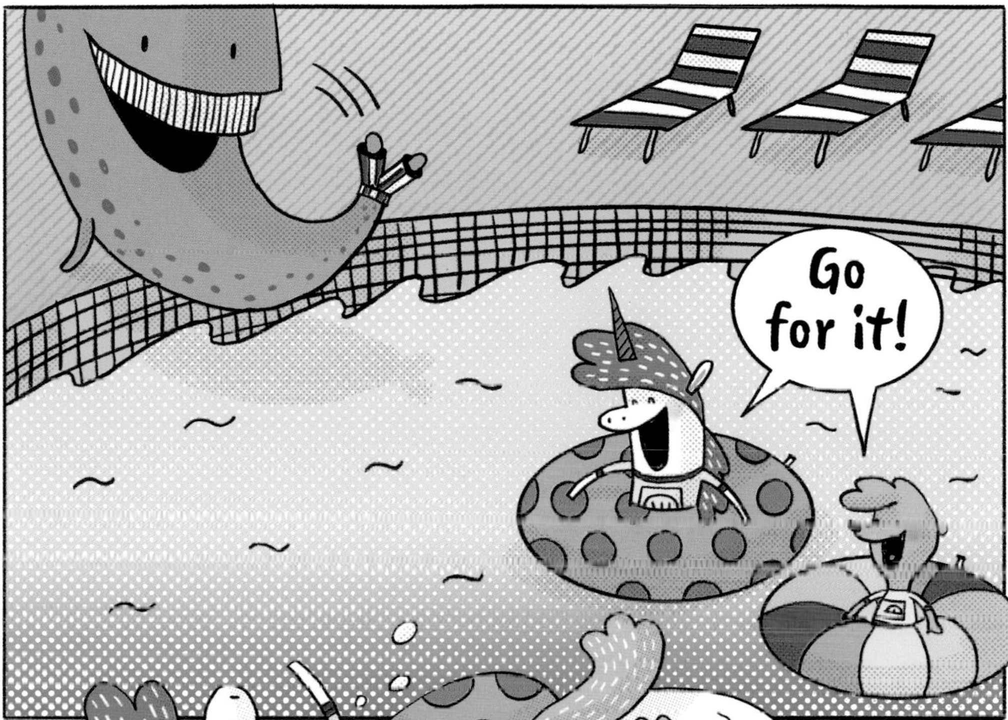
Go for it!

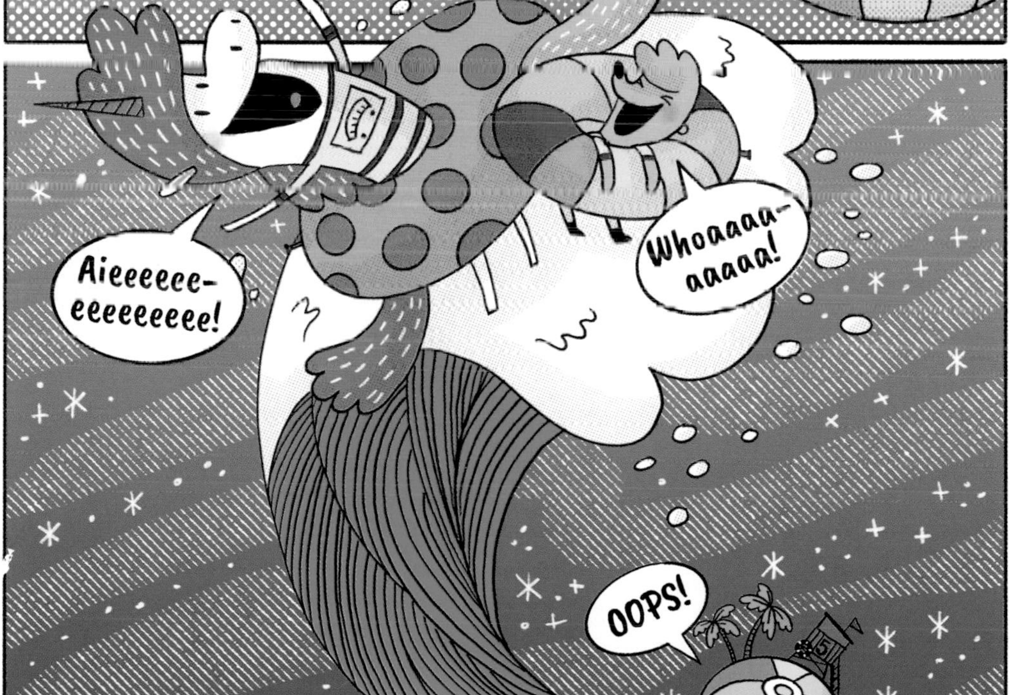
Aieeeeee-eeeeeeeee!
Whoaaaa-aaaaa!
OOPS!

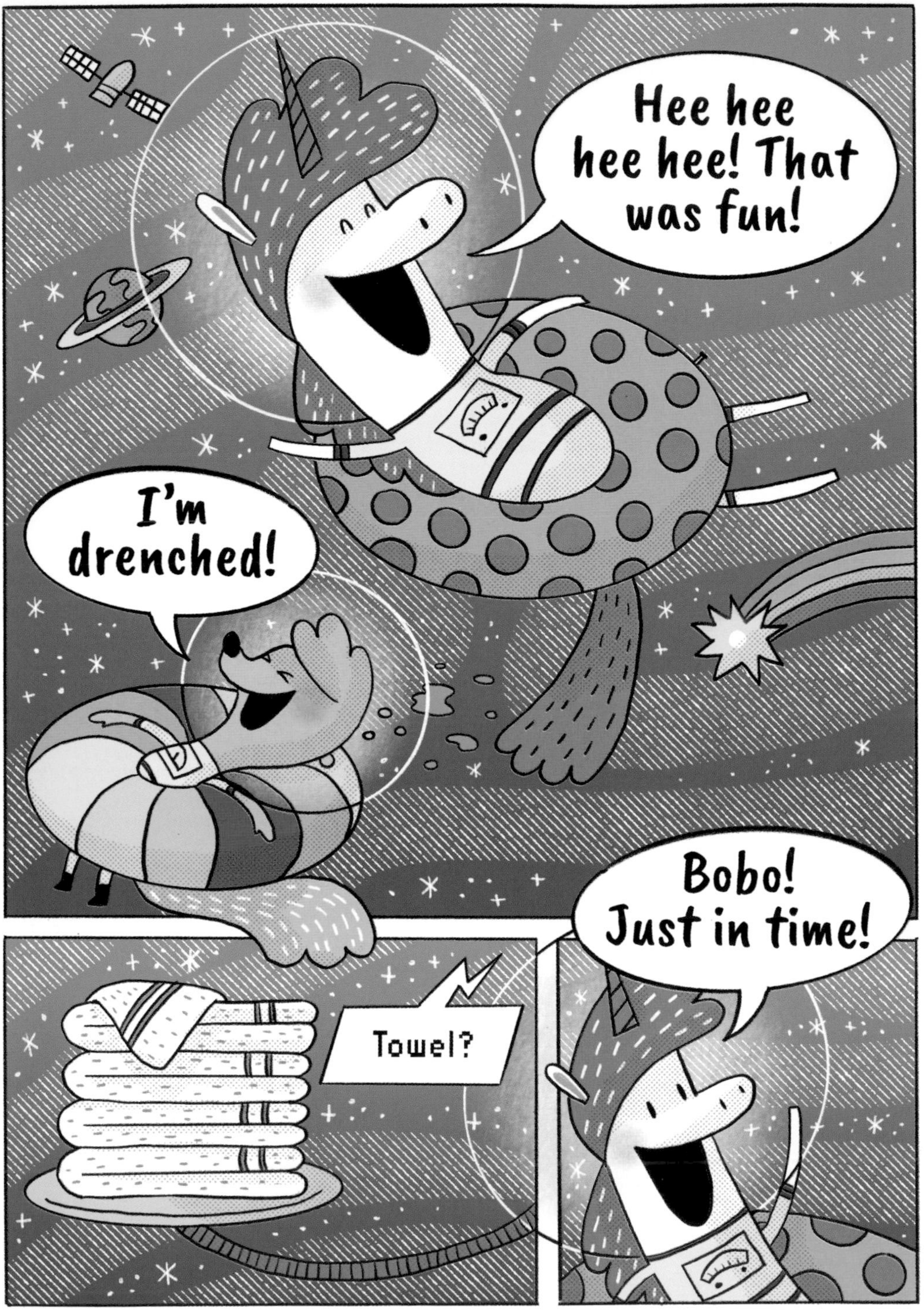

Hee hee hee hee! That was fun!
I'm drenched!
Towel?
Bobo! Just in time!

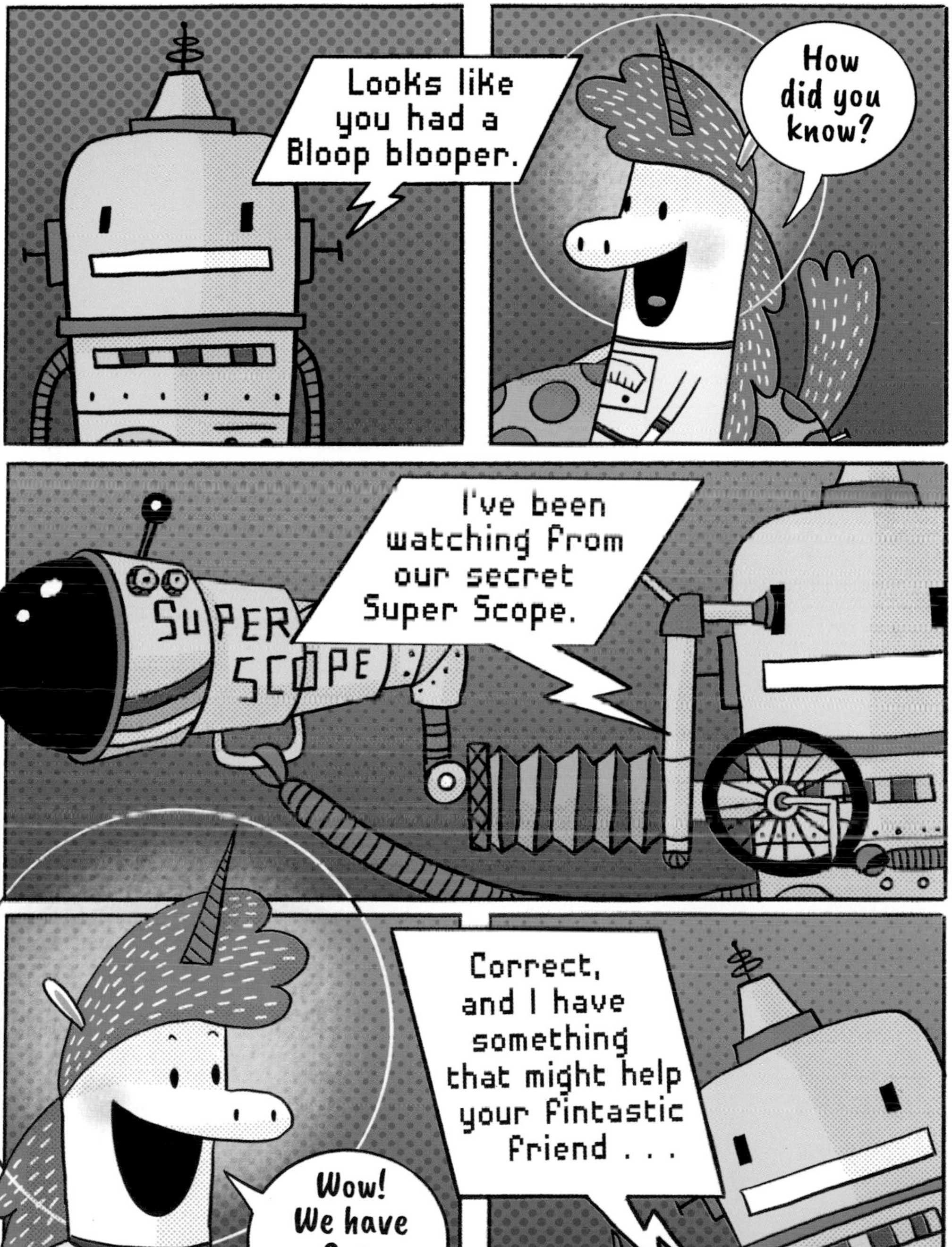

Looks like you had a Bloop blooper.
How did you know?
I've been watching from our secret Super Scope.
SUPER SCOPE
Correct, and I have something that might help your fintastic friend . . .
Wow! We have a Super Scope?!

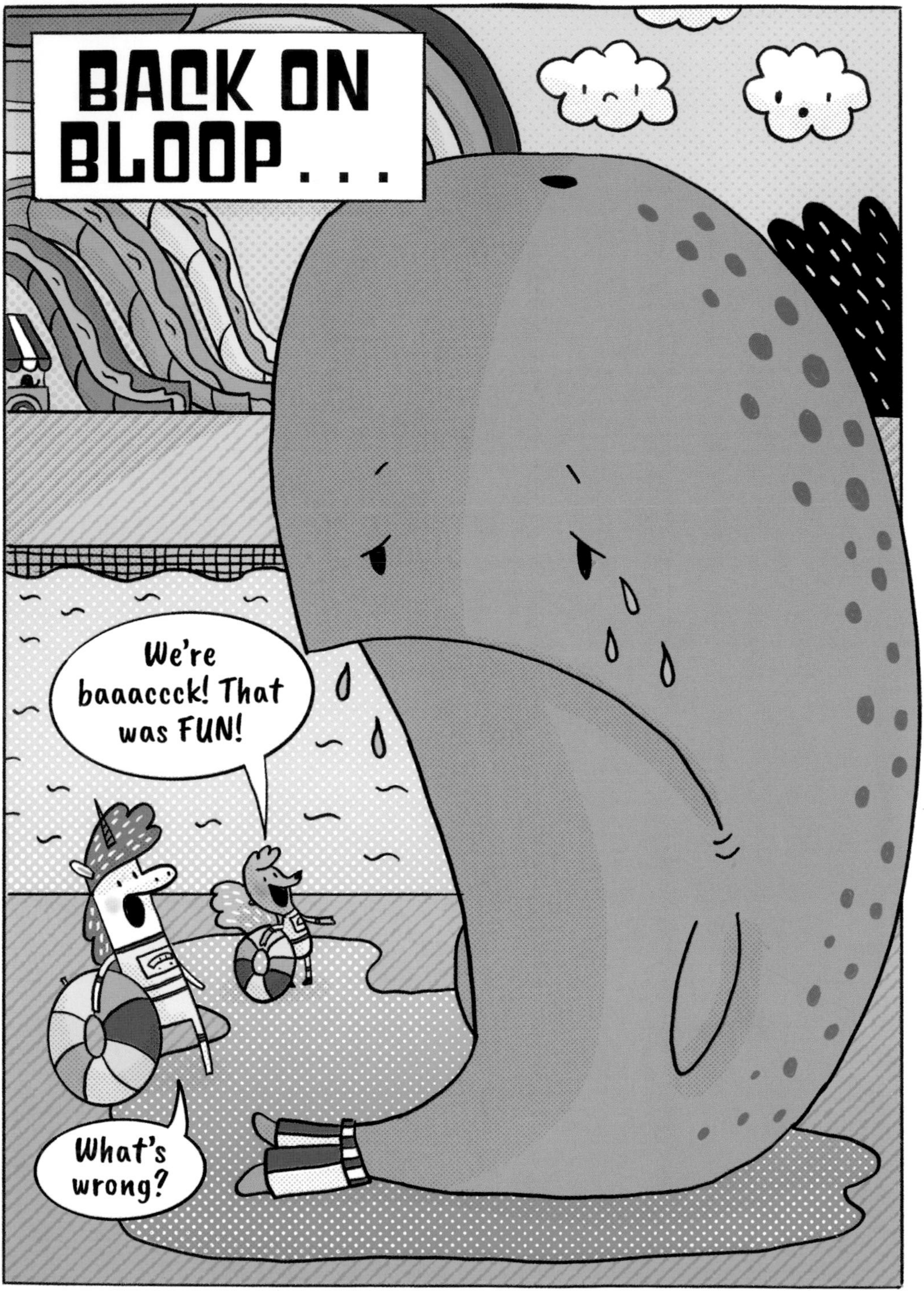
BACK ON BLOOP...
We're baaaccck! That was FUN!
What's wrong?

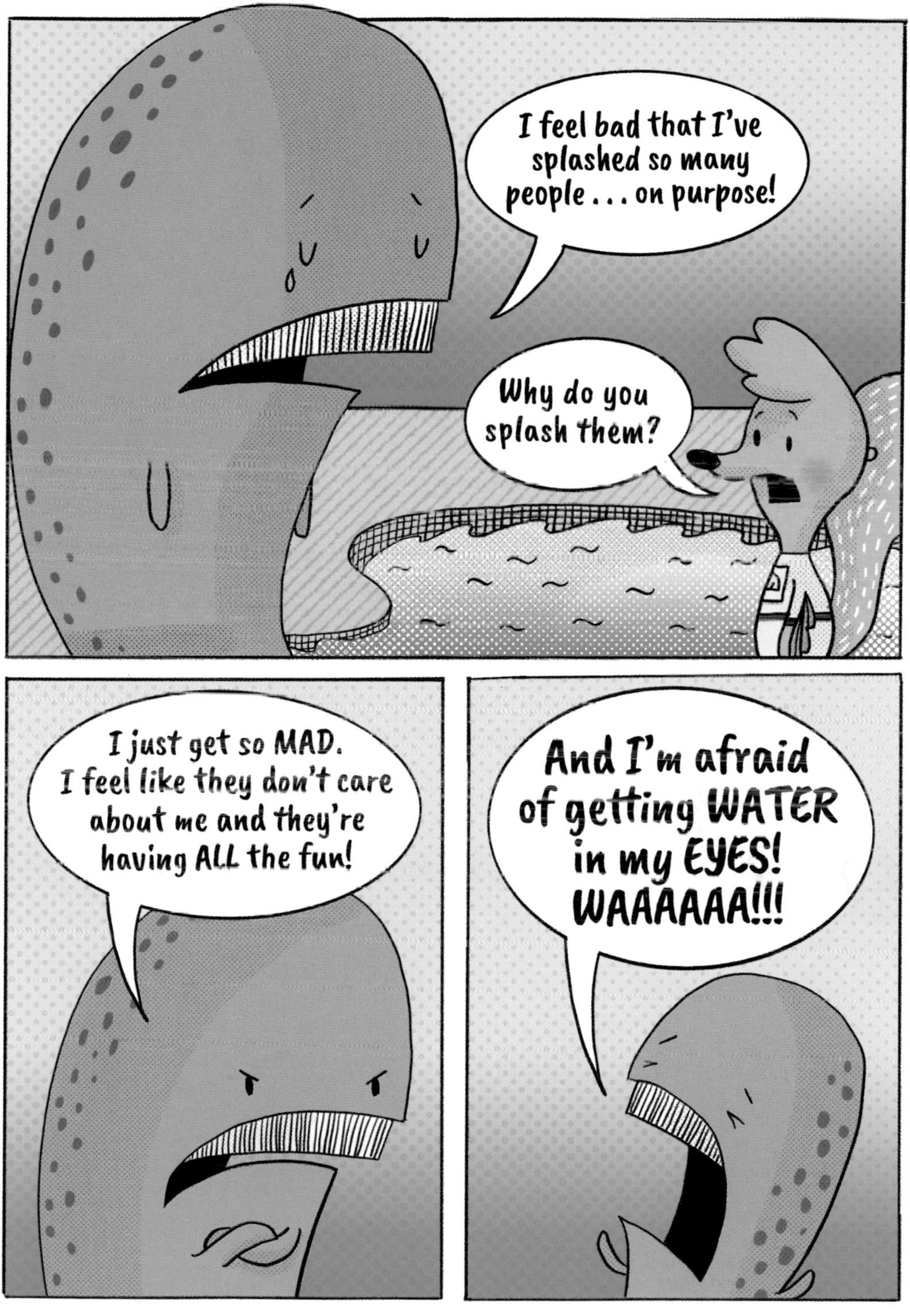
I feel bad that I've splashed so many people . . . on purpose!
Why do you splash them?
I just get so MAD. I feel like they don't care about me and they're having ALL the fun!
And I'm afraid of getting WATER in my EYES! WAAAAAA!!!

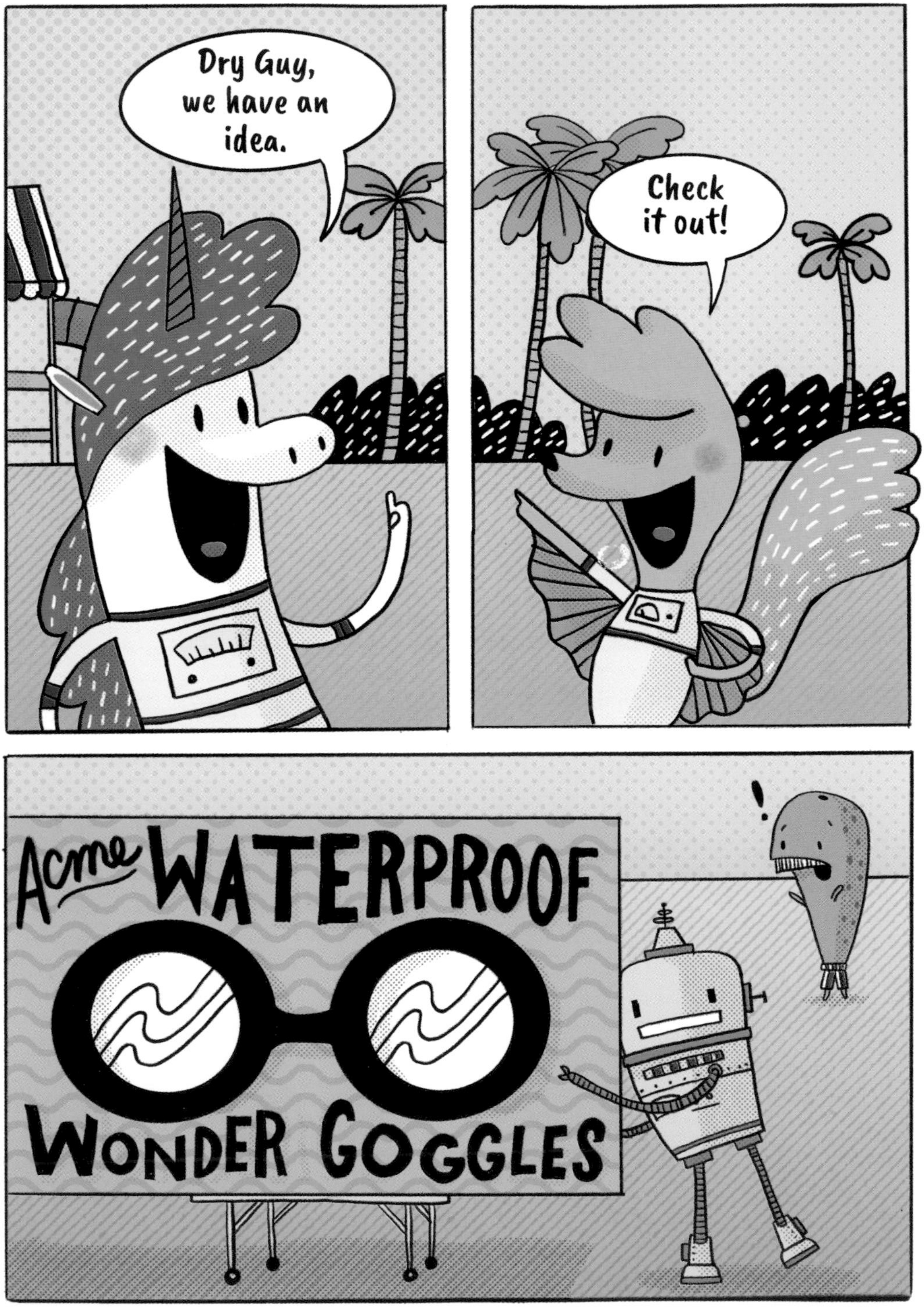

Dry Guy, we have an idea.
Check it out!
Acme WATERPROOF WONDER GOGGLES
!

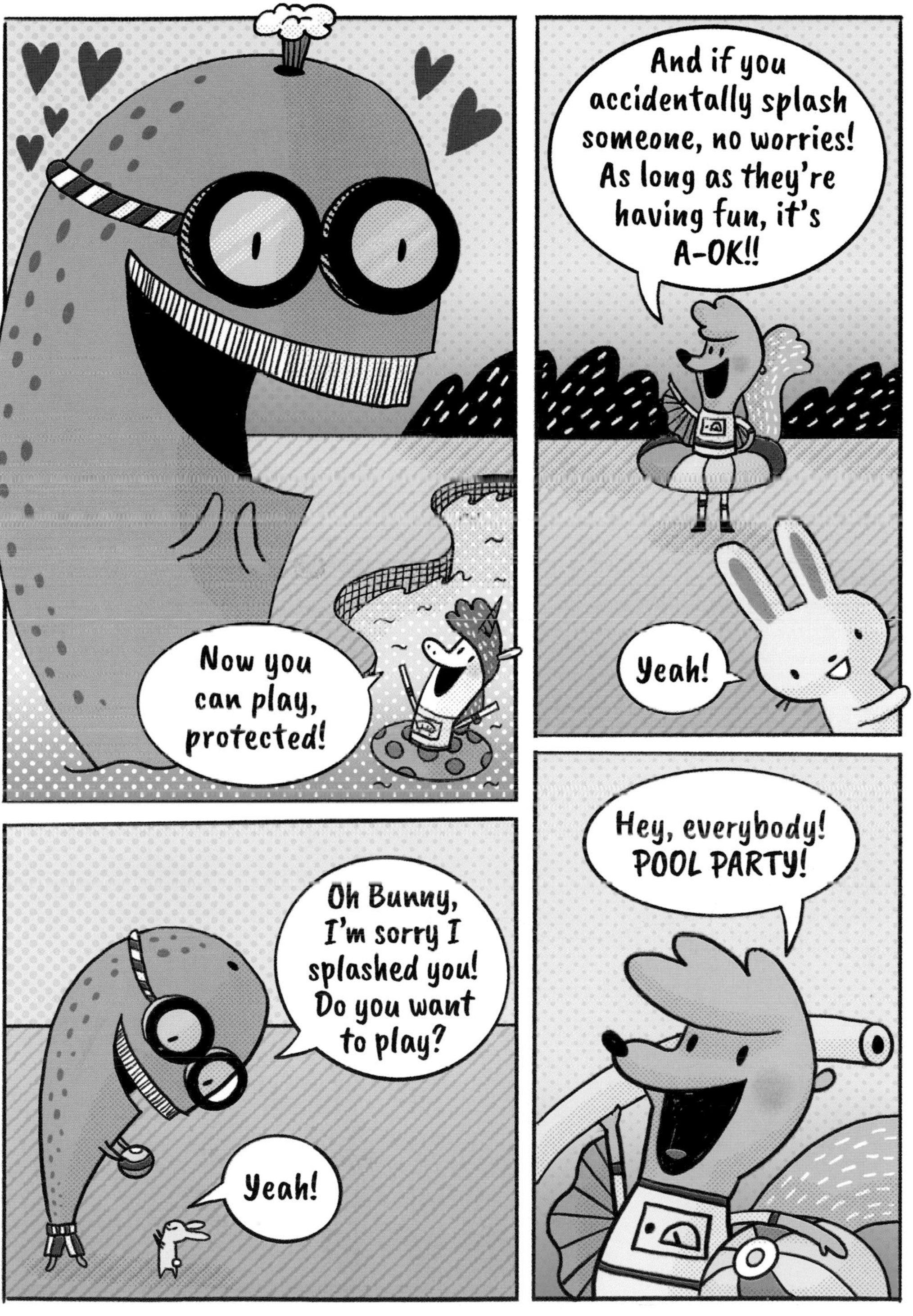
Now you can play, protected!
And if you accidentally splash someone, no worries! As long as they're having fun, it's A-OK!!
Yeah!
Oh Bunny, I'm sorry I splashed you! Do you want to play?
Yeah!
Hey, everybody! POOL PARTY!

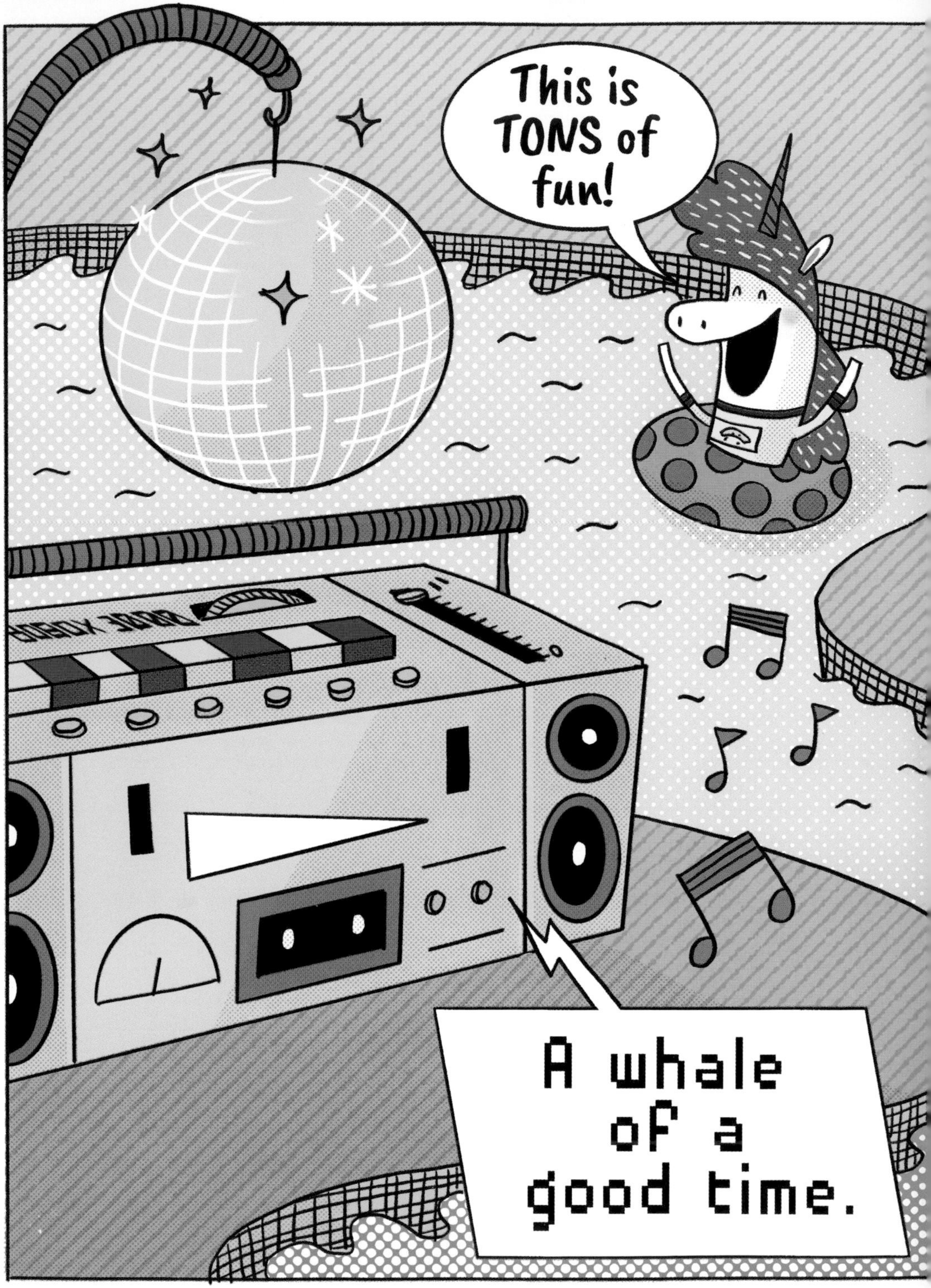
This is TONS of fun!
A whale of a good time.

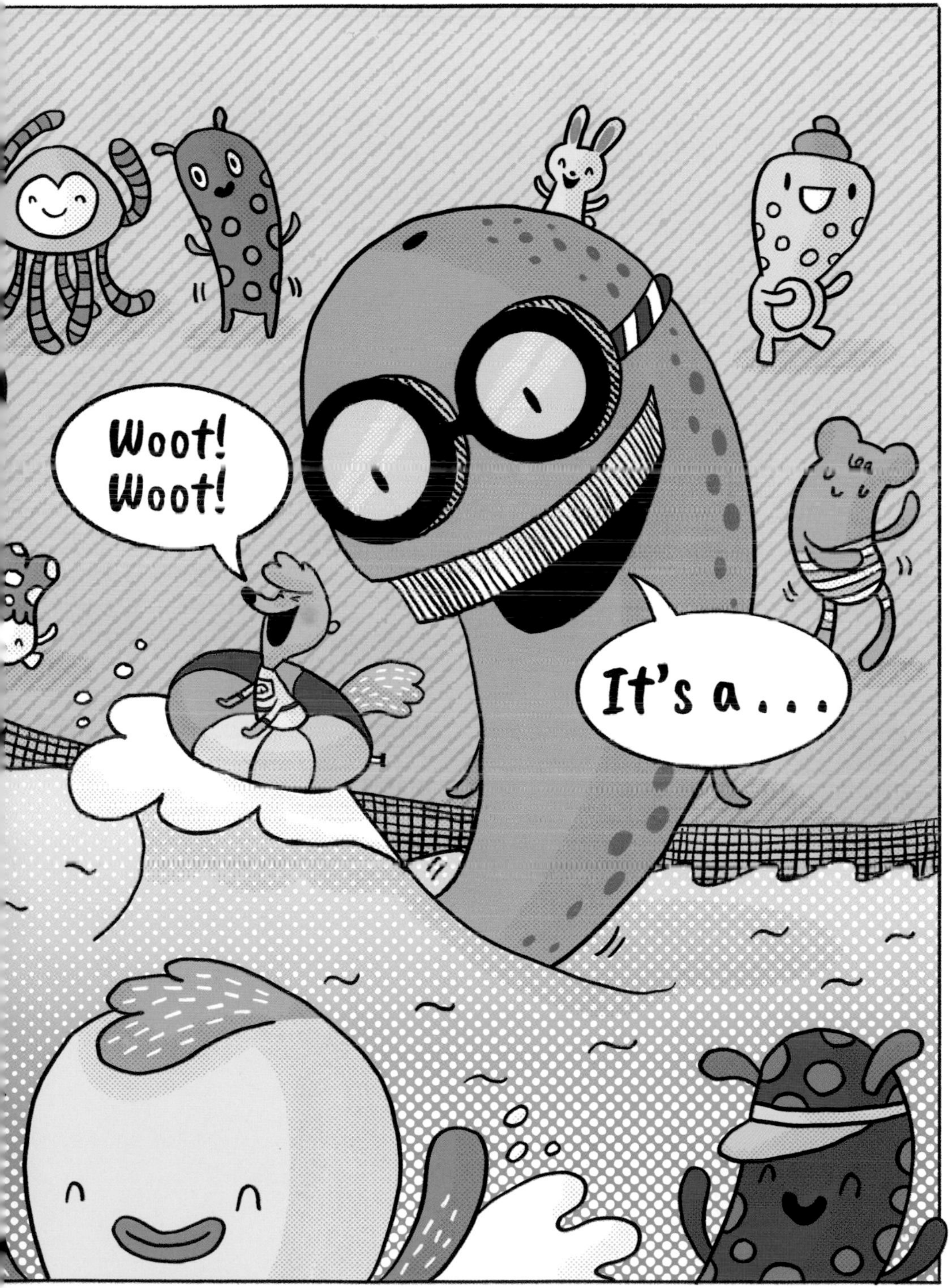
Woot! Woot!
It's a . . .

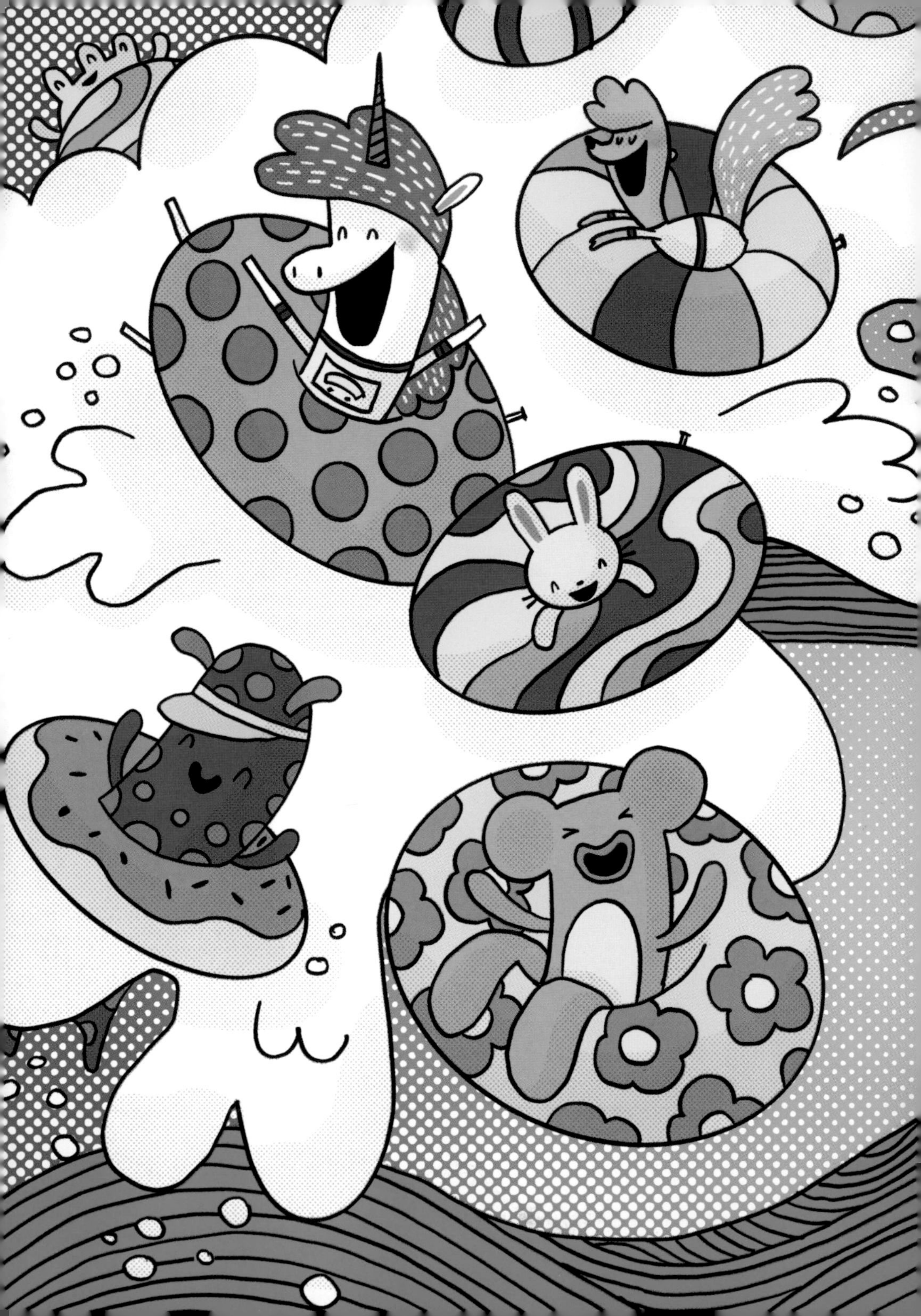

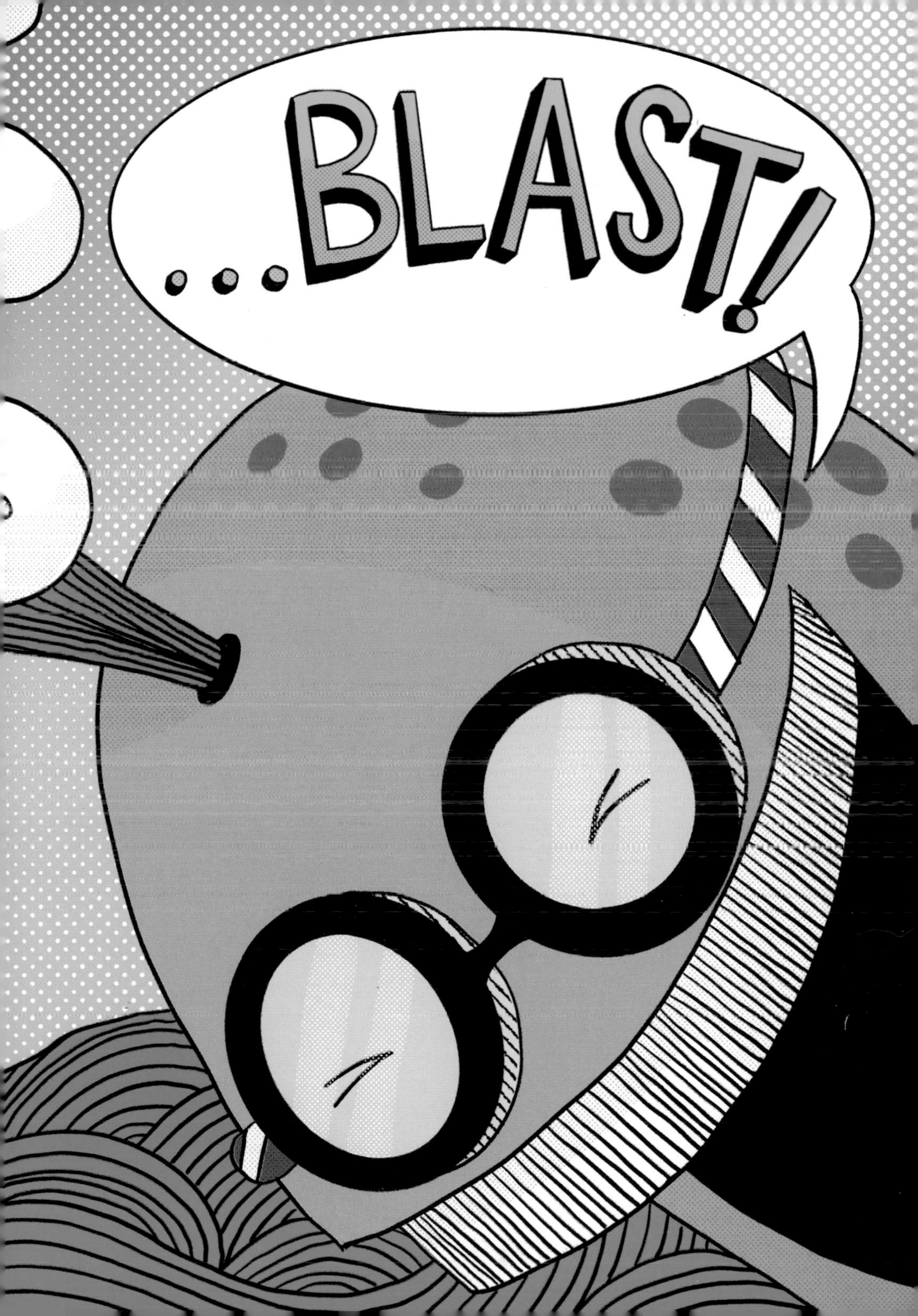
...BLAST!

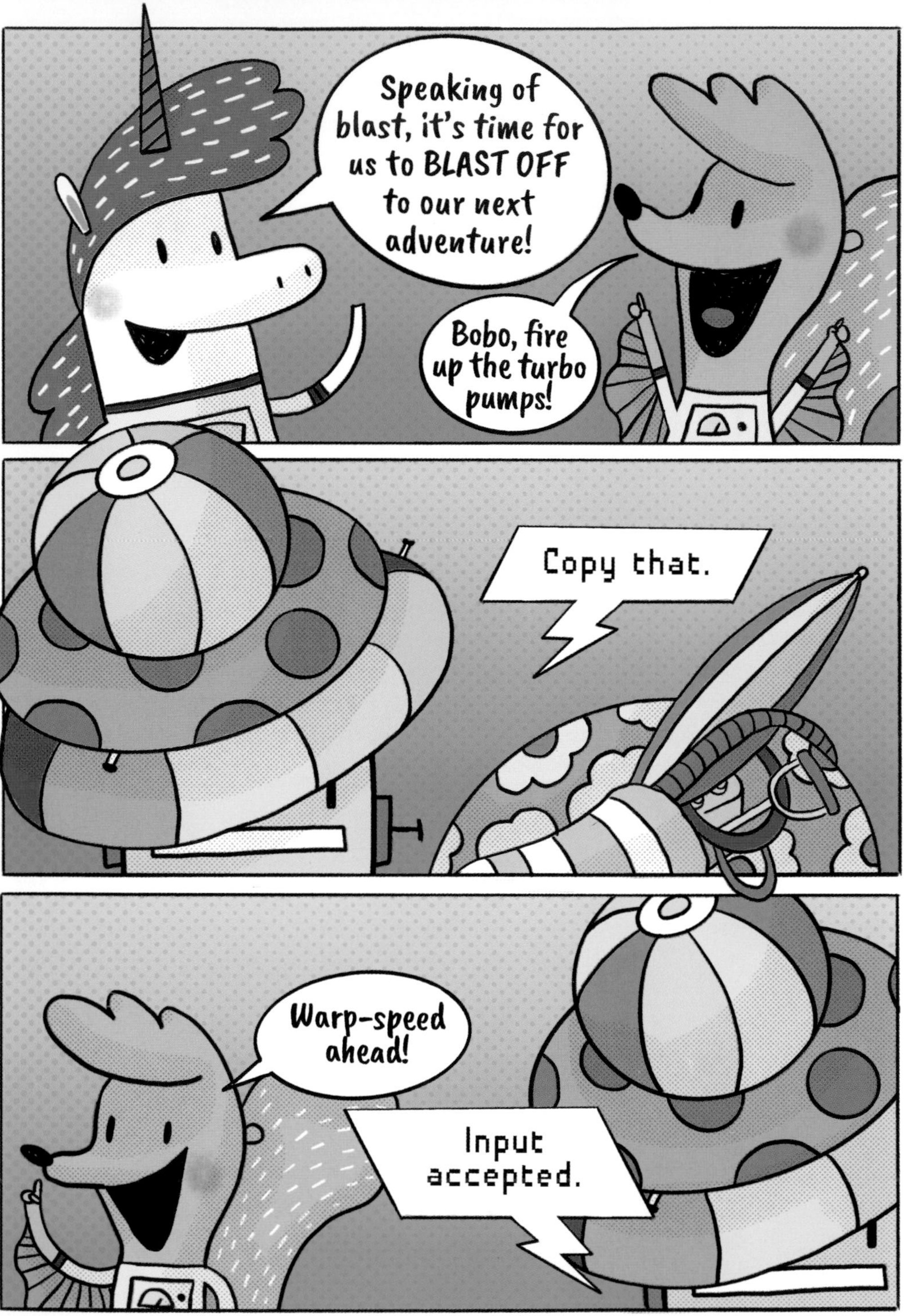
Speaking of blast, it's time for us to BLAST OFF to our next adventure!
Bobo, fire up the turbo pumps!
Copy that.
Warp-speed ahead!
Input accepted.

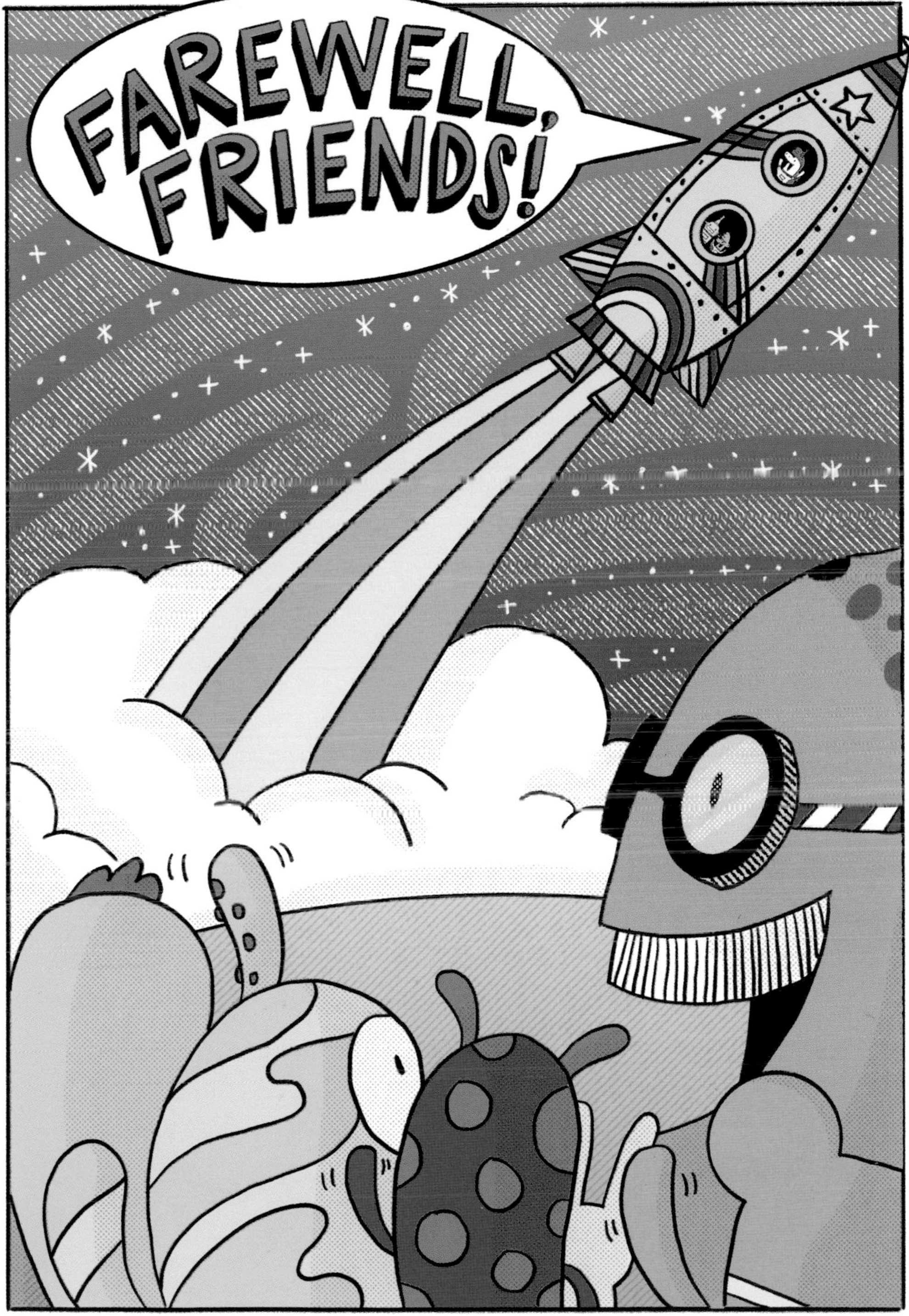
FAREWELL, FRIENDS!

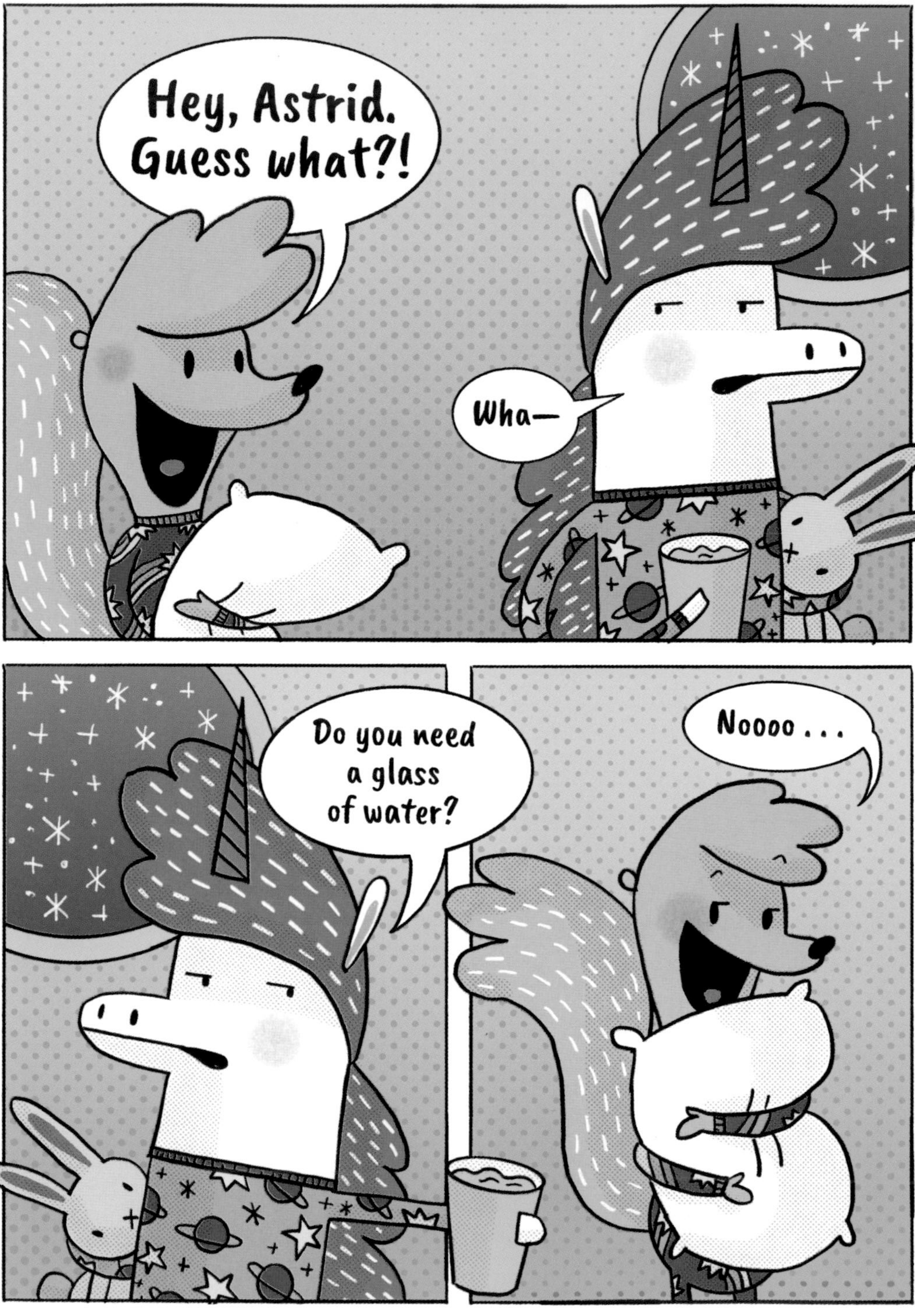
Hey, Astrid. Guess what?!
Wha—
Do you need a glass of water?
Noooo . . .

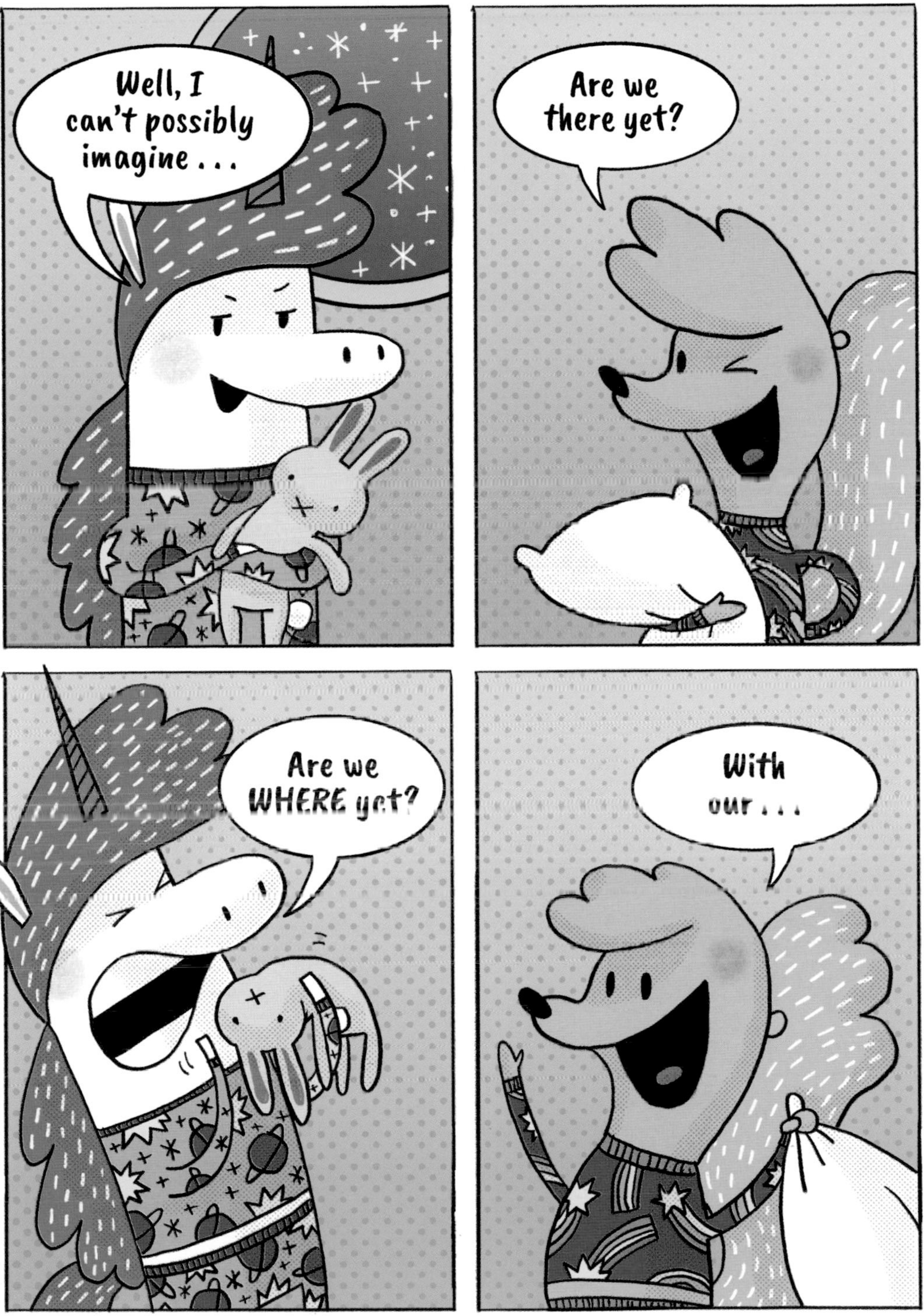
Well, I can't possibly imagine . . .
Are we there yet?
Are we WHERE yet?
With our . . .

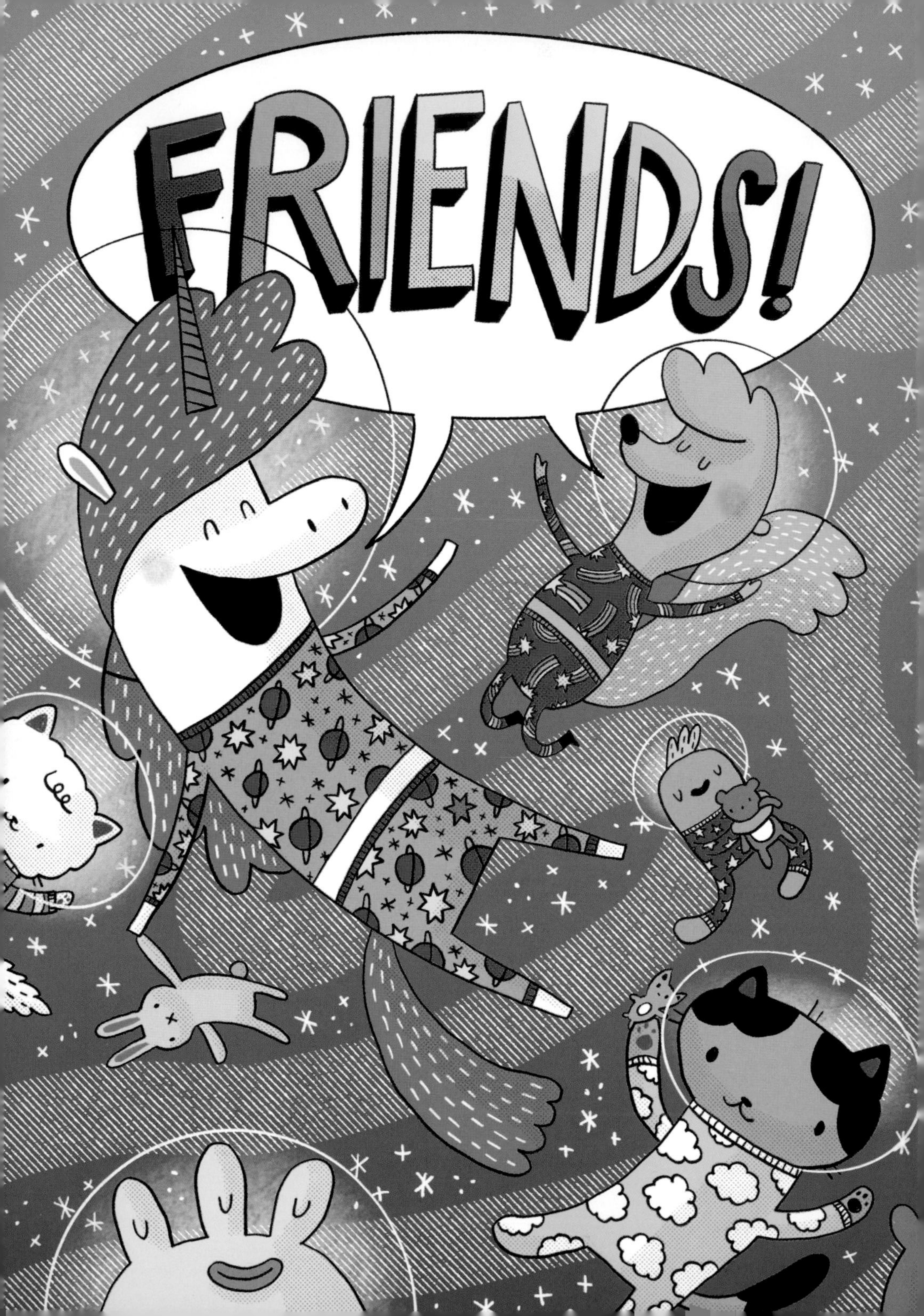
FRIENDS!

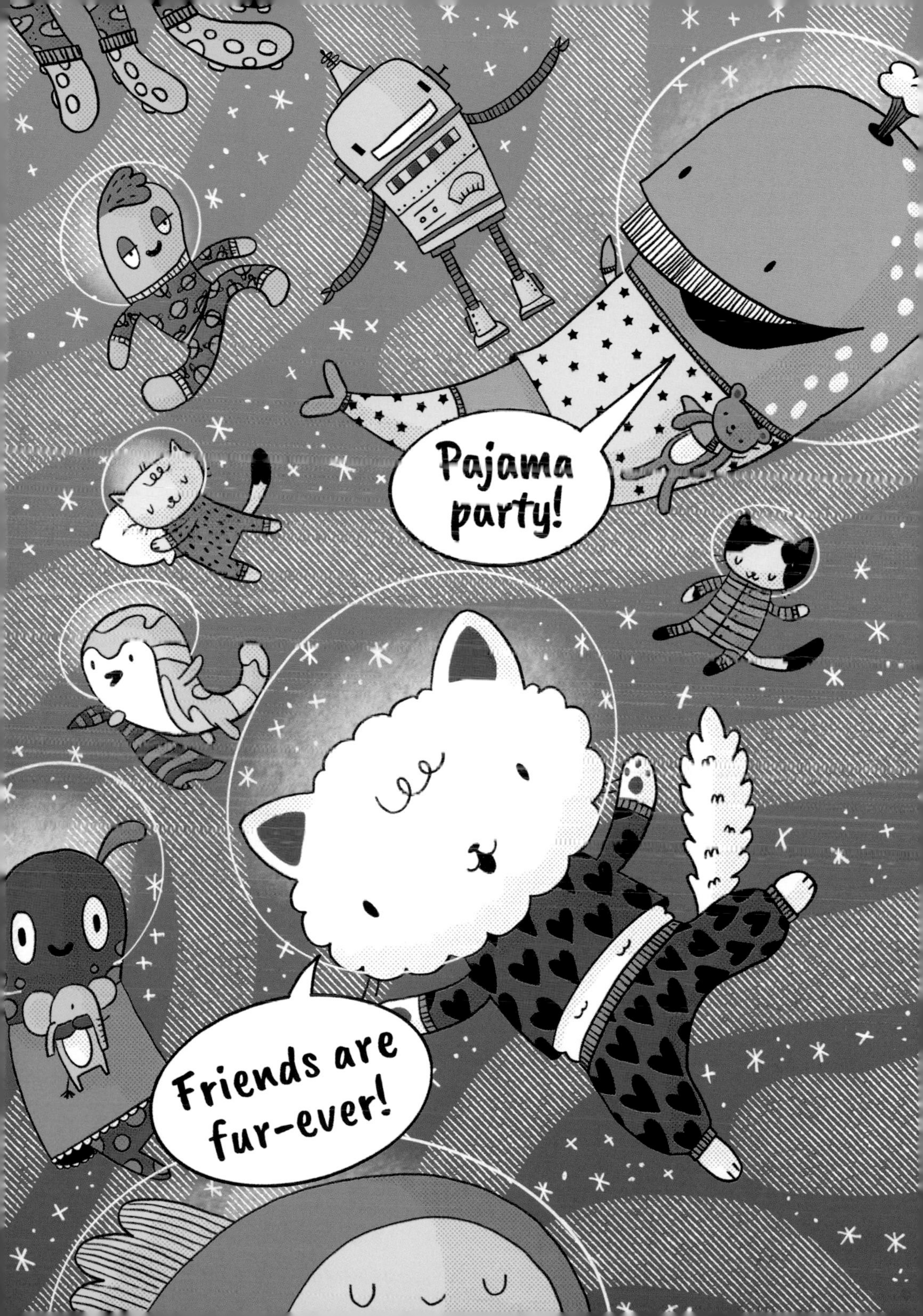
Pajama party!
Friends are fur-ever!

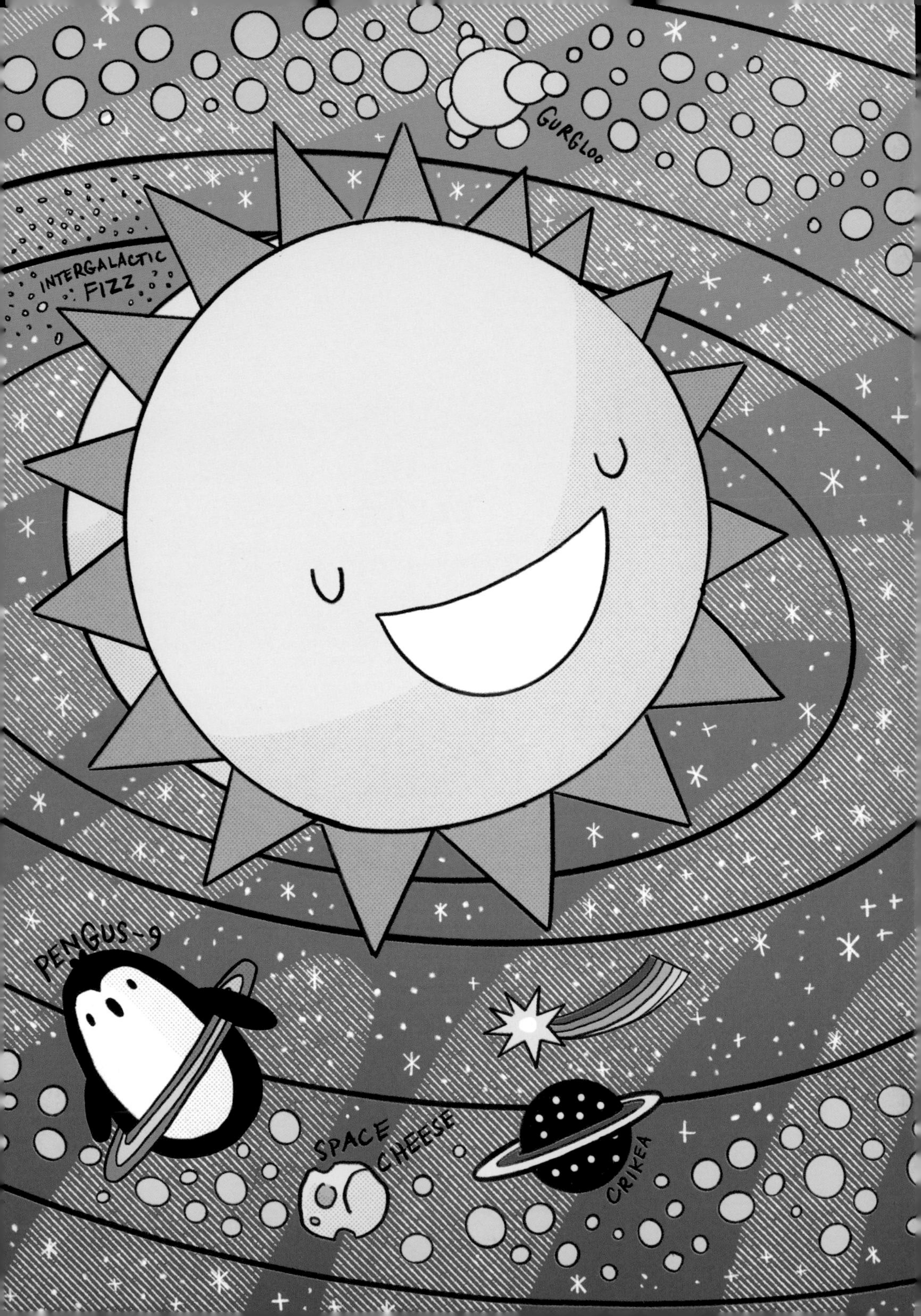
GURGLOO
INTERGALACTIC FIZZ
PENGUS-9
SPACE CHEESE
CRIKEA

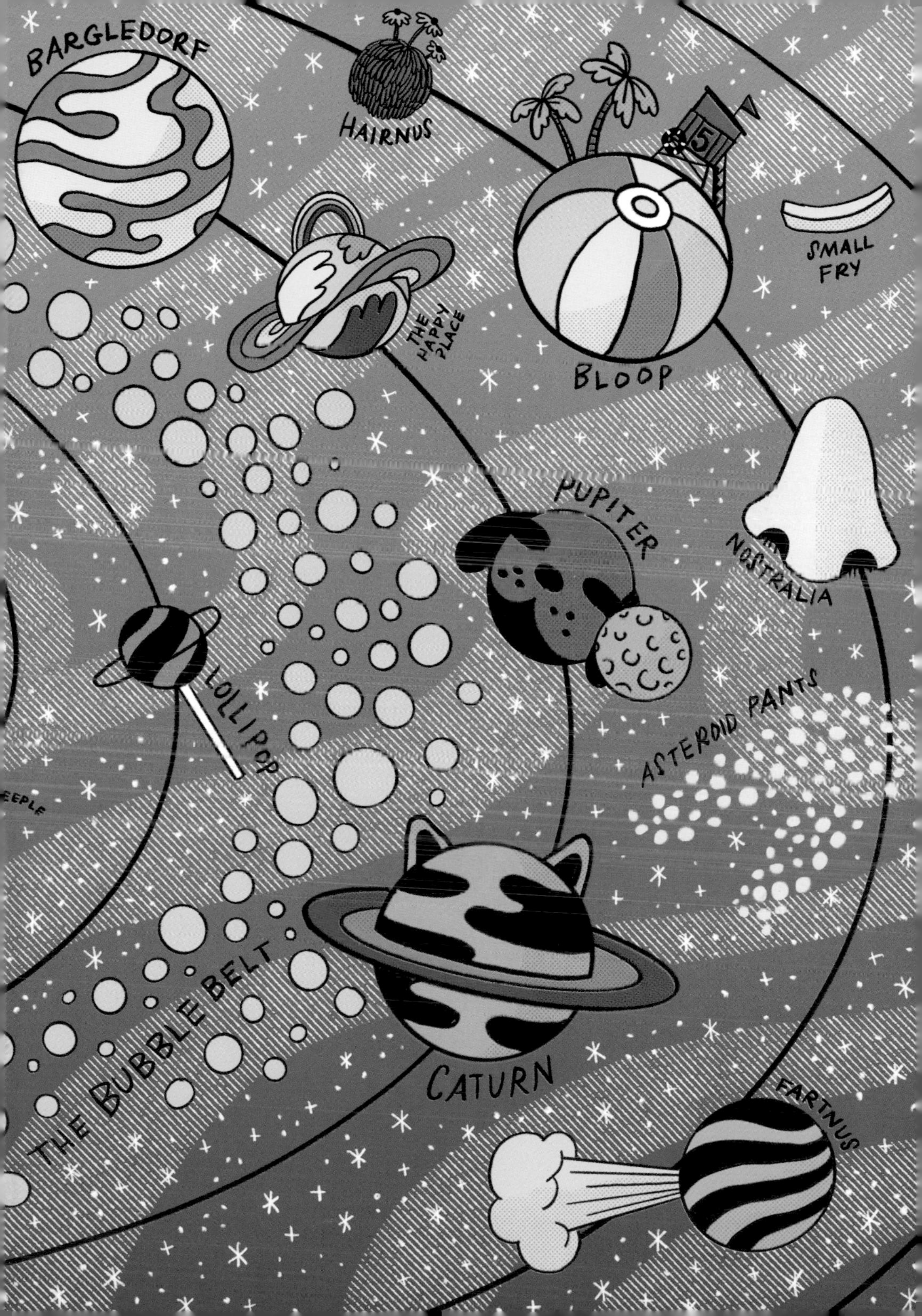
BARGLEDORF
HAIRNUS
5
SMALL FRY
THE HAPPY PLACE
BLOOP
PUPITER
NOSTRALIA
LOLLIPOP
ASTEROID PANTS
EEPLE
THE BUBBLE BELT
CATURN
FARTNUS

FOR FREDDIE, SANS GÊNE, AND LOKI, AND IN LOVING MEMORY OF KYLO AND DASH
–S.M. & E.M.

The illustrations in this book were created using an iPad and digital tools.

Library of Congress Cataloging Number 2021948101
ISBN 978-1-4197-5701-3

Copyright © 2022 Hello Lucky, LLC
Book design by Heather Kelly

Printed and bound in China
10 9 8 7 6 5 4 3 2

Amulet Books are available at special discounts when purchased in quantity for premiums and promotions as well as fundraising or educational use. Special editions can also be created to specification. For details, contact specialsales@abramsbooks.com or the address below.

Amulet Books® is a registered trademark of Harry N. Abrams, Inc.

ABRAMS The Art of Books
195 Broadway, New York, NY 10007
abramsbooks.com